ecct

Pastoral Theology in the Zombie Plague

Rev. Garen Pay

May my humble words be used by Your Spirit to strengthen the faith of Your people. Amen

A certain Pastor's Pre-Sermon Prayer

God is our refuge and strength,
a very present help in trouble.
Therefore we will not fear though the earth gives way,
though the mountains be moved into the heart of the sea . . .

Psalm 46:1-2

Prologue

"What a God-forsaken hell hole."

If you thought or said that when the plague hit, you wouldn't be alone, even amongst clergy. I thought the same thing when I woke up and gathered that, within two weeks, our town of four pastors had been reduced to one: me. One pastor was mistaken for a zombie and shot dead—never wear a red Hawaiian shirt when checking on people's safety. Another, who claimed to be able to perform miracles, had un-miraculously vanished—Gertrude heard his Mercedes peel rubber from two blocks away. It seemed he could get a higher "free will offering" healing zombies elsewhere. Another pastor stayed, asserting she had seen things worse than zombies when she worked in the inner city. I never doubted her bravery, but the neighbors, through the gaps in their boarded-up windows, watched as her husband tore his hair out wondering if he should take his family out of town or honor Ephesians 5 and protect his wife. He took the kids. She got a newfound infectious desire for outreach—and flesh.

Obviously, if you are reading this, you managed to pick up the pieces from a ravaged world, at least enough to make it this far. But the dangers are still there and the horrors and regrets of what you had to do to survive aren't going away anytime soon. Do you still see their twisted faces in your sleep? Do you still miss the ones who didn't make it through and sometimes wish you could join them? I can assure you, you are not alone.

How do you cope? There's a lot of options when every

liquor store or pharmacy's shelves are yours to peruse. There sure is plenty of violence to go around as well if you want to vent some anger at the world, at yourself, at God.

Sure, we can cope. But don't you want something more than a coping mechanism? How about some hope?

Well I found some. Hope in a loving and merciful God. And before you toss this book aside in laughter, hear me out. Let me tell you our story. A story my little girl wants you to know, a story about survival and about finding hope in old promises, but promises that are far from coping mechanisms. No, the promises of God are real, even for people in a plague with all our doubts, fears, and evil.

A Lazy Pastor in a Lazy Town

"This is the day that the Lord has made," I called out to the congregation of seventy or so people.

"Let us rejoice and be glad in it," they, somewhat enthusiastically, responded.

And what a day the Lord had given us that early spring Sunday. The members stared out the windows at the blossoms and the robins while I preached on the Gospel lesson from Luke—Jesus' transfiguration. It wasn't a great sermon in my eyes. I had struggled over it all week, I even remembered to pray about it once or twice, but it just never came together. Even worse for my ego, that old beast, no one complimented me as I shook hands with the members after worship.

I am still ashamed of that sermon. If I, like the Lord coming off the Mount of Transfiguration, knew how near death was, I would have given God's people better. I learned then: it's never a bad idea to preach as if it's your peoples' last sermon.

After taking off my vestments I made my way toward the cookies in the fellowship hall. Before I could make it there, Gertrude, a wrinkly old lady who played organ for our services, called out to me, "Pastor Darren, Pastor Darren!" I smiled and looked down at the wonderful and encouraging old lady, thankful for her work and enthusiasm to try and keep the dwindling choir singing. We talked for a few minutes about a selection she wanted to use for the upcoming Ash Wednesday service that week. After a minute she thanked me, complimented my beard ("Don't listen to them, it's coming in nicely"), and tottered away to hunt down the other choir members. *What a saint.*

Before I made it two more steps toward the fellowship hall, Curtis, an old man, bent nearly double over his cane, hobbled up to me. He was a saint too, technically speaking. He was redeemed by the blood of Christ. He was also the biggest pain in my backside in the entire congregation. I took a deep breath and ran my hand through my short brown hair, preparing for the barrage of complaints. But it turned out it was only one complaint about something we did that we never used to do before. He must have been in a good mood.

After about three more exchanges with other members telling me things that I would try not to forget by lunch, I found myself in the fellowship hall. Before I knew it, I was at the front of the line picking out a cookie with my bare hands that had just shaken seventy others.

I always envied the pastors who fed off the attention and socialization of Sunday mornings. Personally, I found the busy mornings draining. A week's worth of planning come down to a few hours where you prayed your foot-shaped mouth or the sound system wouldn't distract from the message of the Savior, and don't get me started on video screens.

This particular Sunday was even more draining as I forced myself to hold my tongue through the voters' meeting, wondering how everyone who was too busy to stay for Bible Class every week found the time for a voters meeting held in the same time slot. But after the meeting, which was the same as every other voters' meeting —lots of volunteered opinions with no volunteers to do them, and a shrinking bank balance—I headed home and, feeling a bit under the weather, used my four hours of work that morning as an excuse to do absolutely nothing for the rest of the day.

Eventually my wife, Miranda, was able to convince me to go for a walk with our children. Our oldest, Valentine, was fourteen and her long blonde ponytail bobbed back and forth as she lagged behind us staring at her phone through the glasses she never seemed to be happy with. Luke, our eleven year old son, was boisterous and freckle faced. He rode far ahead of us on his bike, swerving in and out of the ditch on the side of the road that separated our town from the endless miles of, still unplanted,

6

cornfields that surrounded us.

I walked hand in hand with my beautiful wife who was talking about something I wasn't paying particular attention to. But I wasn't ignoring her, I said "uh huh" at all the right places and more than once caught myself staring at her short blonde hair and piercing gray eyes.

We sauntered around about half of our small town of four hundred people, isolated several miles from the highway on the plains of what used to be this great nation. The town, Witherton, was just like the hundred other little towns nestled down in what I guess you could call a valley every twenty miles between the plains' rolling hills. We waved at people as we walked around, and I shrugged when Miranda asked me who they were. After five years in town you think I would know their names, but I was more the "stay home at night" type of person and less the "go to every town function" kind.

Miranda and Luke wanted to keep walking, but I knew if we made it to the park Luke would want to play for a while, so I used my slightly scratchy throat as an excuse to cut through the middle of town and go back home. Valentine looked up from her phone long enough to agree with me, mumbling something about bad service.

We turned at the mansion with the solar panels on the north end of town and walked down the highway that bisected Witherton from north to south. And though it made our walk shorter, even I complained about the unusually high amount of traffic on the highway—we saw at least four cars and a tractor.

Our town had only one stoplight, kind of. The flashing yellow light was strung up above the intersection of the highway and Main Street. West of the highway, on Main Street, was the town hub, the fire station, bar, post office, the gas station that doubled as the grocery store, and four hair salons. We turned east, away from downtown and toward our Church near the far end of Main Street. Miranda, still wearing her blue spring dress from church, commented on the Church sign that I hadn't changed in three months. I retorted, only a little defensively, "Don't tempt me or I will put something awful in there about 'knee-mail.'" Miranda scrunched up her face and shuddered, her hair shining as it moved in the sunlight.

Just past the church, on the same property, was our two-story home. The church owned the house and a half dozen families had lived in it as the pastors came and went through the years. I had to admit, it was a little interesting to have a congregation vote on whether you could put a fence up in your backyard, but we were grateful for the cozy old home. To the east we had a great view, the only thing separating us from the rolling prairies and farmland was the road we walked on earlier, train tracks, and a few grain bins. The view out the front was less desirable: the town's nursing home, a large and meandering brick building, squatted across Main Street from us.

Luke and I lingered on the porch for a moment, watching an ambulance speed up to the nursing home. Two volunteer paramedics from town rushed a gurney inside. Luke "oohed" and sat down on the porch to wait for them to come out—things rarely got more exciting than this in our town. I chuckled at him, hoped that all my members at the home were alright, and turned to look out, past the weeds I had yet to pull in our front flower beds, over the fields to the east. I thought about how this town seemed to fit me well. It was quiet and slow. Even Valentine, who often complained about having to drive to the city to shop, liked Witherton. We were happy where God had put us. When I felt up to it, or when Luke nagged me enough, I enjoyed doing a little hunting and fishing, which was readily available and vastly preferable to the hassle of city traffic and congestion that I grew up in. Miranda, who grew up in a small mountain town, felt right at home in our little town, with the exception of how far away we were from her family.

I looked in the house and saw her start getting dinner ready for us and I realized I never did thank her enough for following me across the country to where this church had called me to serve. I didn't have an excuse for my thanklessness either. I was constantly reminded of it as she spent every night cleaning up dinner on the phone with her mother or her sister, while I played catch in the back yard with Luke.

But that night I had to say "no" to Luke, just like I, uncustomarily, did to second helpings of dinner. He didn't protest much, and then went back to his room carrying his football that we usually rough-housed with. The truth was I did feel a little lousy that night. Maybe it was the stress of trying to motivate and teach seventy people when the compliments (which were plenty if I was honest) never seemed to be as powerful as the criticisms. More than likely, I felt crummy because I picked some bug up at church. Whatever the cause of my unease, it still didn't stop me from playing hours of video games with friends from across the country online.

Before bed, as I sat in the dark staring at the fluorescent screen, I clicked through the videos my friends had talked about while we played. Some website was linking a bunch of random acts of violence from around the world to some recent events on the east coast. The website owner, who also apparently believed in aliens, said these videos were proof of a government conspiracy to hide the reality of zombies. Most of my friends joked about the videos, though some genuinely seemed bothered by them. I looked into them, if anything, so I could get in on the jokes next week.

The videos were all unrelated, but strangely similar. Each act was carried out by only a single attacker, unarmed, violently beating random people on the street. Most disturbing was one particular video taken in Florida that showed the victim, beaten and bloodied, being tended to by emergency personnel. The shaky phone camera captured images of the man convulsing violently and then, with a scream, he turned against the people trying to help him. The paramedics tried to restrain the man but were unable to. He threw them off of himself, chased one for a few seconds, before turning toward the person filming. His eyes were wild and blood dripped from his mouth, which snarled at the camera. That was the end of the video, which had been viewed a hundred million times and was even posted on some major news networks.

The internet was not short on theories; it never was. Aliens and zombies were popular memes, but most of the sensible articles called the incidents "coordinated terror attacks," "drug overdoses," or "new popular gang initiations." But soon my scratchy throat and drooping eyes overcame my interest and I went to bed with more examples of the darkness of mankind's hearts, a bit of a runny nose, and with no reason to wake up before noon.

Unfortunately, the phone woke me only two hours later. My head was splitting, and I had already figured out, in my years in the ministry, that no one calls at 3am to give you good news. I sighed and picked myself up to my elbows. The phone call didn't surprise me. Lent, the busiest time of year for a pastor, seemed to be the deadliest for their members. "Figures," I mumbled as I reached over to the phone, bitterly wondering which member dared die and give me more work.

Turned out it wasn't one of my members after all. The nurse from the home across the street apologetically informed me that one of the residents on hospice had died and the family was requesting a pastor as theirs was from a different town. Thankful that I, at least for now, wouldn't have to fit a funeral service into my Lent, I swung my feet out of bed. Getting ready, I grumbled just loud enough to make sure my should-be-sleeping wife knew how unpleasant this task was. I think I even ran into the bed-stand for added effect. I'm sure I told myself I was complaining for a good reason, but the reality was, I did it because that proud beast inside me wanted soft and sympathetic words from my wife, not to mention some sympathy bacon and eggs later.

Minutes later, I stepped out of the glow of my front-porch light into the dark street. The moon was shrouded by clouds that hung so low they seemed to scrape the flickering streetlight near the nursing home. I was halfway across the street when a growl made me spin around. Something was lurking in the church parking lot.

"Stupid Tank," I said, trying to convince myself it was just the dog that the family down the street let roam about the town. Betraying my lack of courage, I walked a little faster the rest of the way to the nursing home, trying not to think about the violence I had seen on my computer just a couple hours before.

I gave one last glance over my shoulder before I entered the nursing home. Nothing seemed to be following me out of the darkness, but, still uneasy, I enjoyed the safety of the nursing home's bright lights and constant smell of steamed broccoli.

Having never met the lady who died, I stopped at the nurse's station to ask some questions about her. The nurse, a small woman, her brown hair streaked with gray, thanked me for coming. She told me the Baptist Pastor from the next town over would meet with the family for funeral arrangements the next day. As she led me to the room, she described how the deceased had been on hospice for weeks.

A third of the way down the dim hall, she led me into a dark and musty room that stank of sweat, old food, and death. I could immediately tell the nurse had been telling the truth about the long hospice stay. The poor family was exhausted from their vigil at the lady's bedside, evidenced by the bags under their eyes and the fast food wrappers overflowing in the garbage can. The nurse kindly introduced me to the family, there were about a half dozen of them crowded into the room. I recognized one of the lady's sons, Jesse, a usually clean-shaven man with shoulder length blonde hair, from the golf course. After the introductions, the nurse excused herself from the room.

All the bloodshot and watery eyes turned to me.

I talked with them for a few minutes, asking them about the deceased, where she grew up, how she fell ill, when she died. The last question made Jesse sob.

"Did you miss her passing?" I asked him.

He wiped his tears on his sleeve and nodded.

"She knew you loved her, Jesse."

He wept harder, "Maybe. The last time we talked before she," he blubbered for a moment, "before she lost consciousness, we fought about the house."

Jesse's sister, with her arm around him, gave a pleading shrug at me, as if they had tried to talk to him about it.

"Death is never good, Jesse, and it never comes at a good time. It sounds like a terrible time for you. But we know who beats death and I assure you, the next time you see your mom, and you will, all will be healed, and all will be forgiven."

I read a passage about how we mourn, but we mourn with hope. Hope found in the Savior who heals our broken relationships, conquers the grave, and gives us a reunion with our loved ones.

I said a prayer with them and the family thanked me before I left. It felt odd being validated by a group of mourners, but I think they actually were thankful, even Jesse. And for the first time in a while, I was happy to be a pastor. As I walked out of the room, I thanked God that He used an often times indifferent and maybe a-little-bit jaded man like me to help His people.

On the way out, I passed by the nursing station, thanked the nurse who had shown me to the room and stopped to talk to Jacob, the funeral director who I had come to know well throughout the years organizing funerals with him. He was a stout man, balding, and generally cheerful despite his profession. A testament to the hope of the Gospel; this man was quite faithful and rarely let the constant death around him bring him despair. But tonight, perhaps it had. He was cordial enough, but I could tell he was tired, more than a 3 a.m. call should show. His combover was disheveled, his suit had a stain on it. "Jacob, you look like you need a vaca-"

His phone interrupted me. He shook his head and squeezed the bridge of his nose, as if suppressing a headache, before apologizing to me and taking the call. I gave him what I hoped was an understanding nod and waved goodbye. He didn't wave back. "Another one?!" he said. "Call Randy, I am picking up a body in Witherton. Well we'll have to make room…"

He was still talking as I walked back into the dark night feeling a bit guilty. I wasn't the only one busy this time of year. And why was I so worried about work when others were losing family members?

Passing underneath the flickering streetlight, the low growl replaced my guilt with fear. I quickened my pace and squinted into the darkness while I crossed the road. *Stop being a coward, it's only Tank.* But the images of growling and violently sick people ran through my head and sped me on into the comfort of my porch light.

My hand was on the door when I wondered what kind of father I would be if I didn't check on the noise underneath my daughter's window. I slowly stepped off the porch and crept toward the church lot. My eyes ached from staring into the dark, searching for the black dog, and just when I was confident there was nothing, its white teeth snapped out of the dark and its bark sent me jumping and tumbling backwards a few steps. I called that dog a few names other than Tank as I shooed it back toward its house. Then I walked back to mine, shaking my head and calling myself a few names as well for being so dumb as to think there might be a zombie outside my house. *There's no such thing as zombies, you dunce.*

Waking up early enough for "good morning" to still technically apply, but late enough that no one would ever say it, I gave Miranda a hug as she unloaded groceries. "Already back from the city?"

"What's wrong?" I asked her when she shot me a nervous glance.

"You haven't heard about the violence on the coasts?"

I relaxed, thankful she wasn't worried about anything important. "I mean, I saw a few videos last night. Is it getting worse?"

"Yeah, some people are saying it's a virus making people go crazy," she said while she stacked cans of green beans. When I laughed, she put the cans down and turned to me. "I'm serious. My mom told us to only drink filtered water from now on."

I laughed even more and started looking through the bags for anything of interest, "You would walk backwards for the rest of your life if your mother said it was good for you."

She glared at me. "Well, it's good for us anyways, so deal with it."

I put my arms up and smiled, "Alright, I surrender."

I grabbed some very uninteresting vegetables and put them in the refrigerator, "How was the city?"

She sighed, "Awful."

"Really? On a weekday?"

"Yeah, it was a mess." She turned and put her hand on her hip, "Like I said, people are really worried about this virus. All the bottled water was gone, along with the filters, and food was flying off the shelves."

I forced a chuckle, "Wow, well, so much for your filtered water plan."

"Oh, don't you worry," she said with a stubborn look on her face and nodded over to a pot of boiling water on the stove.

I shook my head, "You are committed, I will give you that." I kissed her on the cheek, "You're cute when you're stubborn you know that?" Then I pulled a bag of chips out of the groceries and headed for the living room. I collapsed into my recliner and paused when I raised the remote toward the television. I thought for a moment, then shouted back into the kitchen at the back of the house, "Hey hon, were people buying ammunition?"

She shouted back, "No."

That was a relief, I thought, at least people weren't frantic yet. I clicked on the television.

"It was already all gone," she said, finishing her thought.

"Great Scott." I mumbled as I turned my eyes from the basketball game to my growing waistline. At least I had been too lazy to go bird hunting this year—still had a hundred shells or so in the gun safe. Then I shook my head. *People buy up ammo if taxes go up a dollar, this won't come to anything.*

If there was one thing I did well as a pastor, it was taking my day off. No one would ever convict me of being a workaholic. The rest of the day I spent playing video games with Luke, trying to keep Val off her phone, and watching television. And to this day I don't regret it one bit. God was pleased to rest on the seventh day, also in the tomb. Only later did I fully realize that it wasn't just good for me, but for the whole family.

That night I read a few articles on the violence and, admittedly, I got a little worried when I heard that the National Guard had been called in to stop rioting in Boston and that India was in a state of emergency. But ultimately, I had a few services that week to worry about so, uncharacteristically, I went to bed early, said a prayer for the people in India and on the east coast, and fell asleep.

On Tuesday, welcoming another reason to put off the Ash Wednesday Service that I was struggling with, I spent some time driving to the next town to attend the funeral for the family I had met with two nights before. The service was done by Pastor Barnstock, a lanky man with a southern drawl and his graying hair cut military style. He did an admirable job with the service, though, naturally, I silently had some critiques of his sermon, which pleased the proud beast in me. He didn't work any apologetics into his sermon, on a day when the church was, as I always presumed at a funeral, filled with unchurched people.

Later in the service I had to focus on my shoes to stop from cringing when a distant relative of the deceased droned on for ten minutes about how the lady was now an angel in heaven and was probably playing her accordion up there instead of a harp. I plastered a smile on my face while the congregation laughed and I wondered if anyone else knew that angels and people were different creatures. Ultimately, I furthered my resolve to shine my shoes when I got home and to never let family speak during the funeral, but before or after it. Someday, though, I would love to hear a family member speak at a funeral and actually give comfort and assurance from the true promises of God in Jesus. It hasn't happened yet.

When the service was over, I stayed for the luncheon, because, well, free food. I had a bit of an awkward conversation with Wilbur, one of my members who lived a pretty secluded life. He owned a crop-dusting business and other than that spent his time tinkering in his shop and only showed up to church once a quarter. I never yelled at anyone for missing church, though I did try to encourage them, but it always seemed to come off as a guilt trip. He was good natured about it and admitted he could "use a Good Word once in a coon's age." Then I headed home before I had to use the church bathrooms, which had been used by a hundred or so visitors filled up with egg salad and coleslaw.

I spent the rest of Tuesday holed up in my church office working on my sermon for Ash Wednesday the next day. Well, that, and updating my fantasy basketball team. When I was convinced I had done enough to easily be able to finish the next day, I took the minute-long commute walk home. Over dinner I got to chide our daughter, once more, about going over her data limit on her phone, between making silly jokes with Luke that made Miranda "tsk" but smile all the same.

My parents, as usual, tried to call during dinnertime and then again during family devotions, so both their calls went unanswered, though several jokes were made about their bad timing. I did feel a bit guilty however when Miranda talked with her mom half the night, fretting over the news reports of a virus and more violence, and I didn't give my parents a call back. But the basketball game in Cleveland was still going on and my ice cream still tasted good, so I stayed put.

At halftime I dripped some of my dessert onto my shirt, my spoon paused halfway to my mouth, when the broadcast was interrupted by a Public Service Announcement encouraging the nation to use extreme caution to avoid viral and bacterial transmission and around people who seem to be behaving erratically. I eventually wiped off my shirt and resolved to make some disaster preparations. *Not that this craze would reach us way in the middle of the country.*

15

I made good on my promise to make some disaster preparations the next day, though I made them for the wrong reasons. When I got to my office, I checked my email and found a note from our church body's District President, the closest thing I had to a boss, other than the Lord Himself, urging the pastors in the district to use extreme caution when gathering for worship.

Now, don't get me wrong, I loved to worship with God's people, but I hadn't finished my sermon for Ash Wednesday, let alone started on my sermon for Sunday, and the chance of getting an additional service off, well, I would be a liar if I said that didn't interest me.

Which is why, a half hour later I made the calls and canceled church for the night. Most of the members understood, though some of the more independent farmers laughed and thought we were blowing the media reports out of proportion.

I still remember sitting in my office that afternoon, grinning about the games I would get to play that night instead of preaching. I worked on the Sunday service for a few hours and thought about heading home early and calling it a day, but, once more, a tinge of guilt crept up in me. I was supposed to care for God's flock and give them the Word and Sacrament and I wouldn't be doing that at an evening service, so I resolved to do it, even if a little bit, in the day.

Five minutes later I had my communion kit, my prayer book, and was headed for Bertha Wilkens' house. She was an old widow that lived out of town several miles. I was contemplating whether or not I would, once again, follow her children's wishes and urge her to move out of the old farmhouse and into town, but when my phone rang I decided I didn't feel up to starting a conversation that I knew wouldn't result in anything.

I didn't feel up to talking on the phone either, so I let it go to voicemail. But then it rang again. I pulled the phone out of the cup holder of my pickup and saw my mom's picture on it. The picture was taken years ago, her long brown hair had less gray in it, while she was reading a story to my kids. She was probably worried about them. A shadow of fear grew in the back of my mind. They lived on the west coast. *Was the violence there, too?*

"Hi Mom, everything alright?"

My mom was always a worrier, but she seemed even more

tense than usual. "I don't know."

"What's going on?"

"The violence is in town. Shops are closed, people are rioting."

A terrible thought began to enter my mind that perhaps this wouldn't blow over right away. "Alright, is everyone safe?"

"Do you remember Ben Jorgensen?"

"Yeah," he graduated school with me.

"He's missing. And he is just one of dozens."

"What about Junior and his family?"

"Your brother, Kelly, and Emmett are in the desert camping with friends and they might stay there longer because his work might shut down."

"Sounds like a good idea. Maybe you guys should hit the road too?"

"Maybe we will." Her voice trailed off, then she added, choking up, "Why is this happening?"

I spent a few minutes trying to come up with some theological context about wars, rumors of wars, and if the mountains fall into the sea while trying to tell myself that it wasn't that big of a deal.

When I pulled into Bertha's driveway, I told my mom I needed to go. She said they were probably going to leave town for a while with their trailer, maybe with some family friends. She told me she would let me know what they decided.

"Love you, Mom. Tell Dad 'hello,' stay safe, and to never trim that beard."

She forced a laugh, "You stay safe too, buddy. We'll talk to you tomorrow."

I had no clue, as I sat in my pickup in Bertha's driveway, that my mom's call would never come. Instead I sat there thinking: *Thank goodness we aren't on the coast.*

Dust, Ash, and Disease

It seemed unusually quiet at Bertha's, even for a secluded farmhouse outside of town. I should have noticed the usual troop of barn cats wasn't milling about the porch. Knocking on the storm door, I should have noticed her obnoxious, overgrown-rat dogs weren't yipping and wheezing at the door.

As I waited, I flipped through my visitation book and found a reading that I prayed would bring her a little hope as she struggled with her medical conditions and economic troubles. I didn't often pray before visits, but after this visit with Bertha, I hardly ever forget to pray for them and myself.

I settled on Jesus' words, "Do not be anxious about anything."

Thinking she had not yet heard my knock on the glass storm door, I opened it to knock harder on the wooden door behind it. My first knock sent the door swinging open. The hair stood up on the back of my neck and I strained to see into the quiet and gloomy entryway. Something was wrong here.

Should I go in? Had she fallen? Was she dead?

"Bertha?" I whispered. Then I shook my head, cleared my throat and projected into the dark house, "Bertha!? It's Pastor."

The only response was silence.

I stepped over the threshold into her house and the dank odor of the house seemed to have been doubled and mixed with hot garbage since my last visit two weeks prior. The blinds were pulled, which was not unusual for Bertha, her windows all had plastic duct taped on the outside to save on heating bills. Yet the house was still darker than usual. The pitch black, along with the smell, made the air inside the house thick and oppressive. For nearly a minute I peered from the main foyer up the stairway into darkness, wondering if she had been unable to get out of bed.

I shook my head; I would clear the main floor before ever daring to venture upstairs.

I groped down the main hall and mercifully detected faint light piercing through the kitchen blinds. I turned into the kitchen on my right and retched into my sleeve. Resting on the floor was a ball of fur and blood, which, I assumed, used to be one of her toy dogs. The small collar left to the side of the remains confirmed my thoughts.

"Bertha, are you alright?"

I strained my ears. *Was that a knock? Was it the wind?* My own breathing and heartbeat seemed to drown out every other sound. I turned back from the kitchen and continued down the hall even though I dreaded every step I took. Half of me expected to find her dead on the floor, the other expected her to turn the corner alive and well. Both results seemed terrifying to me. The stench grew stronger as I continued down the hall past the kitchen and toward the living room. I held the sleeve of my clerical shirt in front of my nose just to breathe.

In the darkness of the living room I could see a mass on Bertha's favorite chair. "Bertha?"

The mass, like me for several moments, didn't move.

I groped the wall, begging for a light switch.

As I found it, I also found a stack of books on the table below the switch. The switch flipped, along with the books that went crashing to the ground.

Thankfully the light worked and it illuminated a mass of blankets tossed on Bertha's chair.

I breathed a small sigh of relief into my sleeve.

Then I heard the steps above me.

She's here. At least she's alright. I just have to explain why I am in her living room. "Bertha! It's Pastor, I was worried about you."

My explanations seemed to quicken her steps. They fell harder and faster. *Is this eighty year old woman running?* Then I heard the old lady descend the stairs faster than I could have. *Did she fall? Is it even her?* I retreated further into the living room, away from the sound of her crashing down the stairs. I stared, horrified, down the hall toward the stair landing where the front door stood cracked open.

Bertha crashed into the front door, closing it.

I took a step toward her. Before my foot landed, she was up and racing toward me.

"Bertha! It's—"

In seconds she covered the entire distance of the hall. I dodged to my left and Bertha crashed into the wall behind me.

Her face was bloodied, her eyes were red, and her blouse was booger green, matching her drapes.

"Bertha!" I shouted at her, almost a rebuke.

She swiped at me with blood-soaked and bone-exposed hands.

Panicked and confused, I kicked my eighty-year-old member in the stomach and ran for the door.

I heard her scream and then, even over my hyperventilating breath, I heard her crashing down the hall after me. Halfway down the hall I glanced over my shoulder and confirmed what my ears were telling me—she had almost caught up with me. *I know I am out of shape, but really?*

The door ahead of me was closed. I could never open it toward me and still get out without her catching me. Resting against the bottom of the stairwell was Bertha's newspaper retriever, a three-foot pole with a mechanical arm on the end of it. I grabbed my only line of defense, swiveled around and Bertha ran straight into it.

She growled and I screamed.

I didn't know what to do, I just stood there with a three-foot rod impaled six inches into my own member's chest as she swiped at my face and spat blood, saliva, and hot air out of her mouth. *At least her halitosis had improved.*

It seemed like an eternity before Bertha finally collapsed in her hallway.

With one hand on the newspaper retriever and another grasping for the doorway, I opened the door and ran out into the sunlight and fresh air, leaving the retriever impaled in Bertha's chest.

I slammed the door closed behind me and ran ten yards into

the driveway. *What did I just do? What do I do now?* It took me longer than it should have to realize I needed to call the police.

I fumbled in my pocket for my phone and dialed 911. I breathlessly tried to explain to the operator what had just happened. I thought I was destined for jail, who would believe I had to defend myself from an old lady? I was scared. I was angry that no one would believe me. How could they? I was embarrassed. Visions of me being defrocked ran through my mind. What would my wife and kids think of me when I was in prison?

But the operator seemed to know more about what had just happened than I did. After I ran down the driveway to get the address for the operator, she began to question me, "Did she bite you or scratch you anywhere?"

I took a quick survey of my arms, "No. No, I don't think so."

"Did any of her blood or spit, or any other fluid get on you?"

I wiped some blood off the back of my hand, "Yes, some did. Is that bad? Is that bad!?"

"Alright, I need you to wipe that off of you as quickly as possible, and do not, I repeat, do not let it come into contact with your eyes, mouth, or any open wounds."

I put the phone on speaker and set it on the hood of my pickup. Then I ripped my bloody clerical shirt off and threw it on the ground. Then I took the hand sanitizer from the glove compartment of the pickup and spread it across my hands, arms, and face.

At this point I heard the sirens coming down the road. I turned to see a rusty police cruiser slide sideways off the gravel road and into the drive. The cruiser sped up the drive and skidded to a stop some ten yards from me, dust flowing past it.

I took one step toward the officer and his gun was drawn and pointed at me. "Stop right there, Reverend."

I put my hands up and stepped back, "Woah, yes, Tom. I swear it was self-defense."

"How do you feel?"

"What?" *Why would someone pointing a gun at me be wondering about my feelings*, "I don't know, I'm terrified."

"No, no. Fever. Dizzy. Anything like that?" he asked, his

eyes narrowing at me.

The world seemed to be spinning around me and I was sweating like mad, "I don't know, I'm freaked out."

He glanced down at my dirty shirt with its blood-spattered sleeves, "Did any of her blood get in your mouth or eyes?"

"I don't know. I don't think so. Just on my hands."

"Ok. Ok. Ummm." He kept his gun trained on my chest while he gestured with his left hand toward the car. "You're not in trouble, with the law that is, but I have to ask you to get in the back of the cruiser. Slowly." He stepped away from his car, giving me a wide berth as I, still with my hands up, crept toward the back door.

I was near tears at this point. "Tom, what's going on?" I asked as I sat in the back of his cruiser.

He looked pale and shook his head, "Reverend, I wish I knew." Then he slammed the door shut after I got in.

Once I was in the car, he holstered his gun and spoke to me through the window. "So . . . she was just crazy fast and super violent, huh?"

I nodded, "Yeah, crazy is right. She sprinted at me, trying to scrape me and bite me. She was growling like a wolf and," I couldn't suppress a shudder, "I think she ate her animals." I put my hand to my face to stop from gagging once more. Then I remembered the blood on my hands and moved them away from my face quickly.

"Jeepers. It's really here," Tom said, running his hand through his hair.

"What is?" Then it all clicked. *The random acts of violence.* I sat back in my seat. "You mean the violence on the coasts . . . "

Tom hung his head, "It isn't just on the coasts." He turned toward the house. "Is she dead?"

"I think so. I stabbed her in the chest with her newspaper grabber thing. Nothing else would stop her."

He took a step toward the house and I couldn't help but fear for him, "I know it's not my job, but don't you want to wait for backup?"

Tom turned and gave a sad little chuckle. "Out here there isn't any."

Tom was in the house only for a few minutes, then he came out and taped off every entrance and posted a biohazard notice on the door.

When he got back, he studied me closely for a few moments. "Now that you've had a few minutes to calm down, how do you feel?"

I took a few deep breaths, "I mean—I'm still pretty wound up, but I've stopped sweating. I'm not puking. I think it was all adrenaline and emotions."

He nodded and checked a piece of paper that he had in the car. I heard him mumble under his breath, "Not airborne, transferable through bodily fluids and water. Infected have high fever," he looked at me out of the corner of his eye, "and turn violent within one to ten minutes depending on the dosage of virus." He checked his watch then looked at me, "Alright, Reverend, sorry but I had to be careful."

He opened the door for me and I got out of the cruiser, "I understand. I think. So was she dead already? Like, you know," I felt my face redden, "like the movies?"

Tom shook his head, "No, they ain't the walking dead. Just sick. Real sick."

"So a sickness that makes them angry and violent."

Tom shrugged, "They think so. I need to stay here and clean some stuff up and submit a report. You go home and," he looked at me, "actually first, I need those clothes."

I looked around for a moment, "Really?"

"Yeah, no joke. You can keep your skivvies, burn them when you get home, though. Then get cleaned up, oh, and stay in town, they may need a statement from you."

"Who?" I asked as I felt a blush creep into my cheeks while I took off my white undershirt.

"The feds. This is getting bigger."

I took a deep breath and took off my dress shoes, socks, and khakis. Then I walked gingerly on my bare feet through the gravel drive to my pickup.

"Boil your water, and, Reverend," I turned toward him. He looked at me with wide but sad eyes, "Pray."

Only the kids were snickering when I raced into the house with only my briefs on. Miranda, mouth agape, followed after me while I grabbed a plastic bag and raced up the stairs to our room.

23

"Where in the world are your clothes!?" she yelped as I sanitized my hands once more before rifling through my dresser for a new change of underwear and clothes. "And what is the bag for?"

I wasn't ignoring her, I just didn't know what to say as I ran past her to our bathroom and changed, throwing my old briefs into the bag and washing my hands. "It's here," was all I managed as I walked briskly past her and down the stairs to the garage.

The whole family followed me out as I threw the bag into our outdoor patio fireplace. "Is Dad completely crazy now?" Valentine asked, a little less surprised than I would have liked. Miranda raised an eyebrow and shrugged as I poured gas into the fire pit and set it on fire. "That's plastic, Dad, what are you—" Then a more horrifying thought must have come to her mind. She yelped, "Wait? Dad, did anyone see you running around in your underwear? I swear if some of my friends—"

"Everyone back!" I shouted, "Do not go near the smoke." I had no idea if the sickness carried in the smoke.

Luke burst out laughing as I shepherded them back into the house, "That must have been one stinky toot to have to burn your under—"

"Enough!" I cut short his joke that normally would have sent me rolling. He tensed up, and for the first time, the kids started to look uneasy.

"Honey, what is wrong?" Miranda asked, her voice quietly serious and wavering.

I shook my head, "It's here, the virus or sickness or whatever it is."

Miranda leaned against the doorframe of the living room and stared at me. "You're serious, aren't you?"

"Dead serious."

Miranda started pacing, "Alright, alright, no one panic, we will be fine."

Luke's laughter turned to shock, his mouth fell open, "The kids at school said they are monsters—"

Miranda waved a hand at him, "Don't be ridiculous, Luke. They are simply sick and—" she looked at me out of the corner of her eye and then turned slowly toward me. "Did you see one?"

The whole family stared at me. *I couldn't lie, could I?* I slowly nodded. Miranda's eyes went wide. "Kids, to your rooms."

They protested, but I agreed with Miranda. *How do we tell them I killed someone from church?*

When their footsteps and grumbles fell quiet ("Was their blood green?" "No, Luke, go upstairs!" "Did you get it on video?" "Of course not, Val, go *upstairs!*"), Miranda and I talked in the kitchen with hushed voices, not because we thought the kids were listening, but because how else did you talk about something like this?

Ten minutes later Miranda was on the phone with her family, telling them everything I had gleaned from Tom and warning them. I was with the kids in the living room, explaining to them that there was a sickness and to keep them safe they had to follow new rules. I told them I was turning off the water to every sink but the kitchen sink and they were not allowed to use it, only we were. They could use the boiled water. For everything.

Miranda told me her family was doing fine and nothing outside of a few small fights had erupted in their town. Her parents had our niece, Noelle, at their house while Miranda's older sister, Madelyn and her husband, Rob, went back to their house downtown for more supplies.

I knew I had calls to make as well. I had family. I had a District President to report to. I knew I should have called them, but I couldn't find the words and I was afraid. I was afraid of making my mom worry, afraid I couldn't be a pastor anymore, afraid of what I would tell the members, afraid to see their anger and fear when they found out their pastor had harmed one of his flock. Instead, I did what I do best—I did nothing.

Around about the time our Ash Wednesday service would have been starting next door, I stole a glance to the west, checking to see if any cars arrived in the church parking lot next door. Not even Eve, the seventy-year-old widow who hadn't missed a service in her life, showed up. Fifteen minutes after the service was supposed to start, I stopped looking. Even Martha, who always showed up late, didn't seem to be coming either.

I stumbled away from the window and down the hall to my office in a coughing fit. And each cough made the increasing pain behind my eyes throb. Doubled over my desk, trying not to retch, my mind, when not searing with pain, raced. *Was my cold just getting worse from anxiety? Or did a drop of blood make it into my veins? Maybe the virus took longer to incubate than they thought?*

On Ash Wednesday, a day I should have been in the Lord's house, I was locked in my office. When my spirit should have been prostrate, I was soon lying on my back, with an icepack on my head instead of ashes. Regardless, it was all too easy to meditate on my sin and frailty that night.

The verse I never got to share with Bertha was still rattling in my head. "Do not be anxious about anything." *But how, Lord?*

The Wrath to Come

I shot up from the small puddle of drool I left on the floor. I didn't even feel the pain in my stiff neck or the pounding of my headache, I was too afraid. Afraid because I had completely forgotten to hold worship the night before. Only after I tripped and fell in my haste to get to my desk did I realize that I had canceled the service. I laid on the floor and, for half a thought, enjoyed the relief, but soon afterward I was crushed under the freight of the terrible events that led to the worship service being canceled. I cried out in fear and crawled away from the door, afraid that I had contracted the virus, but then calmed myself with the realization that I didn't have a burning desire to rip anyone's throat out. The fever must have just been from a spring cold and the headache from stress. I laid in my office for some time, rubbing my temples and telling myself that if I was infected, I probably wouldn't be thinking the thoughts in my head.

Eventually I pulled my way back into my desk chair and sat with my head in my hands, still trying to process the events of the previous day. I had been exuberant to have the evening off so I could stay up late and sleep in, but now I was up early and wishing everything could go back to normal. I pressed my fingers into my eyes until it hurt, trying to push out the images of Bertha's twisted face. I looked up when I heard a sound ringing over the town like church bells should have the night before: sirens.

I left my office and found the family upstairs looking out the window of our stairway landing. It faced west, giving us a vantage point over the bit of land between our house and the church. At first, I wondered if there was something happening at the church, but soon saw they were looking past the church toward downtown. We could see the backs of the houses that lined the highway and, past them, glimpses of traffic. We watched Tom's police cruiser going up the street, followed by our town ambulance and volunteer fire truck.

Miranda was holding the phone, every minute or so trying a different number, listening to the phone for a minute, then shaking her head in frustration. She looked at me, her eyes puffy, "Our phones still work, but I can't reach anyone, not my parents," she gave me a sad look, "not yours." *So they had it worse than we did. Lord, have mercy on them.*

I could see Luke's freckled face reflected in the window, his face was so close to it—his expression going back and forth between fear and awe—he always loved sirens but was terrified of monsters, even though he was too old to admit it anymore. Valentine stood behind him with a blanket wrapped around her. Her knuckles were white from clutching it so tight, as if it could protect her from everything she saw around her. "It's getting bad isn't it?" she asked.

"No, honey." I put my arm around her and felt her trembling, "It's just a few isolated incidents."

She broke her gaze from the window and set it on me, "I have the internet too, Dad. I know it's getting bad out there. And I know Mom can't get through to Grandpa and Grandma."

"Yeah well, things are always worse on the news and in the big cities. And Grandpa and Grandma Acton said they were leaving the city. They'll be fine. We'll be fine." Then I reached out my hand, "Either way you won't be hearing about it. Give me your phone."

Valentine looked at me like I was infected, "Dad, you can't be—"

"Give it here."

She narrowed her eyes, then let the blanket fall from one shoulder and tossed her phone onto the chair at the top of the stairs and stormed off to her room. "I'll get the news from the kids at school anyways."

But she wouldn't get the chance. Not long afterward the sirens in town were replaced by another sound, a man's voice booming through the house. Miranda and Valentine screamed, Luke went pale white and looked at me. I stared at him for a moment, paralyzed, before I realized the voice was coming from outside the house.

The voice even drew Valentine out of her room and she joined us in our race down the stairs. We congregated in front of our picture window in the living room. A county sheriff's car was slowly rolling down the street with our mayor hanging out the passenger window holding a megaphone. In the backseat two deputies sat, their heads swiveling around looking for some threat, the barrels of their assault rifles hanging out the window.

The mayor repeated the same lines over and over, "School is canceled for the week. Stay in your homes. Boil your water. Conserve your food. Stay calm but stay vigilant. Exercise extreme caution when in contact with others and if there is an emergency, I repeat, only if it is an emergency, report to City Hall."

I looked at Luke next to me, hoping that an excuse to get out of school (I couldn't count how many schemes he had attempted to get out of class) would bring a smile to his face. Instead he turned to me with eyes wide with fear, a look that scared me as much as Bertha's ravenous gaze had. "Dad, what's going on?" he asked.

I looked at Miranda, who had put her arms around Luke, and she shook her head at me.

"Well there's no sense lying to them, especially about the obvious." I looked at my frightened children, wishing I could give them comfort. Instead, I gave them the truth. "Something is wrong. Some people are getting sick and getting really violent and really strong."

Miranda nodded her head and put on a fake smile. "But look," her voice was higher, trying to sound cheery, which only made her seem more afraid, "the authorities know about it and will take care of it." *Lord, I hope she is right.*

Valentine slumped into the wall. "And until they do we have to sit here and do nothing all day?"

Miranda raised her chin up, keeping a hand on Luke's shoulder, cleared her throat, and said, sternly, "No. No. You have homework to do, remember?"

The kids complained, but Miranda and I both agreed angry

29

children were better than terrified ones. Soon they were in the kitchen grumbling about how their projects weren't due for weeks. Only after an hour did Miranda and I decide we couldn't make them work forever, so we let them play some games and I even gave Valentine her phone back, though I had disabled the internet on it.

"The Superintendent sent the same message out that the Mayor did," she said, as she scrolled through two dozen text messages she had received in just a couple hours. She stopped and put her hand over her mouth. "And Jake Robinson is dead."

Miranda took her phone from her, read the message, and asked, "That really tall boy from the basketball team?"

Valentine sniffed, "Yeah. Katelyn's boyfriend. She snuck out to see him and found the police and everyone there."

Miranda, reading the messages, finished the story, "Then the police took her home without letting her see him or telling her what happened." She looked up and hesitated to give Valentine her phone back, but, in the end, she did. "I'm sorry, honey. But he's with Jesus now. If he was, um, *sick*, he isn't anymore."

Val wiped a tear from under her glasses, typed something into her phone, then made for the stairs.

"What are you doing?" Miranda asked, "Why don't you stay with us?"

She stopped on the stairs, "Fine. Dad, tell me a verse about heaven, Katelyn needs to hear it."

The rest of the day was quiet aside from the sirens going up and down the highway. After a dozen passes even Luke stopped looking out the windows at them. Until the afternoon, when we heard a constant hum of cars going down the highway, interspersed with honks and shouts. "What is going on out there? A parade?" Luke wondered aloud.

I peeked out the upstairs window at the highway and, before I could take in the sight of the traffic, the kids had joined me. Cars packed to the roofs, trucks pulling trailers, buses, vans, RV rigs, every sort of car was lined up all down the highway. Their horns honked, some drove on the shoulder to pass, while others sped through the town on the wrong side of the road. They were all headed south, away from the big city an hour north of us.

"Are they all leaving the city?" I asked, trying to hide the quiver in my voice. *Did we need to leave? But where would we even go?* "And why aren't they taking the interstate?" The six-lane interstate was fifteen miles east of us and certainly provided easier travel than the potholed highway we lived on.

Miranda raised an eyebrow at me, "Probably because it's jammed with traffic too." She held up her phone. We put our heads together and watched a news clip of accident after accident on the interstate and traffic on the shoulder; people were even abandoning their cars and heading south on foot, desperate to get out of the city.

For the rest of the afternoon the kids stared out the upstairs window as if it was showing a horror movie they couldn't stop watching. Meanwhile, Miranda stared at the actual television with rapt attention and a note pad. The news feed was full of sightings and reports of the virus, and reports of violence and fires in the city. A ticker on the bottom of the television listed everything the media had learned of the virus, though they admitted they weren't certain about any of it. Miranda stood in front of it scribbling everything down.

I tried, unsuccessfully, to distract the kids until nightfall when they finally seemed to lose interest with the window, even though cars continued to rumble through town. Luke was easy enough to keep busy, I had promised him weeks ago that we would finish painting his model army tank and, on that day, I finally found the time to do it. But Valentine was beyond consolation. She was convinced the Second Coming was happening (I wasn't terribly convinced it wasn't either). She kept biting her nails and crying as she texted her friends who were leaving town, or were speculating how their lives were over, and wondering whose actually were. I tried to talk to her about it, but she slammed her door in my face muttering something about taking a "zombie" to homecoming next year. I thought about demanding her to open the door, but what was I going to do? Ground her? This was hard enough for all of us.

An hour later I carried a plate of food to Valentine's room and knocked on the door.

The only answer was a grunt.

"I brought you some food. Hey, it could be your last meal." I listened for a laugh but didn't hear anything. Typical on a normal day, let alone this one. "Valentine open up, take your food and let me check your window, then I will leave you be."

After a few footfalls on the hardwood floor I heard a slam on the other side of the door. Then a scratch. The sounds brought back a shadow of the horror I felt at Bertha's. *You are being ridiculous, she isn't infected.* "Valentine, answer me right now!"

She cried out in disgust. *Or was it a growl? Did she drink some unboiled water? Lord, please no*, I prayed and threw my shoulder into the door. She swung it open at the same instant and I, along with her plate of food, went flying into her room.

"Ugh, Dad! That isn't funny."

I stumbled to a stop, "I thought you were—" Then I saw the bookcase she had slid out of the way of the door.

She crossed her arms and looked away, "Yeah, I was mad and the bookcase made me feel better. Sorry."

"Never mind it," I said while I cleaned up the food. "Go get a plate of food."

She left without a word while I finished picking potatoes off the floor. She hadn't returned by the time I finished so I made sure her window was locked, drew the blinds, and went back downstairs. I found Val sitting on the counter eating while Miranda told her about how awkward her prom was. I thought about making a corny joke about her prom being awful because she didn't go with me, but Valentine seemed engaged, so I let it go. Instead I did a few terrible impersonations for Luke. He laughed at some of them, did a few of his own, and after fifteen minutes he managed a few bites of dinner. *Poor kid.*

That evening we turned the television off, put the phones away (which even Valentine agreed was a good idea) and played some board games. As we sat there, with our world fraying at the edges, I couldn't help but think of how ungrateful I had been. My beautiful daughter and wife were snuggled under a blanket, scheming to conquer Luke's and my army on the board between us. But even as they plotted in fun, even as Luke had his freckled nose only an inch away from the game piece, lost in thought, I knew fear lurked in all of them. And I wished I could take it away, make it right. I prayed that God would. *If we could go back to normal, Lord, I will never take them for granted again.* It was a bargaining prayer. How many of them had I said, how many had the Lord heard in His infinite days? And how many did we ever uphold? I thanked God that He was faithful to His promises even when we weren't, and then I prayed that, not based on my gratefulness, but based on His Son and His mercy He would keep us safe and give us grace sufficient for the days ahead.

At nighttime devotions it was hard to focus, it was obvious what our worries were. I read the reading meant for Bertha. "Do not be anxious." Maybe the words rang hollow, because we all still worried, but perhaps they, like me, got some comfort that there was still some order, the King of kings still reigned. *This will all work out alright.*

The evening with the family itself would have been idyllic if not for the horror of what I had seen the day before nagging at me. If not for the momentary panic attacks that stole my breath away when I heard a sound in my children's rooms or when I thought of what was to come when I got in touch with my District President the next day. The night would have been a beautiful spring night, with the moon shining high and bright, if not for the darkening storm of fear I saw growing in my wife's eyes, if not for the questions from the children every time a siren screamed across town and brought them out of their rooms.

Miranda and I talked into the night about how we were holding up, how the kids seemed. We wanted to be honest with them but still protect them emotionally, spiritually, and physically. After some time our discussion was joined by the eerie sound of cattle lowing.

It wasn't rare to hear the cows from the cattle yard a quarter mile outside of town, carried by the wind. Miranda shot a sideways glance out the window as we talked, but made no mention of the sound until the lowing turned louder and more desperate. The cows almost sounded like they were screaming when we peered through the blinds on our picture window and looked east. "That's no late-night sorting," I said forebodingly.

"Maybe a coyote got in the yard?" Miranda said with a shudder that betrayed what she really thought was there. I didn't dare haunt her more by describing the images of dead and eaten animals that I had seen at Bertha's.

I let the blinds fall back into place. "If things are wandering around out there, let's make sure they stay out there." We were about to move our couch in front of the door when we heard Luke at the top of the stairs. "Mom, I'm scared." Miranda raced up the stairs to encourage him while I checked each corner of his room twice and put a piece of wood in his window slide to help him feel safer.

Soon we were back down in the living room. "Should you get, you know, your gun out?" Miranda asked, blushing.

"No." I shook my head, took a swig of water and turned to empty the rest into the sink. I caught myself and laughed bitterly, "I should save this water, shouldn't I?"

Miranda nodded at me, but I could tell she never took less joy in being right. We heard a footstep upstairs, "Probably Luke again," she sighed. "Ugh, I wish those cows would shut up."

I nodded in agreement. The squealing was almost constant now, as if the whole herd was aroused. Then the gunshots started.

I jumped when the thumping of the rifle rolled across the fields; Miranda screamed. We both raced out of the kitchen and up the stairs where our children were up and waiting.

"What's going on?" Valentine asked as the gunfire continued to sound from the trees to the north east.

"I don't know what's going on. But I've never had a chance to shoot that many times at a coyote. It's something else."

That was when Valentine, who always pretended to be hard as stone as she navigated awkard situations with her body, her friends, and boys finally clung to me and sobbed.

"Darren, we talked about what we would tell them!" Miranda said as she took Valentine from me and held her.

"That was before I believed this thing would get this big."

The gunfire still went on, Luke, clutching the banister at the top of the stairs, flinched at every shot, and jumped as the sirens started up again.

"Alright kids, everyone is sleeping in Mom and Dad's room tonight," Miranda said. "Luke, be a brave man and get the sleeping bag from the hall closet. Val, you too, bring your sheets into our room and put them on the floor." Miranda looked at me as if to apologize for renting out our room, but I had no objections—I didn't want them out of our sight ever again if I could help it. I nodded at her and stalked off to my office to do what needed to be done.

I eyed my gun case in the corner of the office and got the key out from the pages of one of the western novels on my shelf. My pump shotgun was simple and I never cleaned it as much as I should have, but I had a hundred shells and trusted it much more than my rifle that I could never seem to hit anything with. I pulled the shotgun out, put a few shells in the tube, but never cranked one into the chamber. *These days are dangerous enough without shooting yourself.* With the gun out, loaded, and sitting on my desk, I felt safer. At least if something came to the house I could fight it.

No guns would help me, however, when I had to preach a sermon to Bertha's family. After checking that the kids were safe with Miranda in our room and all the doors and windows were locked in the house, I sat back at my desk and tried to think of what I could possibly say. *"Sorry I stabbed your dear grandmother, she was scaring me."* I put my hands in my hair and groaned. *I cannot do this sermon.* I started to draft an email to my District President asking him to do the service for me. Then I deleted it and asked him to take over with ministering to the family. Then I deleted it a second time.

How could I minister to anyone knowing I killed a member? I put my head in my hands thinking about what a terrible pastor I was.

I drafted, instead, a letter of resignation. *God's people deserved better than me.*

It wasn't terribly long, but by the end of it my chin was quivering and my throat burning as I fought back tears. I hadn't even talked to Miranda about it. What would I do to support my family? I had no other training or skill. Where would we live? The house belonged to the congregation, not to us. But this was bigger than that; I was convinced I was unfit for the ministry. As I worked up the courage to send the e-mail, I reread it one last time. Halfway through, the power went out.

The Shadow of Death

Everything went pitch black behind our drawn blinds that shielded us from moonlight and hungry eyes. I scrambled out of the room, knocking a picture off the wall as I felt my way down the hallway. I stumbled up the stairs toward the children. Luke was trying to fight back sobs, more than likely embarrassed to admit that the night light going out terrified him. Miranda held him with one hand while the other tried to find the flashlight she had in her bed-stand. Valentine was sitting up in her makeshift pile of sheets, trying to help calm her brother, but looking wide-eyed and scared as well.

It took half an hour of me checking dark corners, false comfort, and Miranda's singing to get Luke and Valentine settled back in their beds. Not long after, I, with my shotgun high on the dresser across the room, laid there next to them, sleepless. My mind rattled between resignation, Bertha's growling face, how long it would take the power to come back on, and what it would mean if it never did. After an hour of tossing and turning; after an hour of getting out of bed, checking out a noise, and going back to bed; after an hour of restlessness, I knew I wasn't falling asleep anytime soon. I went back to my office, cleared off my desk by candlelight and dragged it into the living room, where I sat in the dark listening, worrying, and praying. Eventually, long after midnight, the sirens, gunshots, and squealing cattle serenaded me to sleep.

If it had all, blessedly, just been a dream, I would have groaned when my alarm went off in the morning. Instead, I gasped in fright and scrambled up the stairs trying to silence it before it woke the kids sleeping in my room or something more sinister outside our house. Miranda, laying on the bed, was obviously quicker than I and shut it off before I got up the stairs. After I settled down and checked on the kids, I took the batteries out of the alarm. *We might need them sometime.* Then, with a baseball bat in my hand, I crept through the house, jumping only a little bit when I opened the kitchen door into our garage and a neighbor's cat hissed and escaped through an open garage window, which I promptly closed.

Soon I found myself back at my desk in the living room. Unable to concentrate enough for my morning devotions, I skipped straight to the prayers and prayed for peace, a cure, and forgiveness. Then, with a bit of guilt, I remembered to pray for the people suffering from the infection itself, their loved ones, and my family. *Why didn't I call my mom back?* I comforted myself knowing that I would see them again, prayerfully, in this life, but if not, at the feast on the Last Day—where the only things feasting will be healthy and happy.

Miranda and the kids shot me, and my new desk space, puzzled looks when they came down for breakfast, but they didn't say anything. Nor did anyone talk much while they ate breakfast or, more accurately, poked at it. "Neither of you are leaving this table until you finish it," Miranda ordered. "We can't waste anything, not right now," she explained, her voice cracking.

"We have to eat everything? Finally, my time to shine!" I said, patting my belly. The forced joke, while drawing no laughter (something any dad is used to), did get a few smiles and took the edge off the morning.

After breakfast, Miranda took charge, trying to keep the kids busy. She had them do homework again and then chores. She had them storing water, cleaning up, gathering candles and matches. Miranda was wonderful, even though I didn't miss the fact that she kept trying her phone, turning it off and on to conserve the battery we had no way of charging. She kept the children so active they even stopped looking out the windows at sirens and barking dogs.

Everyone noticed when the gunfire returned, however. This time it wasn't far off at the cattle ranch, it was in town. Miranda screamed and I told the kids to get in the closet, which they gladly

37

did. The shots were sporadic at first, resounding from different parts of town and followed by a string of sirens. After an hour, the shots were still going off around town, but I couldn't see any of the fighting from any of our windows. *Did I keep them in a closet forever? Is this the new normal, raising children with gunfire as common as a passing car?* As the day went on the gunfire remained and the sirens stopped chasing them.

Eventually, necessity made us let the kids out of the hall closet, though new house rules banned them from going near the windows and from sitting on chairs. They played their games on the floor, or at least acted like it. Luke never noticed that he had six cards in his poker hand; Val didn't seem to care.

As darkness fell on our little town that night, so did the chaos. The sirens had long since been localized near city hall, across the highway from us. The cracks of gunfire from the neighborhood were reminiscent of the Fourth of July, except instead of lights in the sky, there was smoke. Pillars of it, shaded blue and red from fires and sirens, stretched upward on a night so eerie, so abnormal, the wind didn't even blow through the prairie town.

Miranda and I, tired of forcing the kids back into our room, sat on the floor of the upstairs landing, peering out the blinds toward downtown. We watched spotlights, headlights, and flashing lights flicker between houses and through the trees, but none of them could overcome the growing darkness—darkness of silhouettes running through the town, the darkness of a night blackened by a smoke-filled sky.

Miranda let the curtains fall and sat slumped against the wall. After a moment, she tilted her head to the side. "Why isn't Tank barking?" I strained to see around the church to the neighbor's yard, but it was no good. It was too dark and the angle all wrong. "Why aren't any of them barking?" she asked.

I shuddered and thought about Bertha's dogs, eaten by their ravenous owner.

But there were other sounds in the night, more than sirens and gunfire. They were faint, as there was no wind to carry them, and I think for several hours we tried to ignore them, but they were there: screams.

Around midnight, the rate of gunfire peaked. In a twisted

grand finale, the shots ran together in a furious cacophony. The kids ran out of our room crying and I tackled them to the ground and shouted at them to stay there. Miranda, through her tears, tried to comfort us as we lay on the floor saying, "This is good. This means the good guys are fighting them, err, it, back."

Valentine covered her ears and sobbed, not caring that her eyeshadow smeared down her face; Luke, awkwardly lying next to me, held to me so tightly that my shirt was tearing where his hands clawed into me—I paid it no mind. And I laid with my face pressed into the carpet praying, "Lord, have mercy. Christ, have mercy. Lord, have mercy."

I don't know how many times I said the prayer, and I have no idea how long the shooting went on. But eventually it tapered off enough to hear engines roaring and tires screeching; it tapered off enough to hear screams and shouts. And then it was gone.

Everyone looked up, eyes wide with fear, not knowing if the silence was worse than the sounds of battle raging in our small little town. I pried Luke off of me, stumbled my way to the window and looked out at the same scene as before: fires burned, blue and red sirens flashed through the trees, and silhouettes moved through the streets. Except now they weren't running, they were walking.

I should have felt hopeful. Hopeful that the panic was past and calm was restored. But the hair was still standing on the back of my neck. The walkers weren't walking with a purpose. They were not racing to set up a perimeter. They were not waving to their allies. They were not aiding the wounded to an ambulance.

They milled about aimlessly and they wandered down the alleys between houses. I swallowed a scream when I saw one ripping at a body on the ground. I fell to the floor and shook my head at Miranda. "Oh God! Oh God! Not good, not good!"

She wrenched Luke's hands off her and crawled to me and grabbed my hand. "What did you see?"

I took a ragged breath. "We lost."

She put her hand over her mouth and then crawled the rest of the way to the window and peeled back the curtains. I joined her not long after and whispered, "You may not want to see it, but it's in the gap between the Franklin house and the one to the right of it."

Her gasp told me she had seen what I did.

Then there was a gunshot across town and the silhouettes weren't walking aimlessly anymore, they ran toward the sound. Soon, the small part of the street we could see was empty.

An hour later, the lights were still flashing, haphazard shots echoed through tree and building, and silhouettes walked, ran, or feasted throughout the town. The kids were back in their beds on the floor of our room, but I knew that, at the very least, Luke wasn't asleep; I could hear a sob every now and again and Miranda desperately pleading for him to be strong and to be quiet. Downstairs, I paced with my shotgun in my hands. I went from window to window, looking for any sign of movement and trying not to think about how terrifying it would be to peel back the curtains and see a bloodied face pressed up against the glass.

Miranda stayed upstairs. Sometimes when I glanced up she was gone, in our room comforting Luke and Valentine, other times she was peering out the landing window, other times, mercifully, she had nodded off as she sat up against the wall under the sill. She gave a start and spun toward the window when she heard an engine roar in town. I raced to the side window on the first floor to peer toward downtown as well. Between the houses I caught a glimpse of the mayor's large pickup truck racing out of town and into the countryside.

In spite of all my horror, I felt a grin creep into the side of my mouth as I thought how glad I was I never voted for that mayor. A dozen or so silhouettes chased the mayor's truck down the road, and I could only hope they would keep running. *Run away, run away, and leave us alone.*

I stepped away from the window when I heard Luke crying again. Apparently, the screeching tires startled him, and I could hear Miranda whispering to him as he took deep breaths between cries. But the cries turned to screams when we heard something hit our front window. I crashed into the dining room table in my haste to get to the front of the house. I never glanced up the stairs, but heard Miranda trying to quiet the kids.

But even if she could, it was too late. Something was rhythmically slamming against our front window, steadily harder. I walked up to it, hoping the moon would silhouette whatever was making the sound through the blinds. But it didn't. I slunk to the corner of the blinds and peeled them back ever so slightly.

There was nothing at first, and then a paralyzing fear gripped me when a bloody hand smacked the window once again. A lady from across the street was now free from the nursing home and her wheelchair. I couldn't remember her name, even if I wasn't terrified, but the arthritis ridden lady who played cards while I visited my members now had half her scalp peeled back and was slamming her knobby and twisted hands on my window.

I fell backwards and in a shaky whisper, not daring to take my eyes off the window, called up to Miranda, "It's someone from the home. I think she's sick."

Miranda jumped each time the window was struck. "Like, *sick* sick?"

"Yeah, what do we do?"

Smack.

"Just be quiet, right? They will go away," she called out as loud as she dared down the stairs.

But the kids were still crying.

Her next smack had the sickening sound of glass cracking.

I pulled out my phone and called 911; there was no answer—not that I expected one.

I cursed as I squeezed the shotgun in my hands. The grips were slick with sweat from my palms. "Get down here, Miranda."

She had to shake Luke to get him to let go of her and Val pulled him into her lap to give him comfort and keep him at the top of the stairs. "Come hold on to me, Luke, help me feel safer," the brave girl suggested.

Miranda quickly and quietly walked down the stairs and to my side. In the meantime, I shoved a handful of shotgun shells into my pocket.

"Lock the door behind me and don't open it again 'til I tell you."

"Are you sure about this?" She put a cold and shaky hand on my arm.

There was another smack and a louder crack.

I nodded and then I unlocked our deadbolt and listened.

Smack.

I opened the door and slid out into the smoky still night, my shotgun at my shoulder.

The nursing home's generator was apparently still running and gave me some light to look down to my right at our front window. The window was cracked and each time the lady smacked the window with her arm her dangling scalp swayed and the crack in our window grew larger.

"Excuse me, but—"

The lady turned and growled.

"Leave now, or—"

She ran at me and clawed at me through the porch railing.

"Please no," I pleaded with her and tried to fire a shot in the air, but the gun clicked.

I cursed and cranked a shell into the chamber while she started to climb the porch. I fired a shot into the sky and she threw a twisted leg over the porch railing, still clawing for me.

With tears in my eyes, I cranked in another round, aimed, pulled the trigger, and sent her somersaulting backwards off the porch railing.

"Oh, God, forgive me. Lord have mercy."

What do I tell my kids? I wondered as I heard them screaming inside.

The growls to my left pulled me out of my thoughts.

My chin quivered as I saw a bloodied old man dragging himself toward me. Behind him, silhouetted by the manor's lights, four more residents sprinted at me.

I backed into my front door, I wanted to scream to have Miranda let me in, but I couldn't speak and it wouldn't have helped. *They were coming.*

I took a deep breath, found some semblance of a voice, and shouted—more of a croak, "If you step on my property I will shoot."

None of them listened.

I had missed plenty of pheasants hunting on the Great Plains, and while a man was larger than a pheasant, I had never shot with such nerves and terror. My first shot went wide, missing the closest runner who was on my driveway now. I cranked in another shell and hit him square the next time, he crumpled in the drive. I fumbled in my pockets and jammed another shell in the chamber. The next runner made it to the steps before I put him down, the third was on the steps when I pulled the trigger and nothing happened. *You only put one shell in, dolt.* Counting to two isn't as easy when you are getting run down.

I screamed and dove off the porch. The runner stumbled trying to get over the railing and allowed me time to find a shell that fell out of my pocket and onto the lawn. I slammed the chamber shut and landed a shot in the man's shoulder. He spun around, fell over, but was immediately after me again. I could feel another shell under me, I rolled over and put it in the chamber. My next shot hit the man in the chest.

He fell backwards, growling and working his way to his feet again.

"Why won't you die?" I shouted.

I wheeled around and ran into the street while the runner chased after me. I dropped several shells but was able to get three in before I turned back to see the man, thankfully, slowing. A few steps later he collapsed to his knees and tried to crawl after me. I aimed the gun at his head, but I could tell he was dying. *Do I save the bullet, or put him out of his misery? Do they even feel pain?*

The growling at my feet made me spin away from the dying man. I jumped backwards and saw the man, who had been crawling in my driveway, reach for me. I wouldn't have recognized him if not for his beard and, albeit bloody, football jersey. It was a member of mine from the nursing home. "Chris?" I shot a glance back at the runner who was crawling still. "God, why?" I asked, shaking my head at the man who used to be so full of joy. It had all been replaced with hunger and rage.

I was sick of killing, sick of it. And there was no way I could shoot another member. I ran away from the two crawling men, though the one I had already shot was even having trouble crawling with all the blood left in his wake.

I thought about running around the back of the house in hopes that these two crawlers wouldn't try and get into the house all night, but one look at the darkness covering our side alley and the thought of more infected racing toward the sound of gunfire persuaded me to run around Chris and onto the porch.

"Miranda, let me in now."

I fell into the house and Miranda slammed the door shut and locked it. The kids were staring down at me. I tried to hide my tears. "It's bad. It's bad. It's bad." It was all I could say as I paced around, running my free hand through my hair.

I heard scratching at the door. Miranda looked worried, but I convinced her I didn't think he could get in. I moved the couch in front of the door, just in case, and re-stuffed my pockets with shotgun shells. I stared at the door while Miranda demanded I change my clothes. She used gloves to put them in plastic bags and threw them in the garage. Even after I got new clothes on, I felt dirty. We used a flashlight to look for any blood and used disinfectant wipes on any skin I had exposed. But even reeking of chemicals, I still felt dirty inside and out. Was the virus on me? There certainly was one in me if I could kill people like I just did.

The scratching stopped after a few hours, though I did have to grab Miranda a few times, who, driven mad by the constant scratching, growling, and moaning, wanted to kill the zombie herself. It simply wasn't an option, however, since my fight had made our street the most popular part of town for wandering zombies. There were dozens outside on our block, walking, waiting for some greater indication that there might be food somewhere. Eventually the scratching stopped. I suppose Chris died from his wounds in spite of his bloodlust. That was the only good news of the night, *they can die*. I could think of little more merciful than that, that they would die, for their sake and ours.

Back on the upstairs landing, with all our kitchen furniture on the stairs, and our kids finally back in their beds on the floor, we peered out our side window at town. The fires grew brighter, though some of the spotlights and sirens were waning or extinguished. The silhouettes were closer, though, drawn by my gunfire. We watched several of them milling about the church next door. Then, hearing something, they all turned their heads and crashed through the church's glass front doors, growling.

Miranda fell away from the window, put her hand over her mouth, fought off a sob and said a prayer, "I lift my eyes to the hills, from where does my hope come from, my helps comes from the Lord, the maker of heaven and earth."

I stopped myself from pointing out to her that there wasn't a decent sized hill around for a hundred miles.

Dwelling in Deep Darkness

We slept as much as we could between gunshots, screams, and growls. The wind and the settling of the house—sounds we dismissed in a brighter time, in a different life that seemed impossible and so long ago—were now sounds of horror, convincing one or all of us that there was a zombie lurking somewhere. I must have scanned the whole house five times that night. When the sun finally rose and flooded through our drawn blinds, it painted our walls in a shade of red to match the blood that, no doubt, covered the walls of other homes in our town.

When it rose high and bright enough to give me an ounce of courage, I pulled back the blinds far enough to squint into the street. I don't know what I expected to see, the sheriff and coroner taping the street off? Instead, I saw the ashes of our town falling on the bodies littering the lawn and street. I gasped and turned back from the window to Miranda, who had crept up behind me. "There are literally dead people in the streets. What's going on?" I paced for a minute and ran my hands through my hair. "No. No, this can't be," I said to myself while Miranda looked on. "They will come, they have to come. They are busy in the city is all, they will be here soon." As soon as I said it, I knew it was a lie—the cities would be far worse off than us.

Miranda's bloodshot and gray eyes finally found me. They looked like a storm with red streaks of lightning. She said what I knew to be true, but didn't want to accept, "They might not come, Darren. We need to do what we can to survive this."

I shook my head in denial. "No. They'll come. This is

insane, they can't just leave bodies in the street."

Valentine, still quarantined to the upstairs, called down, "What are we going to do?"

Miranda looked at her and her brother, who was staring through the upstairs guardrail, then back to me, her eyebrows raised at me, pleading.

How could I tell them that I had no idea what to do?

I wound up doing what I always did when a decision seemed hard. Nothing. "We are going to sit tight, stay quiet, and wait this out."

No sirens sounded through town that day and the intermittent gunshots, our town's last gasps at resistance, slowly died out through the morning like, for all we knew, billions of people around the world. And then there was nothing to hear. No thump of helicopters like angels coming to save us. No government officials on megaphones heralding safety. Not even the sound of a passing car or humming air conditioner. There was nothing to hear except our own sobs and whispered prayers.

But there was plenty to see. Too much to see. The kids weren't allowed a peek lest they see Tom, his police uniform bloody and torn, lying ravaged outside our church's back door. Lest they see Chris' body on our front porch or his blood that had begun to seep across the threshold of our front door. Lest they see the dozen other bodies lying in the streets and yards and alleys. Lest they see the bodies that moved.

One thing that didn't change with the plague, we found out, was a child's inability to listen to their parents. I raced up the stairs when I heard Valentine screaming. By the time I got there, Miranda had pulled her away from the window and had one hand clamped firmly over our distraught daughter's mouth and another on Luke, who was wrestling to peek out the window. I glared at them both and Luke stopped struggling, but Valentine didn't notice, her eyes were closed tight and leaking tears. I peeked out the window and saw her Spanish teacher ambling behind the church— no, ambling toward our house, where she heard her student, now food, scream.

I saw three more zombies come out of the church and turn their rigid necks toward our house. That was when I realized I was thinking of them as *zombies,* I nearly laughed at the thought of me as some action hero in one of the dozen zombie movies I had seen. I shook my head. They weren't strictly like the zombies from the movies—they weren't dead, though they sure looked like it. But no, *only One raised the dead.*

Two of them, as far as I could tell from their wounds, I had never seen, the third was a county sheriff, with his leg dragging and his green uniform stained red. His long-rifle's strap was wrapped around his leg and he dragged the rifle along beside him, paying no attention to it, only to where he heard a scream—my house.

I turned back and, after Miranda made Valentine promise not to scream, saw her take her hand off Val's mouth. The poor girl turned, sobbing into Miranda's shoulder, stammering, "It's real . . . zombies are real . . . and they are coming." She shook her head, cussed under her breath, and sobbed some more. Meanwhile, Luke shrank back from the window, his eyes wide, mumbling something about monsters.

If I wasn't so scared, I would have laughed that Miranda, even with zombies coming toward us, still managed to reprimand Valentine for the bad word. Instead I hissed at her, "Stay away from the windows and stay quiet."

I crawled to the window and hoped the zombies had lost interest and heard some other sound. At first, I thought they had, until I looked straight down and saw them not five feet from our back door. It was my turn to curse then, but if Miranda chastised me, I didn't notice.

As quietly and quickly as possible, I ran down the stairs. I checked to make sure my shotgun was loaded and stood by the door, waiting. When we first moved in, I was disappointed we didn't have a large glass sliding door to the backyard from our dining room, but on that day I thanked God for the heavy wooden door with only a little window near the top of it. I pressed myself up against the door. I could hear their feet shuffling and I could hear their breathing, thick with phlegm and blood. But they hadn't assaulted the door of the house yet. *Or did they know how to use doors?*

I leaned against the door, still as I could be, given that I was shaking, until my feet were numb. Part of me wanted to run, part of me wanted to kick open the door and be done with it, one way or the other, but I just stood there, trying not to breathe too loudly. I wondered for a while why these zombies weren't sprinting and beating down the door like the zombies I had seen the night before. Then I remembered the silhouettes milling about until a sound sent them running. *The stronger the evidence of food, the stronger the response.* I didn't want to give them any more evidence with a blast of my shotgun, but if they started scratching on my door I would have to.

Ultimately, someone else gave them more evidence. There was a bang somewhere across town, from gunfire or a car running into something or a burning house collapsing, only the good Lord knows. But I do know that I thanked Him when the zombies turned their gaze from our house and ran off across the town. It was a guilty prayer, one you pray when someone else gets the bad break, when the sick person gets the transplant because someone else lost their life too young. Of course, most Christian prayers are that way, thanking One for dying in our place. But He did so willingly, sacrificially, all I was doing was praying that someone else's neck was stuck out in the putrid wind, not ours. I probably didn't even say a prayer for them, maybe I did.

Either way, my plan of doing nothing was reinforced. There were now strict punishments for loud noises. Punishments such as cleaning the bathroom and boiling water. We hung carpets and towels from ceiling fans, chandeliers, and walls to dampen sound. The kids were forbidden from looking out windows and were only allowed downstairs for a good reason. Most of the days we sat around a candle in the upstairs landing while our house got darker, danker, and hotter.

Miranda and the kids begged to open a window, I denied them, even when we stored our refuse in the garage. *Just stay alive at all costs, for a little while longer*, I thought. *They will die or help will come. We just needed a little time.*

But we didn't get enough of it.

After a few dark days in our home, the only thing that time brought us was less food and more heat, less evidence of civilization and more stench, less peace and more despair. I couldn't fathom why help had not come. This was modern America. *Maybe the government brought all their resources to the cities to control the virus there first, then they would come for us.*

It was the most we could hope for, it was the lie we told the kids, because we all, deep down, wouldn't have traded our lot for someone in the city. Not to mention someone who was sick, or elderly, or, Lord have mercy, expecting. *"But turning to them Jesus said, 'Daughters of Jerusalem, do not weep for me, but weep for yourselves and for your children. For behold, the days are coming when they will say, 'Blessed are the barren and the wombs that never bore and the breasts that never nursed!' Then they will begin to say to the mountains, 'Fall on us,' and to the hills, 'Cover us.'"* Still didn't change the fact that there weren't any damned hills around us.

Night was the worst. We didn't dare make noise to drown out the growls and cries from around town. Luke, with his active imagination, barely slept after seeing a PG13 movie. Now with real monsters outside his window he shared a bed with us. That's not entirely true, however—there were only two sleeping in my bed, Miranda and Luke. I spent nights fitfully sleeping on the couch in the living room with my shotgun across my chest.

Before I took my post downstairs, we still had devotion time. At least, the nights Miranda was collected enough to remember. I remembered; *how could I forget?* How could I forget the God of mercy who seemed entirely absent and distant? Yes, I remembered family devotion, but wouldn't remind anyone else. I hated family devotion. Before the plague, I would have loved for either of the kids to ask me a question during devotion time. Now I dreaded them, and they came each night. "Why is God letting this happen? Is He coming back soon? Would a good God even let this happen at all?" I stammered my way through some answers. I used the canned responses I had heard before that seemed well enough to satisfy their curiosity. But when evil is all you can see, it sure is a lot harder to believe them.

Regardless, nearly every night, we prayed for our families, for a cure. Each night we prayed that they would leave our home alone. Thankfully, the Lord, for the most part, listened to that prayer. Though other homes were not as blessed. One afternoon Miranda and I watched nearly two dozen zombies furiously sieging a house on the highway. We watched as they bashed in the windows and crawled through them, over the furniture the people had put against them. It only took minutes for them to get inside.

49

An hour later they slowly, aimlessly, wandered back out one by one, their faces covered in blood and their bellies larger. We didn't know who lived in the home, but Miranda cried anyway and I spent the night pulling my hair out from guilt. I could have fired a shot, I could have shouted, I could have done something. *And then they would have broken into our home.* I cursed God because of the injustice. Quite literally, my neighbors were suffering, but how was I supposed to help them and not put the family God had charged me to care for in danger?

I consumed myself with protecting my family. I meted out rations on food and water, I triple checked each window and our soundproofing. Miranda was the reason we never got infected in the first place, with her emphasis on clean water. But I never thanked her for that—it shamed me. I was supposed to keep us safe, so while she entertained and cared for the kids, I stood guard with a loaded shotgun and a heavy heart. I was busy brooding over my anger toward God and trying to get over my paralyzing fear so that I could actually do something. On those rare occasions I succeeded, my actions weren't exactly helpful either. I was a trained theologian and there seemed very little use for that in the new world. I could list every Christological heresy, but I had no idea how to make something that ran on AA batteries work on 9 volt. I had a library with books on apologetics, hymns, preaching, biblical languages, and the brave martyrs, but none of them could make me brave enough to try and harness the natural gas that still ran through the furnace. *Though sometimes blowing up the house seemed more merciful than day after day of darkness, heat, and fear.* Soon self-pity was added to my anger and fear.

In my better moments, I plucked up the courage to pull the siding off the house and put it over our windows; the family watching from upstairs to make sure my hammering didn't attract anything. It was Miranda who filled the bathtubs with water, which gave me the idea to put buckets under the downspouts. Meanwhile, Valentine, with the remaining battery left on her phone, took to following us around and recording our conversations and actions. On one particularly warm afternoon, after my, probably, twentieth failed attempt to start a fire without matches or a lighter (we were saving them for winter—if we lived that long), I wiped the sweat off my brow and rounded on her. "It may seem like it, but it is not hot enough to boil water in here, so please, leave me alone!"

She stopped recording and gave me a scalding look. "If we make it out of this, the world, if there is still one, might want to know what we went through."

"Well, go teach them how you clean the upstairs landing, then."

She rolled her eyes at me and left the room.

Cleaning the landing was just another of the many chores and activities Miranda had come up with to keep the kids busy. It was far easier to watch them grumble than tremble. For the most part, we were able to stay active, busy, and not too scared during the daylight hours. But, since I could hardly do handyman work in the daylight, I certainly couldn't by candlelight.

It was the dark hours that, naturally, haunted us most. The family played games by candlelight, but most of the dark hours I spent pacing between the windows, clutching my shotgun. *They can die. They can die. They can die.* It was the constant refrain in my mind. I had seen them bleed out, I had stabbed and shot out their hearts. *They can die.* Death was my savior, my idol. I reveled in infection, not *the* infection, but the kind the infected must be getting from their open sores and rotten meat. *Kill them all.* I praised violence. Each gunshot was another "amen," another chance at life, each fight or reckless pursuit a chance for them to break something, cut something. Yes, death was my idol, my shotgun, my scripture. I clutched it in my few hours of interrupted sleep. I always had it by my side. As long as I had it and enough shells, we had hope, we were safe. *They can die,* I repeated. *We just have to live longer than them.*

"I don't know how much longer we can live like this." Miranda fell into the kitchen chair, tossing her cleaning rag at the sink. She pulled out her, now weathered and crinkled, photo of her whole side of the family, set it on the table, and put her head in her hands.

The photo was taken at our previous summer's vacation at her parent's place out in the western mountains. *If any of us in that picture knew what was coming, none of us would be smiling.*

Her dad, Bryan, with his clerical collar on, was looking

51

askew, but with a grin, at Val who had Luke in a headlock. Bryan's arm was wrapped around Miranda's mom, Mary. The mountains, with their white caps, matched their hair. Miranda and I were in the middle smiling wide. Miranda's older sister, Madelyn, was on our left. She was on her toes, kissing her husband, Rob, on the cheek, while their seven year old daughter, Noelle, with the same fiery red hair as her father, grimaced in disgust.

Are any of them alive? Did the plague spare their town? I wondered if it had spared my family either. *Maybe my mother and father were*, my chin quivered, *gone. Maybe they were worse off.* I shook the image of my brother and his family being infected, walking around aimlessly. *Maybe they are on the way here.* I pushed the reality that the coast had it worse than us out of my mind while I sat down next to Miranda and rubbed my temples as if I could drive the thoughts out of my head by force. Finally, I whispered back to Miranda, "We have water, I got us wood to boil it, you are rationing the food. Why can't we live like this?"

She tucked the photo back in her jean pocket, then leaned forward and grabbed my arm, tight. "Because we are trapped in our house. The kids can't sleep." She got up and, after pacing a moment, walked across to the front window and looked through the crack I left in the boards outside.

"Anything out there?" I said, standing and reaching for my gun.

She shook her head and turned to say something to me, then she paused, furrowed her brow, and looked back out the window slit. "Honey, the bodies are gone."

I stared at her for a minute, puzzling over what she meant. Then I walked over, put my head next to hers, and looked out over our street. Once sprinkled with corpses I had shot, the street was empty aside from the black blood stains the bodies left behind. "You're right. Have you heard a car or anything? Maybe the government—"

Miranda screamed and I fell backwards when the zombie put its face up to the board's slit. Its mouth was still full of flesh it had ripped from the corpses in our yard. Immediately it roared and began banging on the boarded window.

The kids were screaming and Miranda ran upstairs to quiet them while I tore the barricades away from the front door. I opened the door, swung my gun around and killed the zombie with one shot, graffitiing our front boards with its blood.

Movement from the nursing home made me turn toward the street. Seven zombies had seen me and were sprinting toward me. *I can't fight them; the whole town is probably on the way.*

"Lord, have mercy," I prayed, while I ran into the garage and slammed the garage door button. I cursed when I realized there was no electricity. Instead, I heaved open the garage door and shot at the closest zombie. Then I hopped into my pickup truck and fired it up.

The tires screeched when I reversed out of the garage and the trucked heaved when I ran over a zombie. Once in the street, I cranked the truck into drive and sped up the street toward downtown. I craned my neck while I laid on the horn to make sure the zombies were following me. A mixture of fear and relief washed over me when I saw them turn from my house and sprint after me. *What do I do now?*

I stared in my rear-view mirror and forced myself to slow down to keep the zombies' interest. Then the truck lurched and my chest went into the steering wheel. If I had any breath in my chest, I would have screamed at the blood splattered across my windshield from the zombie that must have run headlong into my moving truck. If I had any hope left, it vanished when I saw the street ahead of me. The heart of town was teeming with zombies, like maggots on a corpse. Dozens of them were racing toward me, leaping over abandoned cars and police blockades set up in the street.

I think I was in tears when I hit the gas, hopped the curb, and ran over two more zombies. My chest slammed into the steering wheel once more, even after bracing myself for impact. I got around the abandoned cars and got back on the road. I laughed and cried when I hit the horn again and, filled with some reckless daring, shouted, "Come get me!"

I turned south on the highway, having no interest in trying to weave through the police blockades guarding City Hall on the other side of the highway. I didn't have the time or ability to count the racing zombies, but I guessed that fifty followed me south out of town, between the farming co-ops with their systems of grain bins rising high over the plains and our withering town. A handful of zombies in the south end of town emerged from the houses and co-ops. I thought of running another over and put my seat belt on, but decided against it; a broken radiator could doom me just as much as a bite.

Outside of town, chaos gave way to fields of prairie grass and tilled soil. I wondered if the farmers had gotten their crops planted; if they had, they weren't growing yet. The road was open aside from an abandoned car every mile or so: remnants of the city's exodus days before. One, however, was not completely abandoned. The woman in it was bashing her head bloody against the window, trying to get to me as I drove past. It was hard not to speed up on the open road, but I forced myself to slow down and hold onto the horn, lest the fifty some zombies give up the chase and return to town, and my house.

After three miles I saw a zombie, still running full speed, trip and fall. Then the majority of them began to slow. With joy I realized that, while the zombies will tax their bodies to the limit without regard for pain or weariness, they still couldn't do more than their bodies allowed.

Their hearts still had to pump blood, their lungs still needed air, their muscles still needed energy. So I led them on longer and longer. After ten miles, the pack had halved, as zombies fell to the ground, their legs giving out, and continued the chase on all fours. Some of them fell and lay still. I prayed, for their sake and ours, that they had died. *They can die.*

But I knew humans could run for many more miles, let alone when infected. And my thoughts went back to my family. *What if some of the zombies did the same?* I sped up and when the fastest zombie, even in all its tactical police gear, was out of sight behind a small rise, I turned on a gravel road and sped another mile before turning once more and heading into town on another one of the dusty roads that checkered the mostly flat farmland for miles and miles.

I shut the truck off east of town, just as I saw the treetops and our church's steeple crest the hill ahead of me. Thankful that my house was on the end of the street, and with my shotgun in hand, I walked to the top of the hill and gave a sigh of relief when I saw that no zombies were coming up the road toward where they may have heard the sound of my truck. I hopped into the roadside ditch, prayed their eyesight was weak, and began to jog the quarter mile to my house. A terribly long handful of minutes later I made it to my door without any zombies having seen me.

I got to the door and knocked, in as human a way as I could. *I had never been more thankful for "shave and a haircut."* Miranda got the message and yanked the door open. I rushed in and hugged her.

"Where did you go? I was worried sick!"

"Did they all follow me?"

"Yeah, we watched like fifty of them follow you. How many were out there?"

"Way too many. Hopefully they don't find their way back for a while. But for now, we are safe." *They can die.*

"Yes, but I do have to tell you," Miranda looked like it hurt to say it, "the water's out."

They can die, but so can we.

After a few days of rationing water, we still had a few pots worth in the bathtub. But, much like our water reserves, life was beginning to drain on the family. Try convincing a teenage girl to go to the bathroom in a bucket, mix it with bleach, and toss it out a second story window—I doubt that made it into her documentary. I tried to convince her that it was better than going in the garage, but poor Valentine might have hated me more than the zombies that hobbled past our house two or three times a day looking for leftovers of rotting corpses across town. Luke seemed bipolar. Half the time he was begging me to tell him more about fighting zombies and begging me to take him with me in my next "adventure." The other half of the time, usually at night, he spent in nightmares, panic attacks, and praying that God would make the monsters go away. But I didn't care, the kids were alive and to me, at that point, nothing else mattered.

How little I knew.

After nearly a week, Miranda and more unseasonable heat convinced me to let them open the upstairs windows more than just for dumping refuse. But even that had its downsides, especially when a wind out of the west brought the stench of decay from downtown into our home.

But we continued to make it through each day. One day, as

55

the sun set the family played cards upstairs while I sat at my desk in the middle of the living room, cleaning my two guns by candlelight. When darkness finally settled on the town, Miranda, as usual, whispered down the stairs, and I peered one last time through the windows before reluctantly creeping upstairs to sit on the floor in the landing to have our devotion. I shared a Bible reading, ignoring Luke, who looked puzzled when the Bible lesson talked about God's mercy. I then led us in a hymn and the same prayers for our families, ourselves, and a cure. I started to leave when Miranda grabbed my arm and pulled me back down. "That's it?"

"What do you mean 'that's it'? That's all we ever do."

"Yeah, but I figured since it's, you know, Sunday and all." She shrugged at me.

I whistled quietly. It was Sunday, the second Sunday in Lent already. Lent; where we are reminded that everything gets old, sick, and dies.

I should have offered encouragement, like how God would be with us through the suffering. Like how He suffered too, for us, and conquered it. I could have said something about how He drives back the darkness. But I didn't; I pulled away from Miranda and went back to my post downstairs. I sat down at my desk wondering how the first, and now, second Sunday in Lent went by without me even noticing. *Oh, how life had changed.*

After cleaning a gun a hundred times, you would think I could do it mindlessly. But, delirious, exhausted, and emotionally and spiritually brittle, it would take me ten minutes to disassemble and reassemble my gun with my fumbling fingers and wandering thoughts.

That Tuesday the migraine set in. The candles play tricks with your eyes so, at first, I thought I was blinded by the light. But the blind spot never went away until the pain in the opposite side of my head hit like a dagger. Ten minutes later I puked my rations into a bucket. Miranda gave me some pain medication, but it didn't help. She told me I was almost violent with her when she wrenched my weapons off of me and laid me on the couch next to my desk where I had been sleeping most nights. And that was where I writhed in pain for a day. I had had migraines before, in

56

stressful Holy Weeks where I juggled six services, but this was worse, it took all my strength not to cry out so a zombie would come and infect me. *At least they never felt pain.*

A day later I still couldn't hold food down, but I felt well enough to sit back at my desk and keep my endless watch. I passed the time writing names on a piece of paper by candlelight. Bertha Wilkens; I could still remember her face not four feet from mine trying to bite my face off. Chris Thompson; I will never forget his growls and moans as he died on my front porch. Mike Fleming; his kind eyes were full of rage when I ran him over. And then there were the others I knew I had killed, but I did not know their names.

My eyes watered and my throat stung as I thought about them. They were real people, victims of a sickness they could not control, killed by someone who was supposed to bring hope. I chuckled through my tears, thinking, even though it was all luck, I was a better zombie killer than pastor. *How many people had I helped save?* I just tended a flock. Was anyone storming the gates of heaven on my account? Anyone saved from the jaws of hell? And how many people had stopped coming under my watch? How many people did I say the wrong thing to? *Lord, have mercy, did I push them away?* What more could I have done? Maybe if I wasn't so lazy and gave another phone call. Maybe if I wasn't so lazy my sermons would have been more dynamic and the people would have stayed. But no, the membership list grew thinner. Meanwhile, I stared at a growing list of lives I had ended.

No, I couldn't have slept if I wanted to.

Miranda clanked the pot of boiling water next to the fireplace. I jumped. She apologized profusely. *Had I been that hard on her?* Getting angry with every noise anyone made? I shook my head. "Don't worry about it."

She approached me cautiously. "Darren, I've been wanting to talk to you."

"I know you have. I know you better than you think."

She smiled quickly, but clearly had something on her mind. "You know, the water is getting pretty low. Even at this ration, I think we only have two days left."

I nodded. "I know, I think if I can get the tarp out of the garage I could get some dew going and I already have buckets outs—"

"Yeah, I know, honey. But it hasn't rained, and what if it doesn't?"

I rubbed my temples. "I don't know, honey." *They can die, that's* all *I know.*

She nodded. "Well I was just thinking that, well, you've been outside before, even out of town, maybe—"

I stood up and shook my head. "No, you're crazy. I can't go out there and leave you here."

She stepped closer to me. "Yes, you can, we are alright. And you can teach me how to shoot."

I shook my head. "No, I have to be here. I have to protect you."

"How does that work when we die of thirst?"

I glared at her.

"You are good at this stuff, you're a fighter."

I was crying again, because I knew the truth. "No, I'm not. I got lucky that's all."

"But, honey—"

"You don't get it!" I said, far louder than I would have let anyone else speak in the house. "One screw up, one mistake, hell, even just coincidence—the gun jams, the car stalls—one *anything* and I'm dead. No, not even dead, worse than dead. I'm infected and coming back to eat you guys. No. We don't go anywhere. We wait. End of discussion."

I knew Miranda had more to say, but she bit her tongue and walked up the stairs with the water. I looked up at the kids, who were peering down the stairs with tears in their eyes. But none of them understood.

A day later, the dew collector I set up had produced about half a cup of water and there was still not a sign of rain on the horizon, only haze from the fires still smoldering around town. At nightfall I crept upstairs, cursing the squeaking steps, for devotions. After I read the Bible lesson on being strong and courageous, Miranda started to sweetly sing a hymn. And, as if scales fell from my eyes, I looked around the room at my family.

Valentine was no longer a moody, smart-talking teenager, she was uncaring, thin, and staring off at nothing, as if she, like her phone, was running low on battery. I don't think she would have reacted if a zombie jumped through the window. I had never seen her so distant.

Luke, bless his heart, was trying to sing the words of the hymn, but he was thinner, paler, and jumped at the slightest sound from anything in the house. He would shuffle closer to his mother and only after a few seconds would try and sing again. *Goodness, when was the last time I saw him smile?* He was no longer boisterous and mischievous, he was rigid and concentrating too hard on everything he did. If I didn't know him better I would have thought he was well behaved. *Or sick.*

Miranda was the worst. Her courage and resolve were still strong, but I could tell she was cracking. She looked at our children and, while she smiled at them, her eyes were wide and concerned. Her thin frame was trending more towards skeletal, even though she never admitted to taking less rations. Even sleeping downstairs I could hear her sobbing at night as she cradled her children back to sleep and prayed for her family hundreds of miles away. *If I don't go out, she will.*

After the kids went to sleep, I took up my post downstairs. I thought for a moment on my family and my responsibility to care for them. I thought of my own fear and for the first time in days I opened my desk drawer and pulled out my Bible. I didn't know where to look, so I opened it randomly, it fell on Amos 5:19 "It will be as though a man fled from a lion only to meet a bear, as though he entered his house and rested his hand on the wall only to have a snake bite him."

I laughed.

I put my hand over my mouth I laughed so loud. It was the first genuine laugh since before I believed this plague was real. I laughed and I praised God. I bowed my head and prayed, "Lord God, thank you for letting this fool see the error of his ways." A random verse, *please,* I knew God and His Word better than that. I thanked God that, when I was looking for luck and random chance, He reminded me to remember the truth of His Word. After a bit of thought, I purposely turned the pages of my Bible. I read His promises of hope even if the mountains fall into the sea. I read the Christmas story about how a child was born to be a light in the darkness. I read of the crucifixion, of the resurrection where no virus would ever afflict God's people again.

The first thing I did was go back upstairs. I kissed my

children and then, kneeling by Miranda, as she was still awake looking at her picture in the candlelight, I gave her a kiss like a husband should give a wife.

"Are you alright?" she asked with an eyebrow raised.

"Maybe for the first time in over a week." Then I crawled into bed next to her, my shotgun leaning against the nightstand next to me.

They can die. But we can live.

A Divine Call

"This is the day that the Lord has made," I said.

The kids, sitting at the table over breakfast, looked at each other and then to Miranda. She seemed as puzzled as they were and shrugged. After another moment they all responded, "Let us rejoice and be glad in it?"

"You better believe it. Especially now, a whole lot of people didn't make it to this day."

Valentine mumbled under her breath something about them being lucky.

Earlier that morning I had awoken to check out a noise in the backyard, a zombie was in a fistfight with our garden fence but seemed none the wiser to the four lives in the house next to him. So I wandered down to my office on the first floor and, holding a candle, looked around. I could still see the indentations in the carpet where my desk used to sit, but my focus soon switched to the wall with its pictures of family, friends, and my degrees.

I glanced over each of them, praying for each of the people in the pictures. I nearly passed over my certificate of ordination hanging on the wall, but a few words caught my eye: "A Divine Call." They were written in bold on the top of the certificate. My name and a few signatures from the District President and the Church Chairman were scrawled across the bottom.

"A Divine Call," I whispered.

I had always thought of being a pastor as a job, and it was, to be sure. But it was somehow more. I was the one chosen by these Christians to bring them the good news of hope and forgiveness and life in Jesus. Yet, since there were no more District Presidents and since there were no more paychecks and since there were no more bosses, no one went to work anymore. I had simply done the same. But wasn't my Call different? Wasn't this vocation, the vocation as pastor, something more than a way to get a paycheck?

I pulled a few books off my dusty shelves and brought them to the living room. After some time, I found myself dripping tears on the page when I read about priests in Nazi Germany holding mass even though it was illegal and no one showed up, but they held it because that was what they were called to do. More tears fell when I read about Martin Luther, who, when the black plague came to his town, sent his family off to safety while he stayed behind. Because that was what he was called to do.

And here I was hiding in my home, wishing to be alone in some underground bunker because the plague had come to my town.

I prayed for strength and for wisdom. Then I went upstairs and held the worship that I should have held on the last two Sundays in Lent—for the few congregants available. I preached on Psalm 43:5 "Why are you cast down O my soul, and why are you in turmoil within me? Hope in God; for I shall again praise Him, my salvation and my God." I told them how the church next door might be empty or filled with zombies for all we knew. I talked about how we could get consumed by the plague, but we still had a Savior and we would praise Him again, maybe not up in our upstairs landing, maybe not next door, but definitely in His kingdom. "May that be our hope and our light in the darkness; thanks to the One who died in our place."

The sermon didn't make it all better. It didn't miraculously get us water or safety. But the words gave me courage, and I needed it. And it seemed to do the same for the family too, that or they were just happy to have a father and husband again. Either way, when the gospel is heard, it makes any day a little less gray. I thanked God for that.

After the services Miranda made us all a breakfast of oatmeal with raisins and a quarter cup of water each. We were down to our last bucket. It was then that I told the family I would be going out later in the morning. Miranda almost spilled her water ration and, had times been better, I would have thought by the look in her eye that she would have flirted with me.

But it turned out, she was able to do plenty of that when I showed her how to work my hunting rifle a little while later. Once she was confident in the general mechanics, we stashed it upstairs, along with the longest kitchen knife we had and a few broomsticks I had whittled into spear points. I gave each of the family a kiss, "If I don't see you again, I love you all and I will see you in the Kingdom." Halfway down the stairs I turned back. "And if I come back trying to eat you guys, honey, my heart is yours—pierce it once more with that spear." She didn't think it was funny, but I winked at Val, now recording on my phone, and chuckled when I went through the front door.

My laughter didn't last long, however, in the eerie quiet of the ravaged town. Even in a town of four hundred there was always a dog barking, a child laughing, or tractor engine humming. But today there was nothing but the sound of my footsteps and rapidly beating heart as I paced quickly to my truck.

A few long minutes later, I made it to my truck without being spotted. I checked the bed and backseat before getting in and figured if nothing spooked when I turned the engine over, I would go straight out of town and to my destination: my member and church elder Kevin had a place in the country with a well for water.

I turned the engine on and rolled to the top of the hill. The sound of the engine must have been carried by the wind out of the east, because five zombies were already heading toward me from the nursing home. I crossed myself and drove toward them. I swerved around four of them; the last, however, got a hold of my side mirror and, after dragging for a few seconds, ripped it off. The rear tires jumped as I ran the zombie over. I looked in my rear view and saw the wounded zombie crawling after me, the other four paying him no mind.

I drove past my house and church, hoping to lure anything lurking in my backyard far away. I spared a glance over and thought I saw a light on in the church, shining through the stained glass, *probably just the sunlight.* Soon after my gaze turned toward the town horde, which was beginning to stir across the highway from me. I swerved, much like last time, onto a neighbor's lawn to dodge some abandoned cars in the road and I shouted as the truck lurched. There must have been a body or a wounded zombie in the still fast growing spring grass. Thankful that nothing broke on my truck and not seeing any zombie rise from the grass to chase me, I shrugged and wondered if zombies needed to bed down and sleep somewhere.

Back on the road, I cruised past our block, just slow enough to keep the chasing zombies interested, then I turned south on the highway and as I was about to lay on the horn to attract even more zombies from the city center, I saw, tucked under the long-gone-mayor's tree, his megaphone.

I could use that, I thought.

Before I knew what I was doing, I threw the truck in park and sprinted for it. I grabbed the megaphone and, in my haste to get back to the truck, dropped it. I doubled back to it, picked it up, but had to drop it once more because one of the pursuing zombies was already too close. I shot him, then turned toward the growl by the mayor's house. An infected lady was sprinting at me. *Was it his wife?* I shot her and moved to grab the megaphone again, but as I did, something grabbed my ankle. I could see the depression in the grass where the zombie had crawled through the lawn from the mayor's shrubs. W*hy didn't you learn from the one you ran over?*

I screamed and fell, trying to shake myself free. But his grip was too strong, maybe strong enough to scrape through my jeans and into the skin.

I shot between my legs. The zombie let go, but its blood caked my pant legs. I thought about squirming out of them, but I heard more growls and many more stomping feet.

I grabbed the megaphone, tossed it into the bed of the truck, breaking it for all I knew, and didn't even shut the truck door. I sped away from the forty zombies rounding the corner from downtown. When I got enough space and wits, I slammed the door shut and headed out of town. My foot was a little heavy, I blame the adrenaline from nearly getting eaten alive, so about half the zombies lost interest when I disappeared over the small hill out of town. I had to put the cruise control on to go slow enough to entertain the rest of the zombies for the next ten miles.

The cruise control also let me work my dirty pants off. I tossed the contaminated pants out the window and was thankful for the spare clothes I packed with me. *I may get turned into a zombie, sure, but I was never going to drive home half naked again.*

I was cheered when I saw, starting about six miles out of town, a few devoured or bloated and sun-bleached corpses from my run through town last week. The lady in her car no longer tried to get me, she was slumped over, held in place by her seat belt. She had apparently succumbed to heat or the head wounds she gave herself when I drove by the last time. *They can die.*

But we can live. I sped up to leave the chasing zombies behind. I drove a few miles to ensure I didn't bring any unwelcome visitors to Kevin's. *Maybe I would be unwelcome after this mess.* I shook my head when I turned off the highway a few miles later, only having seen about six corpses out of the fifty chasing me the week before. *They can die, but they don't die easy.*

My gas gauge was at half after I weaved my way back to Kevin's farm, stopping periodically to ensure no zombies were following me. I said a prayer as I pulled slowly down his long drive, a beautiful quarter mile tunnel of gigantic oaks. I hoped that he was safe, and that he was willing to help in these dangerous times.

I was thankful when I pulled up to his house and saw the windows of his two-story farmhouse were still intact. Some, lower to the ground, were even boarded up. But then I wondered what to do next. Did I honk to announce myself so he wouldn't shoot me? Or did I stay quiet as not to attract any zombies?

I opted not to honk. I got out of my truck, hands and gun held in the air and stood there for a few minutes. Sure enough, a side door opened and, swinging his gun around, Kevin came out of his house.

We were never a congregation that hugged a lot, so I was surprised when he smiled and embraced me for a moment. He was big and strong in his work boots, jeans, and, as always, a camouflage shirt and hat. His, usually buzzed, black hair was longer and his beard fuller than when I had seen him last, his belly smaller and his face paler, too.

"Pastor." He almost seemed choked up. "Man, it's good to see you."

"And me you. Your family alright?"

He nodded and scratched his beard. "Yeah, we got food and a well, we are boiling water and doing alright. But you're in town, how is it there?"

I looked down. "Awful, really. I know a lot of people didn't make it and a pack of zombies is living downtown."

Kevin whistled and took his hunting hat off as if to pay respects. "Yeah, dangerous times. I've killed a few of them and burned 'em, but been pretty quiet."

But maybe I was changing that. "I'm sorry if any heard my truck, but I had to come. We have no water."

"Well why didn't you say so?" He turned toward his tractor. "And don't you worry about bringing anything here, Jayce is a crack shot." He gestured toward a dormer window where his son leaned out. He waved at me with one hand and held a rifle in the other. Kevin shook his head as we walked toward his tractor. "To be honest, the scariest thing ain't the sick—it's the healthy."

"You've seen people? I mean, uninfected people?"

He stopped and turned toward me, eyes wide. "Yeah, I mean, you're right. They're all people sick or healthy. But the normal people, had a couple of them stop by on a few occasions. People askin' for something, some wanting to live with us." Maybe I blushed because he pointed at me. "And don't you worry, you can ask for anything, but some of the folks seem dangerous, like they ain't really askin', you know?"

"Matter o' fact, not two days ago, Grant—that big guy from golfin'—was making off with my tractor before I ran out and stopped him. He said, 'I figured you were gone or didn't need it.'" He shook his head, started walking again and hopped onto his tractor. "The worst was when that wagon train from the city came through, people tearing all over the countryside, camping, looking for homes, I bet a bit of healthy blood was shed that night, but we made out alright."

We talked for some time before he fired up his tractor and loaded a sprayer tank full of water into the back of my pickup. When he was done, he hopped down and seemed to be inspecting his work boots. "I'd ask you to stay with us, but some of Jenny's family from the city is with us, we are pretty full up here."

I shook my head and stammered, "Of course, no—I mean, ya, I understand."

"But if you need like a night, by all means, come here." There was an awkward silence for a while before he interrupted it.

"Is there anything else I can do?"

I thought of the hordes ravaging the town and all the people who might be stuck in their homes like my family. *They can die. We can live.* "Jayce is a pretty good shot, huh? How 'bout you?"

Two days later, I was hiking back to the truck with a bucket for water, a rifle and shotgun, and a backpack full of ammunition. Miranda was torn on Kevin's and my plan to fight the town horde. On one hand she was grateful for me to be out of my shell of fear, but I couldn't help but get the sense that she thought I was swinging a bit too far toward recklessness. In the end, her heart for the other families that may be suffering convinced her to support my decision to fight.

The plan was simple: I would meet Kevin and Jayce at the huge co-op with towering grain bins on the south end of town and west of the highway. We would climb up and, from the safety of the high ground, pick them off like we were shooting cans in the backyard.

That plan, however, went out the boarded-up-window when I pulled up short at the top of the hill, horrified to see seven zombies in the bed of my truck splashing around in the water tank. I froze for a moment, then crouched low, using the crest of the hill to hide me from the zombies.

I knelt for a moment, trying to catch my breath and think. I debated whether to fight or run from the infected carjackers. If I left would I walk to meet Kevin and Jayce? Would they try to fight without me? I came out to fight, why not start with these? *Because there's no high ground and the nursing home for zombies was only a stone's throw away.*

I turned and, as quietly as possible, walked away, back toward town and, having reached my house without drawing any attention, followed the ditch south toward the smaller grain bins. *If I could get to them, I just had to run across the street and up a ladder to the safety of the large bins.*

Halfway to the small bins, something saw me. The howling came from the middle of town, between me and the large grain bins on the other side of the highway. I broke into a run, the fifty pounds of gear awkwardly and painfully thrashing around on my back and shoulders. I wasn't making it to the larger grain bins, but the lesser of the co-ops with smaller grain bins was closer to me, on this side of the highway, only a half a block south of me.

I risked a glance behind me and saw five zombies were chasing me from town, along with the seven from my truck, who were now racing down the hill behind me. I turned forward, afraid of stumbling if I looked any longer. The grain bins were looming larger above me. *I can do this.*

My breath, like the roars behind me, grew louder and I told myself to not look back, *it can't help you.* After what seemed like forever, I clambered across the train tracks. Once clear of the tracks, which felt more like snares, I stole a look over my shoulder. One of the zombies, who looked like a man in his twenties, was far ahead of the rest and gaining on me. I swiveled and fired a shotgun round at him. It didn't kill him, but spun him around and off balance. It was enough to slow him, so I didn't complain. I racked another shell as I turned and kept running.

I jumped over the barb wire fence, but, weighed down by my gear, my leg caught the top wire and sent me toppling to the ground. The rifle on my back slammed into the back of my head and my leg blazed where the barb wire ripped my pants and skin. I ripped my pant leg even further pulling free from the fence, forced myself up, slung my shotgun over my shoulder and, encumbered and in a daze, ran the last twenty feet to the grain elevator ladder.

I had no idea if zombies could climb, but I didn't stop to look until I felt I was at least fifteen feet up the ladder. I looked down between my legs and nearly fell off in despair when I saw one of the zombies leap to three rungs below me and grab on.

He began to climb feverishly, I kicked at him once, twice, until, thankfully, the zombie I winged with my shotgun jumped up and, in an attempt to climb over the first zombie, pulled him off the ladder. They both fell to the ground and the mass of, now fifteen zombies, writhed upon itself, making little progress up the ladder. A minute later, I collapsed on the top of the grain bin, breathing heavily. I thanked God and, with a firm grip on the railing, leaned over to see if any of the zombies were on the way up.

A zombie, with open and weeping wounds on his face, was halfway up and gaining. My head spun for a second, trying to figure out why their wounds never festered with infection, and, more importantly, what to do. I knew I didn't have enough ammo to kill the whole mob from downtown; Kevin was supposed to bring his stash. But I had no idea if he would find me on this grain bin. I wished I had heavy rocks to throw down the ladder, but I didn't. Cursing under my breath, I shot down the ladder. It was hard to miss the head when it was coming straight up at you, but somehow I did. Luckily, the shot to his shoulder was just as deadly. He fell thirty feet, knocking another zombie off the ladder below him and, with a crack I could hear over the mob of zombies, he laid still.

I stood and looked across the highway toward the other grain bins—the ones I was supposed to be on. It was impossible to tell if anyone was on them, they were so much taller and a quarter mile away. There certainly wasn't anything moving on their vast network of belts, walkways, and ladders that connected the half dozen tall bins. I envied their height and multiple methods of retreat as I stood atop my forty-foot-tall bin, connected to one even smaller bin a stone's throw away.

I turned and scanned the countryside for a moment wondering where Kevin and Jayce were. *Did I come at the wrong time? That would be just like me.*

Then I heard, in answer, the wonderful growl of an engine. I ran to the other side of the grain bin and looked down. Kevin had steered his tractor up to the ladder, which I didn't know existed, on the other side of my bin. I shuddered to think of the fear I'd experience if a zombie had climbed up without me noticing, or perhaps I wouldn't have felt any fear before the teeth bit into my neck.

The bucket of the loader tractor was lifted high. It was filled with materials and Jayce stood in the bucket next to them with a smile on his pock-marked teenage face.

"You guys are crazy!" I shouted down at him.

Jayce, with black hair like his father, but a bit longer, shrugged and, with a pack on his back and a rope around his shoulder, started climbing up. When he reached the top, he smiled at me. "Happy to see us?"

I nodded my head and chuckled.

Gunshots stopped my laughter. Kevin had crawled out of the tractor cab, shot a zombie with his pistol, and climbed into the bucket. He stood and waved with a smile.

They actually were crazy.

"You are aware this isn't a hunting trip, Kevin."

He clambered up the ladder and stood up next to me. "You sure about that, Pastor? Only question is who's huntin' who?"

"Fair enough."

He started hauling gear up on a rope. "I'll take care of this, you might want to keep an eye on the other ladder."

I nodded and scrambled back across the angled roof. I cried out in shock when I saw a zombie not three feet from the top of the grain bin. It growled at me until the bark of my shotgun sent it tumbling off the ladder. Another shot hit the one behind it who fell, bringing two more down with him.

I fired a few rounds down into the mob at the bottom of the ladder, but seeing little lethal results, I decided to wait until a zombie had reached halfway up the ladder before I shot it. That way, it could knock others off, and if the shot somehow didn't kill it, the fall could do some damage.

After a few minutes of this, Kevin came by. "How many you got down there, Pastor?"

I craned my head over, scanning the mass of zombies at the bottom. "I'd say I'm up to twenty, though I've probably killed ten."

"Hmm, we only got 'bout six on our side. We still haven't got the mob from downtown. Wonder what's holding them?"

I shot a zombie, with a baseball cap still miraculously on its head, off the ladder below me. "Probably just distance. Sorry I couldn't make it to the other grain bins closer to downtown."

He looked to slap me on the back for reassurance, but then glanced at the edge next to us and scratched his beard under a red bandana he had tied on. "Don't worry. We had to kill a pack of three on the way here too." He carefully set some boxes of shotgun ammo down next to me. "We makin' plenty of noise though, they're gonna come. Might even be good they don't all come at once."

"This might entice them." Jayce propped his high power rifle on a box of gear and aimed it toward downtown. "You may want to put your earmuffs on."

I wanted to say thanks for the reminder, but the words caught in my throat. *I hadn't put anything on. No mask, nothing.* I grimaced when I saw blood spatter on the ladder not a foot below me. A drop of that in my mouth or eyes and I would be turning on Kevin and Jayce. I pulled out my shooting glasses and a facemask I had from painting the porch the year before. Then I put on my ear protection and gave Jayce a thumbs up.

He smiled and, after looking through his scope for a few seconds, lobbed a shot off toward downtown.

Kevin paced between the back ladder and Jayce, where he used his binoculars to spot after his son. "If you're aiming to shatter that car window you hit too low and to the right."

"Gotcha," Jayce responded and, as his dad walked back to the ladder, he tinkered with his rifle scope.

"Why are you shooting cars? Don't you want to save some ammo?"

Jayce shrugged. "Got to get them stirred up somehow, and easier to sight it in on a still target. But I think I got her pretty close now." He whipped his hair aside, looked into his scope and cracked off another round. A car alarm started blaring downtown. "Yep, I'm good."

I nodded at my rifle. "Mind swapping spots so I could sight my rifle in? I've never been able to shoot it straight."

Jayce unloaded his rifle and set it aside. "Sure thing. I'll spot for you too."

Five minutes and twenty rounds later, Jayce put the binoculars down and shook his head. "Well I know I shouldn't lie to a pastor, so… Pastor, you're an awful shot."

I took my eye from the scope, where I could see ten perfectly "healthy" and bullet-free zombies rummaging around the honking car and hung my head a bit. "I know, sorry."

Then he looked through the binoculars again. "But it looks like they finally lost interest in the car and are headed this way." He shouted, "Here they come, Dad!"

Kevin, who was watching ladders for us, came over with his binoculars. He peered through them for a second and whistled. "I thought you said there were fifty in town, Pastor."

"Yeah," I answered, squinting toward downtown.

"Then how come I see a hundred?"

I looked through the rifle scope and saw a stampede of zombies sprinting around the corner from downtown, straight toward us. I squeezed off a round and saw some asphalt kick up, the mass of zombies unfazed.

"Alright Jayce, you're up." I unloaded my rifle and scrambled out of the way.

He sat back down behind the box, breathing a bit ragged. He reached for his rifle magazine but fumbled it onto the floor and watched as it slid toward the edge of the grain bin. He made to reach for it.

"Don't you dare, Jayce," Kevin said firmly and grabbed his son's shoulder.

Jayce stopped and stared at where the magazine slid off the roof. "Sorry, Dad. I'm sorry."

Kevin turned him by the shoulder. "Look here. There's a hundred zombies. Have we got more than a hundred bullets?"

Jayce nodded.

"So what's the problem? Load your rounds one at a time and make 'em count son, I know you can." Then he turned to me, "Nothing changes. Watch your ladder, Pastor, and give us," he paused and nodded toward the horde, "and them, a prayer."

I nodded, stuffed my pockets with shells, and was thankful that Kevin's confidence had made my hands shake a bit less.

While Jayce cracked off rounds at the mass of zombies nearly a quarter mile away, I opened up every box of shotgun shells I had and set them, secured from sliding off the roof by my backpack, next to me. *I can shoot these straight,* I thought, infusing myself with confidence. I looked down the ladder and cracked another zombie.

Kevin was still patrolling the roof, congratulating his son with every rifle hit. "Not bad son, he'll bleed out before he gets here."

I looked back and saw Jayce, while his shots were hitting, was having to wipe his eyes before each shot. I waited until his dad wandered away. "Jayce, are you alright?"

He fired a shot, then looked away, sniffed, and wiped his eyes. "I know some of them, is all."

I sighed and, after checking my ladder, scooted closer to him. "Me too. But you have to understand, there is no other way right now. They are sick and we don't have a cure. They can't help their actions and, sadly, we can't help what we have to do, either."

He nodded.

"Try and ignore their faces and know that, ultimately, this is what they would want you to do. And when the twisted faces haunt you anyway, remember that you are helping others live. And so, for this evil you must do in this broken world, I, as your pastor, in the stead and by the command of Jesus, forgive you."

He sniffed. "Thanks, Pastor."

And just like that, on a grain bin with a mass of death looming toward us, I realized I was still a pastor even if I never got another paycheck.

I patted Jayce on the back and soon he was back to lobbing shots into the distance, dropping a line of bodies in the fields and roads far from our grain bin. But the trail he left behind didn't seem to thin the pack at all. Soon the racing horde reached the bottom of our grain bin, where the sight of their numbers, and their stench, seemed overwhelming.

I remember mumbling the Lord's Prayer hoarsely and shakily as we fought off the zombies who, boosted higher by the pile of their fallen comrades, climbed faster. Kevin could no longer leave his ladder to give us reassurance or orders. For a long time, nothing but guns and ghouls spoke.

But eventually my pockets were near empty. I shouted over to Jayce and he left the zombies he was picking off in the back and came to help me with the more immediate threat of zombies less than ten feet below me. The blood spatter was on my pant legs.

He padded my pockets with the last box of shotgun shells and stood next to me. We alternated reloading and firing rounds down the rungs. My barrel was steaming, but still I pressed on, firing round after round. Until my pockets were empty once more.

"Kevin, I need more shotgun ammo," I croaked as loudly as I could across the grain bin.

Between shots he turned to me and shook his head, he didn't have any more.

While Jayce covered the ladder, I grabbed my rifle and, using fingers cracked and slick with my own blood, I worked the scope off the top of my rifle. "I can't use this thing anyways." I shoved the scope in my backpack and, with iron sights, I pushed off the next wave of zombies.

As I reloaded my rifle, Kevin scrambled over and gave me a long iron rod. "Save the rifle ammo if you can, there's more than a hundred here. Jab them in the head, and if they grab it, just let it go. Don't get pulled off." I set my rifle down and took the rod. I jabbed the air a few times to get a feel for the weight and nodded.

Kevin nodded back and then gestured toward town, where a dozen more zombies were racing across the field toward us. "Gotta be two hundred of these things now, at least. God help us."

I wanted so badly to say that He will, but I didn't know if He was going to help us out of this one. So I said what I did know, "He already has."

Kevin lifted his camouflage bandana, spat, then patted Jayce on the shoulder. "Amen. Back to the ladders."

The highest zombie, a girl with her shirt torn to pieces, was only two feet from the top. She looked up at me when I came to the edge and leaped off the rungs toward me and my pointed rod that took her through the eye. She fell, but the one below her kept coming. I jabbed him three times in the head before he fell. I thrust so hard on the third jab, my momentum almost carried me over. "Careful," Jayce said, as he reached for me.

I shook him off. "Don't reach for me if I go, but thanks. And I'll try to go easy."

I prodded two more zombies off the ladder and, just when I was starting to feel proficient, a large burly zombie in overalls grabbed the rod and yanked. I let the rod go, not before I was leaning off the grain bin and over a writhing mass of death. I grabbed the handrail and swallowed a scream as I pulled myself, with Jayce's help, back on top.

While I composed myself, Jayce held the next wave off with his rifle. The large caliber would tear through two of them at a time if he aimed it straight down. When he fumbled his reload, I knew I needed to step back in, this time with my baseball bat.

The first zombie was two feet from the top when I cracked its head with the bat. It went limp immediately, one of the nails sinking through his skull. The metal and bone creaked as the man fell into the arms of his peers. Two zombies later and all the nails were bent and useless. Even worse, while the zombies may have been dazed or concussed, they only fell when I heard a skull crack. After a half dozen, I started trying to break their hands, but, between the stress and exhaustion, I missed too many times and found them reaching up at me. Besides, a broken hand wouldn't

74

kill them, just move them back in the queue.

I was sweating, I was getting dizzy from bending over and swinging the bat, which felt like thirty pounds. I was praying, I was cursing. I didn't know how much longer I could last when I heard Kevin say to Jayce, "It's time."

Between swings I saw Kevin hoist open a box and pull out two gas cans. After my next swing I saw him unscrew one and pour the whole thing down his ladder. Jayce grabbed a can and did the same at our ladder—he didn't protest when I held the back of his trousers to make sure he didn't fall off balance.

Then there was a sizzle as two cheap fireworks were lit. Kevin handed one to Jayce and tossed his down his ladder. "Fire in the hole."

Most of you know the stench of zombie. It is rotting; faintly sweet, but completely putrid. Two hundred burning zombies is exponentially worse. Even with my facemask on I had to retch off to the side of the grain bin.

Along with the stench came the smoke. As the viscous black smoke whirled around us, we all stood back and heard the crackle of the flames overtake the growls from below. Not much later I jumped in fright, wondering if the smoke could infect us, but then I realized it already would have.

"It stinks, but at least it doesn't spread the virus." Jayce voiced what I was thinking.

Kevin looked at him and chuckled. "At least we got that goin' for us." But then, even through his smudged glasses, I saw his eyes go back to the fire and open wide.

I turned to where he was looking and saw the flaming arm reaching out of the smoke for us. Jayce panicked, shot, and missed the burning zombie as it staggered toward us. Kevin cursed and drove his long rod through its chest and sent it back into the flames.

I picked up my rifle and glanced at the ladder behind us, which Kevin was guarding earlier. I shouted and shot my rifle at the body crawling at us out of the flames. It slumped to the ground. But another figure in the flames rose up behind it. And another.

"Are they immune to it?" Jayce shouted.

"No," Kevin roared, "but they are damn tough." He had a mask on, but I have no doubt he didn't blush like he normally did when he cussed in front of me, but I didn't care. I was busy, sitting on my backside, keeping our ladder clear. But then my backside started to hurt. I had no idea how long I ignored it, but I couldn't any longer. It was hot.

I pressed a hand to the metal grain bin roof and, even with a glove on, had to pull it back after a second. "Is there grain in this thing?"

Kevin spun around and we could all see white smoke pouring out the opening of the roof above us. "We gotta move."

I started jamming my pockets and backpack with smoking hot gear. "Should we throw the ammo over, the heat will set it off, right?"

Kevin shook his head. "And one in a hundred of them will hit something."

There was only one way to go. We climbed further up the grain bin roof. Then up the ladder that went even higher, up to the overhead lights and the top of the belt that went down to the next grain bin over. I went up first and flushed with guilt halfway up, realizing I should have let the kid up first. But it was too late and Jayce was right behind me. Kevin put down three blazing zombies with his pistol before following us up.

At the top, there was barely room for two of us. Kevin held onto the ladder. So I stepped out onto the conveyor belt, which led down to the next, smaller bin, and sat precariously overlooking the burning grain bin and the town. "Well even if they get us, boys—"

I stopped when the scaffolding we were on heaved to the side three feet. Jayce shouted and I nearly dropped my rifle trying to hang on.

"The grain bin's gonna burn down!" I shouted at Kevin.

"Time to go, old guys." Jayce pointed behind me.

I turned to look fifty feet down a, now listing, conveyor belt to the top of the other, shorter-but-not-ablaze, grain bin. I knew it had to be done. The few zombies who made it through the flames were below us, along with a melting grain bin.

I crab-walked down toward the next grain bin. The others followed. It was easier than I thought, the height was the most intimidating thing about it. The elevator belt was easily two feet wide and gave plenty of grip to stop from slipping, even with the sideways slant from our leaning tower. Within a few minutes we were on the next grain bin. We scrambled to secure the ladders, but soon saw we had little need. The city horde was smoldering a stone's throw away from us.

We hugged, cheered, and shook hands. I even said a prayer of thanksgiving aloud. Then we waited for a few hours, picking off a few stragglers with our rifles and watching the grain bin in front of us, that we had just been on, collapse, along with two hundred of our fears, into flames.

As we sat on the awkwardly steep grain bin roof, our facemasks and bandanas keeping the full weight of the stench of two hundred burning bodies from our lungs, we celebrated that no more bodies crawled or ran at us through the flames. We had conquered the Witherton horde. It was bittersweet, putting down so many people we recognized, but when raving masses are only a few feet away, the relief of victory was infectious—too much so for Jayce, who broke down in his dad's shoulder. "You did good, kid," he encouraged him. "And you did what you had to," he reminded him.

I choked up behind my safety glasses and facemask as well. I thanked God for getting us through that battle and had the audacity to ask Him for more: to see us through the many more we had coming. But I knew God never grew tired of His people's prayers, and I assumed that those future battles would be smaller. So, with a thankful and hopeful heart, I prayed. Yes, *they can die. But we can live.*

Kevin's tractor was buried beneath a pile of smoldering corpses, so I lent him my pickup, now free of zombies, to get back home. He promised, in return, to return it with a new water tank free from zombie infection. I thanked him and, before turning to head home, asked him, "So, will I see you in church on Sunday?"

Commission

"This is the day that the Lord has made," I said.

The assembly of, I was elated to see, twenty people responded, "Let us rejoice and be glad in it."

A few days earlier, Kevin brought my pickup back and, after unloading the water in our garage to keep thirsty zombies unaware of it, we drove through town shouting a simple message. "Redeemer Lutheran is holding worship on Sunday in Jacobson field at 10am. Town meeting to follow. Use extreme caution when traveling and keep one hand in the air when approaching the field. The majority of the horde downtown has been eliminated, but there are still infected about."

The message attracted about fifteen zombies from around the town, nothing Kevin and Jayce, riding in the bed of my truck, couldn't deal with. We thought of checking on people but worried it might be too dangerous. We saw a few people wave out of windows at us, cheered to see people in town.

I originally planned on holding the service at the beautiful brick church with its high steeple right next to our house. But when I worked up the nerve to finally go and clear it, I never made it past the narthex. The church smelled like death, and the sunlight filtering through the stained glass windows cast a red and green hue over the dark building. The shadows seemed to move and the wind made the building creak. I figured if I, the pastor, was too scared to venture into the building full of fifty pews anything could be hiding in or under, I imagined no one else would be too eager to enter the seemingly haunted structure either.

To be honest, I wasn't sure anyone would be bold enough to

leave their homes at all—for a field or a church. But just in case, on Sunday, Kevin, Jayce, and I showed up early, made some noise, and put down a few zombies that sprinted out of town toward our spot in the field. Kevin had towed in a flatbed trailer and unhitched it in the middle of the untended, but surprisingly healthy, alfalfa field. We formed some makeshift stairs out of hay bales and I, taking a table, a cloth, and a cross from the house, erected a makeshift altar on top of it.

I stood on top of the trailer and looked around. We chose the field because it was on the top of a gently rolling hill so no one, infected or not, would surprise us or the people who wanted to attend. Looking south, I never would have guessed anything was wrong in the world. The fields were green and growing with corn and soybeans and alfalfa. Even the fields that weren't planted had their own beauty: a mixture of prairie grasses, flowering weeds, and volunteer crops created a bouquet fitting for the gorgeous and sunny day the Lord had given us.

But then I turned to the north. Toward town. Toward the city an hour away. Black and thick haze, fueled by the city's fires, rolled toward us like a summer storm. Sitting helpless before the incoming front was our little town. Smoke still billowed from the grain bins near our home, smoldering grain and flesh ascending into the sky. Other beacons of smoke rose from our town as well: a few houses and cars set ablaze from fighting, or gas leaks, or some other chaos spawned from the plague. Garbage and bodies littered the streets and for a moment I wondered if we should have picked up the bodies, lest they scare off any of the people who might venture out to join us in the fields.

Kevin checked his watch and coughed awkwardly when he saw that I caught him looking. But we all perked up when we heard the entirely out of place sound of an engine humming. Not a minute later, several trucks and cars made their way out of town. Some, who had clearly seen enough zombies in the past weeks, were calm and calculated, steering around bodies as they made their way toward the field. Others were panicked and sped toward us, erratically steering and driving over bodies, desperate to flee the handful of zombies trailing them out of town. But Kevin and Jayce made sure none of the followers made it to the makeshift parking lot on the edge of the field. It had a large plywood sign the kids helped me paint in the garage. It not only marked the field as a meeting spot, but also gave directions to approach with caution and a hand raised in the air, something no zombie would ever do, at least from what we had seen.

I shook my head as I turned and weighed down a corner of the altar cloth with a box of shotgun shells. Maybe it was because of my own previous cowardice, but I was shocked by the people's bravery. They willingly walked out of their homes for maybe the first time since the outbreak. And they walked to a field holding one hand up high, while a seventeen year old fired rifle shots around the countryside. These people risked their lives to come to church, or maybe just for some human contact; it didn't matter to me at the time. Most of the people held weapons in their free hands, but by the time they reached the trailer and the chairs we set up in the field, they had put them away and they held each other instead. Apparently, our presence, and Jayce sitting on the top of a pickup with a rifle, made them feel safe enough to let their guard down.

Soon I saw even my own family coming through the field. Miranda carried our rifle in one hand and held the other high, our children followed behind her, hands in the air. I had pleaded with them to stay behind, but Miranda, much like the others coming, I suppose, was desperate for interaction, tired of being trapped in her own home, tired of being helpless, and tired of being afraid. *We can live,* and she was going to. I shot a glance at Jayce, but I didn't need to, it was obvious no one hopping out of a car and walking from the parking lot was infected. His rifle never even pointed toward the families coming from the parking lot.

As the people gathered, they talked animatedly about the past weeks. They embraced and cried over horrific news of lost loved ones and sighed with relief when the few glimmers of good news passed around. It was a beautiful sight to see people coming together; it is truly not good for man to be alone. And the children! They ran, they laughed, they squealed with each other, and for once we parents didn't have to quiet them. If the zombies weren't coming for the gunshots that reverberated through town, they wouldn't come for a shout. Luke, along with some of the older kids, hit rocks with sticks in the field and ran, and I got a catch in my throat when he, brave once again, talked with the kids about how he was going to go hunt zombies like his dad did. *I'm no hero, son,*

I thought to myself, but I didn't say it, maybe because I liked it, maybe because I was just happy to see him smiling instead of cowering.

That morning, it seemed like life had come back to us.

Gertrude gave me a big hug and an 'alleluia', "I know it's Lent, but I don't care," she said—after she parked her big Cadillac on the edge of the field. She was even willing to a sing a song for the service. I gladly accepted. Seeing as we had no hymnals, I was happy to settle for a little music, even if it was a bit off key.

Apparently not even a zombie plague could keep Curtis from being a pain in my backside. He caned his way across the field, refusing our offers to let him drive in closer, and complained the whole way out about not having a path that was easier to walk on while scowling down at the tennis ball on the end of his cane that was now covered in mud. In spite of his complaints, I was genuinely happy to see him as well as a handful of other church families that had survived the hard weeks.

By the time worship was supposed to start, nearly forty people were there. Most weren't even members, but people who were coming for interaction and news. The conversations went on for nearly an hour as the people continued to share news and speculate about others in the town and about the virus. I could tell there was no way we could go right into the service. I looked at Rebecca, a member of ours in her mid-50s, who was dressed like church was in a cathedral, not a field. Her husband, Rick, was an usher and was up, in his boots, shirt, and hat, on the truck with Jayce, helping him keep watch. I asked her, "Still want to be secretary?"

She smiled and took the paper and pen I handed her. Valentine, who overheard me, pulled out her phone and bustled over to Rebecca. "Mind if I help? I'm—er—working on something."

"Certainly, sweetheart, pull up a chair." When Valentine settled in next to Rebecca, she added, "Gonna have to find you a generator if you hope to record anything."

Valentine nodded. "That's a good idea. Better than taking batteries from my family member's phones like I have been. But for now I'll take pictures of your notes if that's alright."

Happy to see my daughter engaged, I spoke up, "Can I have

your attention?!"

After a few seconds, people wrapped up their discussions and turned to me. "I know there is much to talk about, so I think we will hold a quick meeting before the service so we can sort some things out.

"First, I think it's important to figure out what we know for sure. I'll start." I paused for a moment, thinking. "Well, the news said it was a viral infection, and officer Tom told me it will hit a person within seconds to ten minutes of contamination. Anyone know if antibiotics can nuke it?" I looked into a lot of blank faces and shrugs. "Well, might be worth testing out is all, seeing as the alternative is—well, you know." I coughed awkwardly and pressed on. "We know from the news you can get it through water, yes?"

Many people nodded.

"And you definitely get it if you are bit."

"Or if any blood or saliva touches you," a voice in the back put forward.

I put a finger up. "Actually, that's not entirely true. I killed a zombie and got their blood on my skin. So, I think it's only if their blood or saliva gets *in* you."

"So we're calling them zombies then?" a young father with a green ball cap interjected. When all eyes turned to him, he flushed. "Just seems a little 'Hollywood' don't it?"

I balked a little bit. "I suppose. I guess—erm—'infected' would probably be more accurate. But they certainly fit many of the stereotypes—other than being dead of course."

"They do have super strength, though. I saw one jump twenty feet," a voice from the back blurted out.

Out of the murmurs Kevin retorted, "It's not super strength, it's normal strength but not held back by fear or pain or nuthin'. They go all out. So the younger ones sure look superhuman, but they ain't."

I nodded and gestured at Kevin. "He's right. Don't underestimate them; Bertha Wilkens ran me down in a foot race. But she couldn't fly or anything. They are entirely human—"

"Shoot 'em in the head. I'm sure of it," a young man in the front said.

Kevin and I shook our heads before he said, "There's a pile of bodies by the grain elevator that were killed with shots all over them."

Jayce added in from the bed of the truck, his voice a bit higher than normal, "And a few at the edge of this field that I put down with single chest shots if you wanna see for yourself."

I agreed with them both and drew the crowds' eyes off the nervous kid and back to me. "They are human. They are entirely us, but sickened to the point of rage. They need legs to run, they need lungs to breathe, they need eyes to see, and they need blood circulating. They die just like we do, but are overcome by hunger so they think only of violence and will do anything to eat you."

A thought occurred to me. "Has anyone seen them use a tool or a weapon?"

The crowd chatted for a while, but no one spoke up to say they had seen any.

I pointed to Rebecca. "Put that down. They don't use tools. Really, they aren't that smart, they just chase, madly."

"Anything else?" Kevin asked.

A young lady, no more than a sophomore, stepped forward. "Animals can get it too." The crowd turned to her. "Our dog must have got it in the water, then he bit my sis' and we had to, you know . . . " Her father, next to her, hugged her tight and they both cried.

"I'm so sorry," I said as sincerely as I could, "but was the dog like a zombie, or was it acting normal when it bit your sister?"

She shook her head. "He was normal, just rowdy and cooped up and snipped at her hand and that was it."

I nodded. "So that means animals can carry the virus, but it doesn't affect them like us."

"No sir." a farmer from north of town stepped through the crowd. "Sure, the cows didn't act any different, but the pigs got it and went mad."

"Like, zombie mad?"

"Yessum, lucky I just sold half of 'em or the buggers woulda got me before I could put 'em down."

I sighed, as if we needed more things to worry about hunting us. "Does anyone know of any other animals reacting to the virus?"

Everyone shook their heads, but one other did confirm that he saw pigs with it.

"Keep an eye out. And, well, if the animals can carry the virus, can you eat their meat?"

There was silence. "Anyone tried meat from an animal that was killed after the virus spread?"

"There ain't exactly a lot of livestock left," a rancher in coveralls interjected.

"True, but it would be good to know."

Jesse stepped forward, the same man who had lost his mother at the nursing home the night before this chaos all started. *At least she didn't live long enough to see this.* His poor dad did, though. He pushed his hair to the side and said, solemnly, "I think I can help us find out." He looked up for a moment, flushed, then looked back down. "My dad isn't exactly getting his dialysis treatments. I don't know how long he will last without them. He says he won't let me risk taking him to town to do it myself, but I think he just doesn't much care now that Mom is gone." He was quiet for a moment, then seemed to remember why he was talking. He looked up. "But I bet he would be willing to have a nice steak before he goes."

Trudy, a young mother, looking worn but still pretty, called out to him, "Jesse, you sure? It ain't easy seein' someone you love get infected."

He studied her for a minute, "No, I suppose not. But if it could help us, give us a clue for some more food to eat—" He cut himself off, shoved his hands in his pockets and stepped back into the crowd.

There was silence and a few people reached out reassuring hands toward the man, understanding the tremendous burden on him and his father.

"That's up to you, just," I could hardly look at the poor guy, "Just let us know." I changed the subject. "They need water."

The crowd looked at me blankly.

I frowned. "I know it's obvious, but they have to find it somewhere, they stole some from a water tank I had filled. And I wonder if they can tell whether the water has poison in it or not."

Now the crowd was interested.

Rick, still atop the truck, cleared his throat. "I have a well, tanks, and a whole lot of chemicals I was fixin' to put on my crops." A handful of farmers said they had similar resources and wouldn't mind experimenting.

Kevin turned to Rick. "Could you get 'em to town? Then put a sign on them so the uninfected know not to drink any of it?"

I tempered their expectations. "Well, we know they die, but it seems pretty apparent that the virus makes them resistant to infection, otherwise they would be dead from their wounds and the rotting meat they eat, so we don't know if poison, or what poison, will actually work."

Rick nodded. "Well, it couldn't hurt to find out, and I won't use much water."

Trudy held her three year old in her arms and, with tears in her eyes, turned to Rick. "Do ya think, maybe, you could bring some un-poisoned water to town?"

Rick looked at Rebecca, who nodded at him. "Of course we can."

Several others in the crowd came forward then, asking for aid and Rick started to look a bit overwhelmed. In a few minutes voices started raising. Curtis naturally added his typical untactful opinion. "Just 'cuz we got wells doesn't mean we have to water the whole town. They don't last forever y'know."

Trudy looked down, "I know, I just—"

I raised my voice. "Come on people. If we are going to get through this, we have to stick together. All we got that the zombies don't is a brain and each other. Let's use 'em. Use our humanity and bear with one another. Let's get people to places where they don't need your well. Let's see what they have that you need." I looked at Curtis. "We have been alone for weeks and what's it got us? This, this meeting, is huge for us. This is what humans do, we work together, we care, we share, and we get to a better place—"

A rifle shot rang through the field, almost punctuating my point.

Most of the crowd jumped, some of them screamed. I swirled around and saw Jayce on the top of the truck. He winked at me. "Sorry, Pastor."

I fought back a smile as I looked to where his rifle was pointing, I couldn't see any zombies.

"After this meeting, everyone who needs water let Rebecca know. Anyone who can spare some water, do the same and we will figure it out. In the meantime, people might still be in town, too scared to come here today, maybe trapped, maybe hurt."

Curtis furrowed his brow even more than usual. "Maybe infected and waiting for us."

"Yeah, that too. But someone needs to help. I have to. I'm supposed to be a shepherd, so you can bet I'm checking on my members. But, I figure, why stop there? If we can get a group of people brave enough, we can band together and clear this town in maybe only a couple days."

"Is this the right time?" Grant, the town mechanic, famous for his big build, equally big mouth, and questionable diagnostics asked with a raised eyebrow.

"No," Kevin answered him, "Yesterday was. Or the day before. If they don't have water, they are in trouble. I got a water tank and plenty of rounds left over. I'll go."

Grant didn't look terribly excited, but mumbled something along the lines of, "Well, I never said I wouldn't go . . . "

Seven more people volunteered to clear the houses over the next few minutes. "Alright, get your affairs and gear in order, we go tomorrow at, say, 9 a.m. Everyone got a working watch?" They nodded. "Alright, the sun should be up and bright by then."

After we had our search parties organized, Grant noticeably absent from them, we soon figured out who had wells, and what homes might be vacant that had wells in them. We got volunteers to bring the water to town that afternoon and guard it for a few hours while people drew from it.

The meeting took hours and I hadn't even done worship. I announced that we would meet again next week and told the people they were welcome to stay for a church service. While half of them turned to walk away I shouted, "Wait! I know you guys may not be church goers, but I'm sure you know people who have died. If you would like me to do a funeral service for them, let me know." They seemed receptive to the idea. "I am going to put a list on that board." I pointed to the one at the edge of the field. "If you know someone is dead, put it on there. And every Wednesday I will hold funerals for Christians and memorials for non-Christians. They will start at noon."

I was still happy that twenty people stayed for the service, even a few of the ones who had turned to leave, stayed. So I was still trying to wipe the grin off my face when we started worship on the third Sunday in Lent. I preached that in Lent we are reminded of our sinfulness, our frailty; it was not hard to draw illustrations. But then I preached about the One who came to undo the brokenness, who, even though we deserve death because of the infection of sin, let Himself be killed so that our infections, of sin or otherwise, might be conquered.

Near the end of my sermon, something horrible happened. Someone asked a question.

Obviously, it was no one from my Lutheran Church, but I looked at George, the old banker who went to the Evangelical Church in town and stared at him for a few seconds. "Um, sorry, what did you say?"

He repeated himself. "What of those who die infected? Can they be saved?"

I saw the tears welling in his eyes and knew he had lost someone in the plague. "Why wouldn't they?"

He looked down at the alfalfa. "Well, they heed no word of Christ or His name. They are inflamed with sin."

I paused for a moment, noticing that his wife and daughter were not with him, and pitied this poor man who had been robbed of his comfort. "Well, perhaps I should ask you. How is anyone saved?"

"By making a decision for Jesus, to sincerely be His disciple, and to feel the presence of the Spirit."

"So the tiny child who dies, or the man who struggles with sin, or the man who screams and shoves his wife of fifty years because of his Alzheimer's… None of these can be saved?"

"I didn't say—"

"But you did. You have stated that salvation, even if in the slightest, rests on us and our decision or ability. You said it rests on our sincerity. You said its assurance is in our feelings. And if that is the case, it is not just the children and those with mental illness that cannot be saved. It is all of us. We are insincere, our feelings come and go, and we don't know all the answers."

I felt a bit guilty saying the man was wrong in front of so many people, but the true teaching of the gospel would be the only way these people, and he, could find hope. I pressed on, trying to sound as sympathetic as I could. "Salvation is not some effort we make, nor is it measured by our ability, nor is it reassured by our age, or feelings."

I spoke to the congregation now, "These people have an illness. It is a virus; it is an infection. And it is, sadly, a virus that steeps them in sin and causes them to lose their mental capacity to remember anyone, much less Christ. But salvation is not about us remembering Him, it is about Him remembering us. And this virus doesn't change that. They are united with Christ through the only experience that matters, the Holy Spirit claiming them, giving them faith through the Word, or the Wet Word of baptism, which is His Work, not ours."

I turned to the assembly. Some, who were not members, were bristling about my reference to baptism, I was sure, so I put it more generally. "Those who are united with Christ in faith are His children and they remain that way regardless of cancer, or Alzheimer's. Why would this infection be any different? Paul reminds us, "those He predestines, He calls." He has called many who have been infected, He has not rescinded that call, they are just fine. Faith is not a work, it is a gift, so is salvation."

Another voice in the back spoke up, "I know they are fine, but what about us?" Trudy stood there with tears in her eyes. "I had to do something bad, something really bad, but he just came right at me..." She cried louder.

My heart went out to her when I looked at her. "I hope that we, like you, will never forget the fact that the infected are actually people, but we do have to understand that in their sickness they will hurt others. And we as humans, as Christians, have a responsibility to care for our neighbor, like that little girl in your arms." I paused as she wiped her eyes on a tissue someone had given her. "It isn't good, it isn't fun, but it is right to stop the sick from hurting others. And short of locking them in a jail cell, the only way to stop them, at least that we know right now, is to kill them."

She still cried.

"Let me ask you this. If you were infected, what would you want us to do?"

She sniffled and looked at her little girl.

I nodded and raised my voice. "Raise your hand if—if you were infected, you would want us to put you down before you attacked or hurt or killed or ate someone else?"

I raised my hand and the whole congregation did the same.

"And your husband would have raised his hand, too." I spoke to the congregation now, "You've heard the commandment, 'You shall not murder.' It means just that, don't murder, but not all killing is murder. Ask the soldier who defends the defenseless, the police officer who stops the terrorist, the father who defends his family. Or, in our cases, the scared citizen, stopping a ruthless infection. It is an evil that we must kill, but it is a lesser of two evils. How much worse if we let them run rampant and hurt others?" I shuddered, thinking of the hordes ravaging the house behind ours. "And for these evils we must do or have fallen short of I announce the word of God to you: that Jesus, who let Himself be taken by an angry horde, has taken your sin away. You are forgiven."

Ritual Cleansing

The next morning I didn't eat much. Partly because we had long since burned all the meat we were unable to eat before it rotted—and we sure weren't going to just toss it aside for zombies to feed on. But that morning, none of us were exactly shoveling down our oatmeal that we had had for dinner the night before. So no one noticed I wasn't eating because I knew in a few hours I would be clearing houses and the dark haze from the city had overtaken our town, making an already scary day that much darker. I dropped my spoon on the table to mask a shudder when I glanced at all the shadowy corners of our kitchen and imagined how many in town might have zombies hiding in them. Yes, there was no room for oatmeal in my stomach that morning, it felt like it was already full; like a large pit of fear had settled inside.

But the search needed to be done. A few hours, a few cheers from my son who thought me a hero, and a few bathroom trips later, I waited in Jacobson field. The sun was higher, but it made little difference, our town was blanketed in ash and gray. Soon Kevin, Jayce, and Rick joined me, and we killed four unknown zombies that trailed them from the country. We pondered for a moment whether they had come from the next town over, but soon we heard the rumble of a car engine coming from town and the moans of its pursuers and we were back to work.

We must have killed twenty zombies by the time we had our team wholly accounted for. Charlotte, a single woman from town, and ever the optimist, cheered some of the team, noting how we had drawn twenty zombies from town and that there probably weren't many left in the houses. The pessimist in me worried that since we couldn't identify any of them, they must be coming from elsewhere, and that meant there could be far more of them than a small town of four hundred could ever supply. *How big would the city's horde be?* But I didn't mention any of it. No one needed that, not now. Instead, I forced a smile that I hoped didn't come off too insincere.

Derek and his wife Linda came a bit after Charlotte, a sporting couple dressed in softball gear and looking almost a bit too eager to hunt zombies. Last of all was Jesse.

I waited to see if anyone else from the meeting had changed their mind and decided to help us out. I knew it was a foolish thought—I couldn't get extra people to help dust the church, how could I get extra people to risk their lives? To be honest, I was thankful so many people, while not willing to fight, had at least offered us ammunition; that was not an easy offering in these days.

Finally, when nothing was moving on the horizons but smoke and the prairie grass swaying in the wind, I suggested we clear Bertha's house first since there was a working well in it and, hopefully, no zombies. We could practice clearing and make certain that some of our needy families could move in. The team agreed and started gearing up. I stepped into my coveralls, buttoned up my trench coat, and put on a motorcycle helmet and goggles that Rebecca, Rick's wife, had given me the day before. She cried when she did, saying her nephew didn't need them anymore.

Kevin and Jayce, in camouflage coveralls, helped themselves into their four-wheeler chest guards, helmets and boots. Derek and Linda sauntered off to their pickup, arm in arm, and started putting on bike helmets, shooting glasses, and facemasks. Jesse had painter's coveralls on, complete with a hood that covered his head except for a clear mask at the front.

"Hey Pastor, wanna ride with me?" Rick asked from the edge of the field. I shrugged and walked toward him. He spat out the window and chuckled. "Might be a good idea, you know, gas is mighty expensive these days."

I nodded in agreement and hopped in his passenger side, looking at him through my motorcycle glasses.

He raised an eyebrow at me. "I don't fault you guys for the armor, I think it's smart." He looked down at his work boots, jeans, and a long sleeve cowboy shirt. "But I'm slow enough as it is, I want to move, and," he put on a pair of goggles and a bandana, "see."

"Can we ride too?" a voice called out from the field.

Rick waved at Jesse and Charlotte, who hopped in the bed of the truck with their assortment of guns and bats and armor. I had to twist to see them settle in. Charlotte was putting her long curly hair up under a ballcap. "Don't need anything grabbin' hold of this," she told Jesse, who nodded in agreement and, despite the shade of nervous green, forced a smile at her, and the machete in his hands stopped shaking so violently.

Not a few minutes later, the team, like some sort of twisted group of trick-or-treaters in low budget costumes, stood outside Bertha's home. It looked much the same as it did a few weeks ago, except now the spring grass had grown tall enough to cover the bottom half of the tires on the burned out cars in her yard. The caravan of three trucks had gotten the attention of a few wandering zombies, which Jayce, steadying his gun on the pickup bed, put down before they got halfway up Bertha's long dirt drive.

Kevin held his shotgun up to the house, his head cocked to the side, listening for a moment. "Well, if those shots didn't wake anything up, I don't think there's anything in there."

Rick shook his head. "I ain't lettin' a family in there without being sure."

Kevin nodded.

Meanwhile, I had paced over to the zombies Jayce had just killed. I felt I should say something. I rehashed a few thoughts from my earlier funeral and memorial services.

The rest of the team wandered over as well.

Jesse, his trembling shadow falling on the corpses, looked at them for a moment then turned away. "That's Frank Meddles, from Riverdale."

Derek leaned in and shook his head. "Damn. Sure is. What they doin' all the way over here?"

"Lookin' for food I s'pose," Kevin said sadly. "Makes you wonder when the ones from the city will make it this far."

Rick shivered. "I'd rather not think about that."

"Maybe we—"

I stopped when I saw Charlotte walk over to us, holding a bottle of whiskey. She pulled out the stop and raised the bottle. "Here's to you Riverdale folks." She took a long pull and then poured the rest of the bottle on the zombies.

We all stepped back and watched as she dropped a match on all of them.

I thought sitting on a grain bin with a horde of zombies racing at me was scary, but it was nowhere near as frightening as clearing a dark house. At least on a grain bin you saw the horde coming at you. But in an unlit house, you had no idea which shadows, lengthened by a darkened sky and twisted by whatever shifting flashlights we could find, held a zombie or not. Your heart stopped as you looked behind every door or chair, you prayed whenever someone stuck their head into an attic or crawl space, you hated the sound of your own breathing and heartbeat that seemed deafeningly loud, and you jumped whenever a team member bumped a channel changer off a table.

By the time we finished clearing Bertha's house, we discovered it was best to be as loud as possible to try and draw any zombies to us, but also to calm our nerves. The silence and shuffling were far more frightening than communication, which, if nothing else, reminded you where the other people were. It seemed we didn't jump at every creak of the floorboards when we were louder.

I couldn't smell, thankfully, through my facemask, which saved me from retching once more at the smeared blood and hair on the ground. I couldn't say the same for Jesse, who had to run out of the house and rip his, now vomit laden, painter's hood off. I pitied him and realized that perhaps I was getting used to the gore of the new world. Part of that thought reassured me, the other part horrified me. *Blood and guts are normal now? Lord have mercy.*

Bertha's body had apparently been taken by Jacob, the funeral director, or someone, but other than taping off the house, nothing had been done to clean the stains and the, now gelatinous, pooled blood inside.

After twenty minutes of checking rooms, closets, under beds and in attics, we pronounced the house clear. And the knots in our stomachs started to unwind themselves.

"But no one can live with all this infected blood in there," Kevin said as he leaned on his pickup and swished the bottom of his boots in the bucket of bleach.

"We can bleach the place," his son suggested.

Kevin looked at his feet suspiciously. "Son, we don't even know if bleach works."

"It's the best we can do, other than burning the whole place down," Jesse said as he sat, taking deep breaths on the tailgate of a truck, getting some of his color back.

Rick nodded. "Yeah, and they probably shouldn't have supper on the floor."

A few of the team members snickered at that. It was the first laughter I'd seen from them all day. The mood had lightened since the house had been cleared, but the burden of a whole withering town full of dark closets and corners still weighed on us all.

The rest of the team tried to figure out how Bertha got the virus, while I volunteered to haul a few gallons of bleach into the house for the new residents to use; assuming the house would still be clear when they got there. I paused before I stepped over the congealed puddle of Bertha's blood in the entryway that I had spilled. *Sorry, Bertha.* I shook my head and set the jugs of bleach on the kitchen counter, then headed back through the blood-spattered hallway, anxious to finally be rid of this house. I paused, however, when I saw, tucked behind the open door, my prayer book.

I stooped and picked it up with my gloved hand. I turned it over and saw Bertha's blood had smeared the side of the pages. My stomach lurched and I held it away from me, then I tossed the book into her hall trash can. I stared at it for a moment, wondering if in fact, this corrupted blood, this corrupted virus was stronger than all our prayers. Before I could quiet my conscience and doubt, Rick called me over to the trucks while he put his cowboy hat back on. "We're burning daylight."

Soon the caravan of pickups was heading back toward the smokestack that used to be our quiet little town and toward a hundred houses that, unlike Bertha's, we had no clue whether there was anything waiting for us in them or not.

Only minutes later, we were driving slowly through the five or six (depending on whether or not you counted the dirt side roads) blocks of our little town. I was on the megaphone. "Signal to us if you need help," I repeated. The first people we contacted were about three dozen infected that we put down pretty quickly, though two of them made it into the back of one of the trucks. Jesse, who I was afraid would lock up in shock, buried his machete into the side of one of their necks and kicked it out of the truck. The other was vaulted backwards by a shotgun blast.

As terrifying as it was, I thought it was good to let some of the crew who hadn't seen any fighting get a few of the nerves out of the way. I immediately felt guilty about that thought as Derek and Linda hugged each other. "You guys alright?" Jesse asked them.

Linda sniffed, nodded, and gestured to one of the bodies. "That was my aunt." Neither of them looked as if zombie hunting was an adventure anymore.

I pulled a little notepad out and marked her aunt's name down, then turned to the team with their shaking hands and puffy eyes. "It's not easy to put down people you know. And when it gets easy, well, that's when you have to be afraid, I think." I looked at Linda, who nodded. "I'll do her service on Wednesday if you would like."

She reloaded her shotgun, fidgeted with her goggles, and stood up straight. "That would be fine, Pastor, thanks. Let's just keep going, though."

As we started rolling again, Kevin shouted some orders out his window, "You don't have to hit the head, take a breath and hit 'em in the chest." He swerved around a few burned out cars before leaning out the window again and adding, "Wait 'til they are close enough to put 'em down if you have a shotgun, we're gonna need every round we got."

Rick leaned out his window, one hand holding his cowboy hat in place, and helpfully shouted, "And make sure it's a zombie before you pull that trigger."

Not two blocks later, we found our first uninfected family. The wife waved us down from the upstairs window and the husband, holding a shovel, ran out to us. Charlotte knew them and their three kids and talked with them a while as the rest of us ferried a few buckets of water from the tank in the back of Kevin's truck into their house. The husband thanked us and said he would try to make it to the next meeting on Sunday.

We pulled away from his house with our heads held pretty high; we had helped someone today in some little way. I hoped it would give us the push we needed to brave the darkness of the houses we actually had to go into.

A block later, we found more uninfected. We couldn't see anyone from the upstairs window, we could only hear yelling—a man and woman shouting for help. The downstairs windows had been busted out. I picked up my megaphone to try and contact the people inside, but before I could say a thing, Jesse was jumping out of the truck and racing toward the house. "That's my sister's house!" he shouted.

Before he even reached the shattered glass on the front porch, three bodies burst through the door at him. He screamed and fell down in his attempt to run away. Some of our team, who were better shots than me, fired at the zombies over Jesse, who was crawling back to the street.

And then there were more.

Seven more zombies vaulted through the windows, crawled out the doors, and sprinted toward us. I screamed and dropped the megaphone, fumbling for my shotgun. Our skirmishing line of farmers, ranchers, and a pastor held. The firefight probably only lasted a few seconds, only one zombie managed to make it to the street—the only zombie I got my gun up in time to shoot. It rolled to the ground a few feet in front of me.

"Blast it all, Jesse!" Rick shouted. "We all got kin in town we worried about. Run in there alone and you're gonna get eaten."

"Or shot if someone's in there with a gun," Linda added.

Jesse was back on his feet, stepping over the bodies. His face, what little of it I could see through his mask, was white, twisted in panic, and streaks of his blonde hair were wet with sweat and stuck to it. I had no idea if the reprimands affected him or not. "She's not here," he panted.

"Then let's go see if we can find her." Kevin grabbed Jesse by the shoulder and pulled him back. "But you stay behind until you can keep your head on."

Jayce and Charlotte stayed in the trucks to keep an eye out for any zombies that may have wanted to check out the noise, if they didn't have more appetizing options right in front of them. The rest of us filed in, some through the windows, into the dark house, where the screams for help had started up again. It was hard to see in the dim building, especially through goggles and having just been out in the sun. But we followed the screams and found two zombies at the end of what used to be the staircase trying to clamber up to the second floor. Kevin shot them both, then yelled up the staircase, "Are you alright?"

The woman at the top of the stairs, I was pretty sure, used to be the receptionist at the local bank. It was hard to tell with how emaciated and pale she was. Her husband held her in one arm and a sledgehammer in the other. When he saw us, he dropped the hammer and the two sobbed into each other's shoulders for a minute before letting us help them to the ground floor.

The husband explained to us how he had torn down the staircase when the zombies started to break through the boards on his windows. He laddered his way up and pulled the ladder up after him. "And then we sat there for two weeks. Two weeks of hardly any food or water." He sipped on the bottle of water we had given him; "BOILED" was taped on the side of it. "But that wasn't the worst. It was the groans, the scratching, the fact that, every once in a while, one boosted itself on the others close enough to reach the second floor. I should have gone out a window, tried to run, something . . . " he trailed off.

"Believe me," I said, "every single one of us wishes we did something a little bit different. You did enough to keep your family alive. And that is incredible in itself."

He nodded. "Thanks."

We gave them some supplies, a handgun with some ammunition, and enough water to last until Sunday, our next meeting. They thanked us for the help and seemed confident, having made it through that, they could make it on their own until the meeting. He assured us he would be there.

We gave Jesse a minute with his sister. The poor guy was desperate for good news, we were happy to be able to give him some. But soon we were back in our trucks. The rest of the short drive through town yielded, sadly, no more encounters with survivors, at least none that we could contact from the road. We stopped at the edge of town. "Seven people?" Derek said, disgusted. "That's all that made it." He shook his head as if he had been betrayed.

"There's still hope," Charlotte retorted, though she wouldn't look up from the ground. "Maybe people couldn't get to a window or something." She kicked a pebble on the street, then looked up, more hopeful. "Or maybe they are too scared to make any noise and attract any zombies."

Jesse leaned up against the truck and fiddled with his helmet. "That's a fair point, actually."

"So we check the houses, then?" I asked, looking up from my notebook of names and addresses that had woefully little information in it.

With plenty of muted daylight left, we loaded up and headed for a new block. We had thought about doing the clearing more methodically, going house by house, block by block. But it's impossible to separate your feelings and fears, and the reality was most of the team, aside from me, who didn't grow up here, had family in town. The need for answers ultimately steered us toward the homes of people we knew, and we braced ourselves for the worst. We still had plans to clear the whole town; between the eight of us we probably knew the whole town, but we all had people we really wanted to know about. Maybe it was unfair, but we needed a place to start.

I wish we hadn't.

First was Derek's brother's house. We made him stay in the trucks after no one responded to our hails from the roadside. The broken living room window had already dampened our hopes and he was already trying not to cry. When we kicked in the door, we heard the groans from upstairs and knew it was bad news.

We found Derek's brother and his daughter dead and half eaten. His empty handgun was on the floor next to him, the wall across from him peppered with bullets and the floor covered with a half dozen zombie corpses.

As we went up the stairs, the groans got louder. I kicked in the door and dove at the feet of the three men with guns raised behind me. The blasts didn't last long and then they were helping me to my feet. The wife fell back into the bedroom, twitching for a few moments before she completely expired.

I stood up and looked at the twisted corpse. "I'm the pastor, I'll tell him."

No one said anything.

I had delivered bad news as a pastor before. It's tempting to try to say "at least." *At least you still got your wife.* But it's never worth it, it never helps. Eventually, my seemingly numb-with-dread legs led me down to the truck and I just told him sorry. Then I told him exactly what we found.

He sniffed and leaned into Linda who had her arm around him. "He went out swingin', huh?" he asked.

"Yessir, fighting for his daughter," Jesse said.

He nodded. "Figures he wouldn't have the heart to put Traci down, he was always a softy." The man chuckled through his tears.

"You guys went to the Baptist Church, yeah?"

He nodded.

"I'll do the funerals on Wednesday."

"Thanks Preacher." He looked up to the ashen sky and shook his head. "How am I gonna tell Pa, Linda? Might kill him."

She shrugged and put her head on his shoulder.

"Want me to?" I offered.

He shook his head. "Nah, you got yours to take care of after this. I'll tell him, but maybe do the funeral at our place?"

"Of course." I nodded, walked away, and put three Xs next to their address in my notebook.

The rest of the men had, wisely, dragged all the corpses, using ropes, out the back door to burn them. Derek refused to go look at them, none of us could blame him. While seeing a deceased loved one can help the grieving process, seeing a loved one like *that,* well that's something I never advise.

Soon the group was gearing up to head to a house across the street, where Rick's sister, Vickie, lived. Derek wiped his eyes and nose, put his bike helmet back on, and grabbed his gun.

Kevin looked over at him. "We got a lot of people here. You could go. No one would blame you."

Derek looked at Kevin for a moment, then shook his head. "No. It's like Rick said, everyone's got this stuff. Let's go." Then he marched across the street toward Vickie's.

A few seconds later, I caught up with the rest of the team on the lawn. I shouted into Rick's sister's house, but heard no reply through the broken windows. When we made to move in, Rick refused to stay with the trucks, but he agreed to stay in the back of the search party.

The house was, like many others, silent, still, and dark. So dark your eyes hurt. We searched the ground floor with our lights, jumping at a pack of rats we disturbed. The place was a mess, and there was dried or congealed blood everywhere, but we found no bodies. We had agreed to talk loudly and clearly in the houses, to help our nerves and communication, but it seemed wrong, almost insincere, with Rick's hope dying faster with every step. We worked our way up the stairs as quietly as we could. They creaked and we all jumped when one of the crew's bulky armor knocked a picture off the wall. That was when someone started screaming.

The screams came from down the hall and Kevin, at the front of the line, shook with fright and fell into the wall. I helped him up while Derek took the front of the line.

"No! You can't take her! No!" the screaming woman shouted.

Derek kicked down the door at the end of the hall and Rick barreled me over running to the front.

I braced for the gunfire but only heard yelling.

Rick boomed, "Vickie, it's me! It's alright, Sis. Stop!"

I got up and ran into the room behind the others.

Vickie, Rick's sister, held a pillow over her struggling daughter's face. "I won't let you monsters turn her!"

Rick yelled at Vickie while Linda and I, having shoved through the others, who were frozen in shock, tried to pry Vickie's hands off the pillow. Her daughter, who was struggling a moment ago, was laying still on the bed now.

Rick picked Vickie up and tossed her halfway across the room. She screamed harder and ran at her daughter. Rick grabbed her, yelled at her, but she would not relent until Rick slapped Vickie on the cheek.

Derek, his wits about him once more, pushed me out of the way and checked the daughter's pulse. "She's alright, she's breathing now."

Vickie, now in Rick's arms, had stopped fighting, but she wouldn't look us in the eye. She sat on the floor mumbling and wouldn't acknowledge us, no matter how we tried to get her attention. After a few minutes, her daughter woke up and ran to her, which caused us alarm at first, but apparently the terror had passed and Vickie just held her, mumbling and stroking her hair.

The terror had passed, yes, but what was left?
They could die, but could we live after all?

The sky was blood red when we quit checking houses that day. Miranda cried when I walked in the door and went to hug me, but I waved her off. Who knows how much blood was on my coveralls? None of it was ours I assured her. She backed off and put her hand over her mouth, nodding that she understood. It was a long process to undress and sanitize everything. Halfway through I wondered if I shouldn't just burn the whole outfit instead to save time. But the reality was that we had the time. Time sitting in a house with nothing much to do. Also, there was the terrifying fact that, depending on how things were going in the cities—judging by the cloud of debris that moved in the night before, it wasn't going well—we might not be able to just buy new gear again.

While we bleached out all my clothes, I tried, somehow, to share with Miranda and the kids the events of the day. I told her about how we split into teams and cleared block after block of dark, broken houses. I told her who we found alive, who we found dead, and how half the town seemed to be missing entirely. Val recorded parts of the story, had me retell others, and kept notes. I was too fried to care to stop her. But I did have to, after a half hour, tell Luke to stop asking about the gory details. He liked them now, but wouldn't when he was trying to sleep.

Over dinner, I tried to be as normal as possible with Val's phone recording, but the food that I barely touched probably gave it all away—my nerves and spirit were shot. When Val pointed it out, I said something sarcastic about wanting a steak. And only later did I realize how much it probably hurt Miranda, she did everything she could to make the constant schedule of oatmeal and canned soups taste good. But I couldn't work up an appetite, not that night, not after what we had all seen that day.

It was a day full of darkness and screaming and shouting. A day full of terror, wondering what waited behind every door or chair. A day of tears as team members saw loved ones half eaten, or enraged by a virus, or dead from dehydration. A day of guilt as we wondered who we could have saved if we'd come earlier. And there was another day just like it ahead of us.

Maybe it was depression or lack of sleep, but the haze seemed thicker the next day. And our ranks were thinner. Rick didn't show, having told Kevin he was having a hard time settling his sister, Vickie, into their home. And Charlotte, who seemed ever hopeful, said she couldn't take another day of bad news. I didn't blame either of them. I couldn't ask anyone to go through all that again. But some of them, for some reason, did. And we pressed back into town.

Hours later, fifty houses of terror and tragedy later, forty zombies later and, thanks be to God, five-more-people-who-needed-help-and-got-it later, I was up late at my desk by candlelight. It was still hard to sleep. It was odd that after weeks of fear and desperate survival, you feel less nervous, but you really aren't, it's still there, you just get a little more used to it. And so, like every night, I was still awake debating whether to inspect every creak or rustle of the wind. I was still awake going over every scenario that played throughout the day, trying to forget the strands of intestines on the floor, every person dead with horror and thirst written all over their face, every person killed by disease, exposure, or their own hands. *What if we'd done this sooner? What if I hadn't sat for so long, cowering in fear? God have mercy on me.*

I pulled out the tattered list of names from the board out in the field. I drew a few lines on it from top to bottom, hoping a few new columns would fit all the names of the people we had discovered dead or infected that day. Between the two teams, we had nearly fifty people identified. Most I didn't know and any guilt about not being active enough in the community was outweighed by the sweet bliss of anonymity. I didn't know what Theresa Huntsman's laugh sounded like. I didn't know what Maxwell Clary's favorite football team was. And, Lord help me, I was thankful. Because the handful of people I did know tore me up inside. I cried when we shot Jacob, the funeral director, and his family. They came racing out of his house, which sat on top of the funeral home, along with two dozen other zombies. Poor family didn't have a chance with all the bodies piled up in his basement. That was one place we didn't clear. We shot the group that came running out, I said a prayer, and we set the whole place on fire.

Several of the houses of my members were completely

abandoned, like half the houses we cleared that day. Those were the easy houses. We could hope for the best for them. But three other families weren't as lucky: the Rensons, the Schwarbers, and the Montgomerys were all dead or infected. All people I was supposed to care for, all people I knew and prayed for, all people I now grieved for.

I put my head down and cried for a while after writing their names down. *Why them and not us?* Why were they rotted and forced to kill each other, turn on each other, or die in pure terror? Why did God let that happen even after my prayers for them?

After the tears refused to fall anymore, I went into the kitchen and found my vodka, *what sweet relief could it bring.* I knew it couldn't bring any answers, but that night God didn't seem to be giving me any either, at least the alcohol would bring some numbness.

By the grace of God, I put it back. Better to save it for burning zombies than bringing on more dehydration and burning us down from the inside out. I stumbled back to my desk and watched the wax dribble down the candle stick and onto the paper, covering some of the names on my paper. If only it could cover the pain.

Eventually I fell asleep with my head on my desk.

Signs of the Church

"This is the day that the Lord has made," I said, trying to sound sincere on the fourth Sunday in Lent.

"Let us rejoice and be glad in it," the congregation of forty people responded without me. I wasn't glad or rejoicing that morning.

It had been a hard week on all of us. The families were stressed because many of us were out clearing houses, though, by the grace of God we managed it without anyone getting killed or worse. It was a lot of work to only find about a dozen or so people who needed help, but, in a time where there were plenty of reasons not to sleep at night, easing our consciences took one of them away. We didn't have to stay up wondering if other people in town needed our help, we only stayed up wondering who would be next.

But wasn't that enough? Wasn't that worth it? Wasn't any amount of fear and trouble worth it for one life, let alone a dozen? So we had cleared them.

Wednesday, I had held a half dozen memorial services, one at Derek and Linda's, where his father wept over a scrap of his granddaughter's clothes. In spite of the bliss of anonymity, I regretted not knowing her or many of the people I spoke of that day. The town was small, and most people knew or were related to everyone else. All except me, a transplant from the coast, who was too lazy to get to know more people in the community. But I spoke with the families, asking if the deceased was a Christian; if they knew Jesus, or more accurately, if He knew them and had called them by the gospel or through baptism. For those who were, I gave a Christian funeral and sermon packed with all of the promises of the Empty Tomb: eternal peace, full and complete healing, resurrection, reunion, forgiveness. For the rest, I gave a memorial message.

And what a difference that made. A sermon or a eulogy. A eulogy looked back with no hope of a future, a sermon looked back at the person and at their Savior through whom there was a promised reunion. In a eulogy we highlighted only the good things of a person, glossing over the fact that they may have been an alcoholic or ill-tempered. Of the few people I knew well enough to know that what the family told me were blatant lies, well, I felt slimy talking about how great they were when we all knew they were jerks. But in a sermon, I could honestly proclaim their struggles and sins, because then I could proudly proclaim their Savior, who took their sin away. It was freeing, it was the truth.

Regardless, there were tears at all the services. The gospel doesn't take away tears, well it will one day, but in these days there is still mourning, but mourning with hope. Hope that wasn't like our vain hopes at a cure, or in the military. Hope in the gospel is certain and strong; there will be a fulfillment, we, the church, simply are waiting until the fullness of that time. And how often did we pray for that time to come quickly? Because one look at anyone in the Jacobson's field on a Wednesday and you could tell we were a people in need of hope.

The Good Lord knows how many hours I spent in that alfalfa field, but I sure lost count as family after family trudged in and out of the field. Most of them seemed to appreciate the words, which meant a lot to me, and hopefully, to my family. Miranda, desperate to be out of the house, brought the kids out to the field. Luke brought a hammer and nails and put together crosses that we gave each family. He was becoming a better handyman than I, though that didn't necessarily mean much. Val, with permission, recorded snippets of funerals, even interviewed some of the families, or just spent the afternoon laying in the alfalfa watching the dark haze go by. Miranda sang a song at each service, a song of hope and life.

This was probably why I was frustrated even though church attendance doubled in one week. Because we, not just me, but my whole family sacrificed so much to serve the people, to bring them God's word, yet it seemed so taken for granted. No, that's a lie; like I said, so many appreciated it, but a few did not. And sadly, the voices of criticism always sounded louder in my ears, even before the plague. I never would have guessed how much of being a leader of God's people involved learning from criticism while not letting it devour you like a ravenous zombie. Easier said than done, as that Sunday morning made abundantly clear.

Clearing the field took a little longer than usual on that fourth Sunday of Lent. Transient zombies seemed to be drawn to our town. Maybe because smoke was still rising from burned out houses and the grain bins we set on fire a couple weeks before. We tried to ignore the fact that if dozens of zombies from the small towns scattered across the plains were making it to our town, perhaps the thousands from the city would also.

I started the meeting with an update on what we had done in the last week, then Rebecca, today wearing a fancy broad hat, read the minutes from the last meeting, which many of the newcomers appreciated. After a few questions on what we talked about last week, Jesse came forward. "Well, everyone, Tyler and I found a wild and clearly infected pig. We shot it and, very carefully, cut some meat off of it. We tied Pa up, said a few prayers, and fed him some bacon." He paused for a moment, then smiled. "And Pa said it was the best he ever had."

The crowd relaxed, a few chuckled.

The man next to him, who I assumed was Tyler, nodded with a smile. "We had Donald tied up for a whole day, and nothin'."

I nodded at them. "Great news, everyone. Your meat's good. Rebecca note it in the minutes, please, that you cannot get infected through cooked meat."

A voice chimed in from the audience, "But I wouldn't eat it rare."

"Agreed. Still use caution." I strode over to my lectern and looked at my notes. "Alright, next order of business. We cleared Bertha's old house, the water is working, but we must assume it is contaminated. Furthermore, there was infected blood on several surfaces, but we left enough bleach at the house to cover the floor and walls three times over."

There were some murmurs in the crowd.

"So we gotta figure out who gets to live in it. Let's first decide who doesn't have running water. Raise your hand." Miranda and I kept our hands down, we had already agreed it would look bad if we took the first open house. About two thirds of the families, all those living in town, raised their hands. "Sheesh," I exclaimed even though I didn't want to. I coughed to cover up my disconcert. Frankly, I should have known no one in town had water. "Alright, well, who honestly is worried about their water supply even with the truck coming to town once a week?"

About half the hands went down. "Good, thank you. The house has four bedrooms, are any families willing to live with another family until we clear an adequate amount of houses?"

Now only three people's hands were up. *These were the neediest ones*, I thought. Anyone desperate enough to be inconvenienced is truly desperate. "Well then, that makes things simple. Trudy and Evelyn," I motioned to the young mother holding her daughter in her arms so tightly her hands were white, "would only take one room. Could you guys figure out how to split up the other three rooms?"

The other two families nodded and a wave of relief washed over me. Until Curtis spoke up.

"Who says that's the criteria we gotta go by?"

I closed my eyes and rubbed my temples at the sound of Curtis' raspy voice.

"Well," I stammered, "Water is a big deal-"

"So is my house that has no windows on the bottom floor."

"That's true," I assented, "maybe we can get you some boards or some—"

He caned forward and interrupted me again. "And let's not forget Bertha was my second cousin! It should go to family, should it not? Or are you just making up laws all by yourself now?"

Inspired by the curmudgeon, Grant, after he finished lighting his cigarette with his skull and crossbones lighter, chimed in, probably just to spite me. "Yeah, who made you judge and jury of us anyways?" He shouldered his big frame through the crowd. "Just 'cus you think you're better than us, it don't mean you are."

"Well, I don't think—Um, we could have an election I 'spose," I said, wiping sweat off my brow.

"Yeah with a bunch of your members here, some election that would be," Grant snapped and crossed his arms.

"I never meant—" I coughed again, "I mean, I was just thinking if we organized, we could survive better. Sure, we may not get everything we want—"

"Well, unless you're you, then you get everything." He spat in my general direction.

"Enough!" Rick bellowed. I don't think anyone had seen Rick angry before. He was a big man, but always gentle. Angry, he was truly intimidating. He rose up to his full height, his weathered hands balled into fists and his face redder than when he'd worked all day in the fields. "Enough of this nonsense. Pastor doesn't have running water either, and you don't see him giving himself a house." He spat his chew even farther afield and pointed toward the dissenters. "And last I checked, neither of you were on the grain bin fighting the horde with Pastor and the Krenshaws. Or cleaning houses with us this week." He turned to the crowd. "Pastor Darren put this together to try and help, if you want to take part in it, good, help us work it out. If you don't, you are free to leave." He eyed Curtis and Grant. "But don't come bitching to us when a zombie is breaking down your door while you die of thirst." He turned back to me, nodded, and added, "Forgive the language, Pastor."

I nodded to him and scratched the stubble on my chin to hide the grin that I could feel growing on my face. After a moment I collected myself. "Yeah, I don't want to be a dictator or anything. We can vote on this stuff. But come on people," I pleaded, "most of the people we know are dead. Dead!" I let it sink in for a moment. "If we cannot band together in common humanity now, how can we survive? Can we not sacrifice something for someone else? Can we not give of what we have, and help each other? And especially those of us here who are Christians, we have a Savior who gave up His life for us, can we not give up something? And even if we get the short end of the stick, wouldn't you rather be wronged, knowing that we are working together to live? Wouldn't we rather be wronged than tear apart our humanity? We can do so much! We can live!"

Linda, who had been standing in the back next to Derek, rocked onto her toes and spoke up, "I propose a motion. To let

Trudy, the Knutsons, and the Bensons live in Bertha's old house."

Rebecca looked up. "Do I have a second?"

There was one from back in the crowd.

"Show of hands, then?" she asked coolly.

It was unanimous, even Grant and Curtis, mumbling under their breath, voted for them.

The meeting went on for some time while we discussed some ammo conservation tactics. One man mentioned that he had already cleared out the ammunition from the parts store in town. There was a suggestion to check the police office and the supply store in the next town, a few volunteers said they would look into it. Some farmers discussed what crops to grow and one of their wives brought a few dozen eggs to share with the group. A part of me swelled with pride to see people working together. I prayed it made an impression on Grant and Curtis, but perhaps nothing would.

After hours, the sun was getting high in the prairie sky and I moved to end the meeting so we could get on with the Church service. "Well, I know there is much to talk about, but I would like to start worship for those who would like it. If you want to keep chatting, could you please go back to the other side of the field?" I felt bad making the other people move, but I really did want to use the altar I had set up on the trailer. Most of the people started saying their goodbyes, but I kept an eye on Grant and his friends out of the corner of my eye.

I sighed when I saw him laugh and, after shooting me a glance, turn to his friends. "Ain't that cute, fellas, they're playing church."

To their credit, a few of the men around him shook their heads and walked away, but some laughed along with him. He knew I heard him, everyone heard, Grant always spoke loud enough for people to hear him. A few of my members looked down, perhaps in shame. I could feel my cheeks getting warm, out of anger and frustration that I didn't have a great answer. Were we a church? A smattering of Christians in a field with a flatbed trailer?

I tried to ignore him and shuffled some of the papers on the lectern. But Grant went on. "After this plague, damn, if there's a God, He sure ain't anything I'd be bowin' to. But if Reverend Acton here wants to put a pope hat on and these people'll listen, well maybe he is onto something." He howled along with a few of his friends as they turned back toward the trucks.

One of the men who had come last week, while he didn't laugh, turned along with them.

I put my papers down and stepped in front of the lectern. "Hey Grant!" I called out. I stared at him and, though I was angry, I had him to thank for reminding me of something I should have known all along. I had been wrestling with it ever since the plague hit and toppled all our institutions. It was true there were no District Presidents. I had no salary. There were no bishops. But, while helpful for good order, those structures didn't make the church at all. Jesus did.

We were the people who believed in Jesus. We were the people who gathered to hear His Word of hope in the darkest days. We were the ones who received with faith and joy His gifts where He gave us the Spirit and forgiveness and strength. That's what the church was.

I should have known it all along. Jesus called disciples because He would send them to proclaim His Word. He made a Church for a reason, to tell the world about Him and to give them His gifts, He made a Church to baptize, to teach. And for thousands of years, He sent people with His Word and gifts to the world, to be the Church. And that is what we were doing, this was the Church, God's people gathered to hear His Word and Sacrament. And it was my calling to give it to them.

So when the muscly man turned and cocked his head at me, I spoke up, "Forgive me, Grant, but we are not playing."

"Hey, I don't care if you wanna believe there's a God and he's actually good, that's cool, you can be crazy. But in case you haven't noticed, there ain't no church, just like there ain't no government. If somethin's gonna get done, we gotta do it. So—"

"Exactly, and I'm doing it. I am proclaiming the Word of God who is still real and still cares for His people."

He laughed again. "Now that's a crock riper than a three week zombie." He put his hands up and turned back toward the trucks. "But have it your way."

The congregation was silent for a minute. And many of the stragglers waved sheepishly and walked back to the trucks. But forty or so people stayed for worship. They scattered about the chairs in the field murmuring, some were shaking their heads.

After a few deep breaths, I started the service, but maybe it was just my annoyance, or it was their downcast expression, I couldn't ignore what they all had heard. When it came time for the sermon I said, "We know the church is not a building, or a club, but it's God's people." I looked at my notes to buy myself some time, even though what I was saying had nothing to do with what I had written on them. "Yes, the church is people claimed by God and given the gift of faith."

Their blank faces seemed ill convinced. "Think of it this way, if you were traveling, well, before the plague, of course." I hoped I didn't lose them. "If you were traveling, where would you look for Christians? In a barn, or a church?"

A few people in the seats muttered, "Church."

"Right, but let's suppose you go into that church building and the preacher proclaimed that God was dead and we are all doomed and the people shouted in agreement, 'amen!' Is that *the* Church?"

Several people were shaking their heads.

I affirmed them. "Of course not. But what if you go into a field like this and found a sinful preacher standing next to a cross," I motioned to the one on the makeshift altar next to me, "and what if he stood in front of an altar, proclaiming that God is life and gives victory over sin, death, and the devil and gives eternal life to His people who believe in Him, purchased by the blood of the Savior, Jesus, and proven by His empty tomb? What if that pastor preached that Christ offered victory even in the face of sin, disease, zombie virus, and death? And what if the people said, 'amen' to that!? Are those Christians?"

The people nodded.

"Is that group of people, that group of Christians united in that one true faith, are they the Church?"

Some people nodded even more, saying "Yes."

"Yes they are. And so are we. The Church is where God's people do what Jesus told them to do, to baptize, to preach, to, as Jesus said, 'do this in remembrance of me.' That's what the Church does, and its members are those who believe the promises and gifts are for them. So no, there is no government and there are no denominational presidents around, but the church still has a leader, Jesus, the King. And the church is alive and well."

The people seemed calmer, more upbeat.

"Let's do what the Church does, let's worship, let's pray, let's take a little time to be strengthened by the Word of our Savior. There's no building, but," I motioned once more to the altar, "this isn't a bunch of stuff for playin' cards, this is a bunch of church stuff, the signs of the Church. And you are the ones who gather around it, God's people, His body, His bride, His Church."

Yes, I was still frustrated when I started church. Frustrated that the criticisms were so vocal, so oppressive, hitting on our identity as God's people and His goodness. Frustrated that everything I worked so hard on and risked so much for was being attacked from inside and out. Frustrated that I hadn't thought to give a good answer to Grant's face or the half dozen people who left with him.

But by the end of the service, the mood had noticeably shifted. We weren't drifters, we weren't second rate children of God, left behind in a twisted rapture. We were refreshed by the Word of God, absolved by His grace, and sent to fulfill His commission.

That's not to say the church was without its struggles. It got awkward when one of my elders asked about taking Communion. The bread and wine, body and blood, is a gift of God so that His people might know that everything He did on the cross, He did for them—they could taste it on their lips. But it was also to be celebrated in unity and how were we supposed to do that with a conglomeration of five different denominations? I told them it would probably be best if we held a separate communion service later in the week for Lutheran members and anyone who was willing to talk to me about their public confession beforehand. I gave a little speech on unity, I quoted from 1 Corinthians, I asked the people to honor our request to be unified while we celebrate it and reassured them we didn't consider them second rate Christians. And many of the people from the other churches in town, respectfully, simply nodded in agreement. Some seemed wary simply because, as everyone knew now, though it was kind of the point of communion, that blood was powerful. But I did recall one lady saying something to the effect of, "I wish a Baptist pastor had survived."

Discord in the body, like a sore toe that affects your entire demeanor, grieved me. Even worse, it grieved me because I knew that, in several of the conversations leaving the field that Sunday, I was the "bad guy," the "judgmental one." And the latter I suppose I was, but it was also my calling, to judge rightly the Word of God and make sure it was applied. But I was still grieved when I prayed God would give me grace to speak that truth in love. I was still grieved when I wondered, in spite of my captive conscience and church practice, *how many people wouldn't stay next week?* So many had left with Grant, before the service had even started, would I cause more harm to the body than even Grant did?

I tried to shake hands with the grumblers first. I wished them well, answered a few questions, and was sure to welcome them back to worship. Some of them seemed responsive, others short, still others walked away before I had a chance. I found it hard to laugh while the children ran up and down the rows of chairs while the parents talked.

I prayed that the Lord would bring them back, that He would preserve and unify His Church in our little town and around the world. But then doubt slithered into my mind. I couldn't help but wonder: this is the Church, but what if something happened to me? Could it go on? It was a foolish question of course, because Christ is the head of the Church and the gates of hell cannot overcome it. But I found myself jogging after Kevin.

"Hey Kevin," I said. He stopped and looked at me, so I continued, "This new world is pretty crazy, and I am not ignorant to the fact that something might happen to me. If it does, would you keep this," I gestured around, "and especially worship, going?"

Kevin took his hat off and ran his hand through his hair. "Man, I don't know Pastor. I'm not great at speakin' and what not."

I chuckled. "You've faced a horde of zombies and you talk at our meetings just fine."

He smiled. "Yeah, true. People are trickier than zombies, though. So is theology."

"Then come by a couple times a week and learn some more."

He scrunched his face for a moment, then turned, "Alright, but eventually you gotta stop asking me to do all this terrifyin' stuff."

I laughed. "Come by after you bring the water truck in."

He ambled to the passenger side of his truck. "Will do."

Jayce, in the driver's seat, smiled and waved at me before they pulled away.

The noise made me shoot up in bed like I did three times every single night. The same questions ran through my head like they did so many times every night: *Was that the house settling? The prairie wind? Or something creeping?* Knowing I couldn't go back to sleep until I investigated the noise, I picked up my gun and flashlight and hopped over the kids' sleeping bags on the stair landing. The stairs squeaked as I crept down them, straining my ears for any sound and my eyes to dodge the obstacles we had placed on the stairs.

I did my routine, sweeping each dark corner with my light and gun barrel. After I knew the inside of my house was clear, I stopped and listened for a moment, closing my eyes and trying to ignore my breathing, my heartbeat. Were there scratches? Were there moans? My eyes popped open when I heard it—howls. Howls from the countryside. *Humanity isn't the only thing fighting this plague.*

I went back upstairs, hoping the coyotes were feasting on zombies. Though, as I slipped under the covers, I shivered at how bad things had gotten. Here I was, hoping the wild animals would save us. *They can die.*

The thought left my mind as I put my arm around Miranda and felt the cold plastic in her hand. I didn't have to guess what it was, she slept with the picture of her family in her hand every night. She tried to hide her worry, but she clung to that picture for a reason, the same reason she turned on her phone every night before bed to check for any messages, even though we hadn't had service in weeks. As I settled in beside her, I said a prayer for our families. It was odd, because they very well might be dead, but the Lord knew and I didn't, as in most cases, so I prayed anyway, that He would keep them safe. That He would somehow, some way, bring them back to us.

I had more hope than Miranda; my family was mobile. Maybe they were on their way here. Each engine I heard in town made me look out the window for their rigs. But it was never them. I would never tell Miranda, but I wondered if knowing my family was traveling made the longing worse. Sure, they never said they were coming here, but wouldn't they if they were traveling anyways? They could get further from the coast and find out how we were doing. *They would come.* If they could. If they made it off the coast in time. If they stayed away from thieves.

I prayed for them, and I prayed for patience while we waited. We were a people who were waiting: expectantly for family, dreadfully for a horde from the city, desperately for the Lord.

Lord, come quickly.

Daily Bread

"This is the day that the Lord has made," Kevin said.

"Let us rejoice and be glad in it," I replied, trying to hide my grin.

Kevin shook his head across my desk, which I had moved back into my office. "I don't know, I mean it seems easy enough, but there aren't all those people looking at us when I do it here."

"Sure, and it's easier to shoot a target than a zombie running at you, but you do that fine. You just practice it until it's second nature."

"I s'pose," he said, with a slight grimace.

"Speaking of which, did you see a lot of 'em when you were checking the poison?"

He nodded. "Yeah, not enough to make us really worry." His eyes lit up. "But some of the poison is working."

"Really?" I asked. "That could save us a ton of ammunition."

He nodded. "Yeah, but it appears only the pesticide harms them. There's vomit and bodies all over those tanks." He frowned. "The herbicide, though, no such luck."

"That's a shame," I said, while I swatted at a fly on the hymnal in front of me, "especially because we could maybe use the pesticide for these bugger flies."

Kevin chortled, but then looked pensive for a moment. "You know, Pastor, I woulda thought there'd be a whole lot more of them things flying around, you know, for obvious reasons."

I shuddered, thinking about the thousands of dead bodies

116

breeding maggots and the thousand walking zombies feeding mosquitoes and ticks, completely unaware of the parasites gorging on them. But Kevin was right, there seemed to be less mosquitoes than any previous year. "Have we had less rain than normal?"

"Not any less to be worth mentionin'." He shrugged. "Maybe they are getting full on the hordes and leaving us well alone."

I screwed up my face, thinking. "Never known bugs to be so particular . . . but what if the virus is killing the bugs? Just like it kills off the infections these zombies should be getting from their wounds."

Kevin gave a low whistle. "Now that sure would be a kindness." Then after a moment he added, "But I'm gonna keep my spray on just in case."

I laughed at that and agreed. None of us knew for sure if the virus could be transferred through insects.

He stood up. "Tomorrow when I come in, if I don't see any bodies by the herbicide tanks, I'm gonna drain 'em. Could use the tanks and I'm not too keen on watering the zombies."

"Good thinking," I said, as I stood and shook his hand and walked him to the front door. "Keep reading a chapter a day in your Old Testament study book, practice your Hebrew alphabet, and get me a devotion for next time."

"Yes sir," he said and, putting his cap on, he tipped it to Miranda. "Thanks for the tea, ma'am."

"Well, it's your water in it, so I'll take half the thanks." She smiled and waved at him.

He chuckled and eased out the door, checking all around for zombies. Seeing none, he headed down the road to his pickup and headed out of town.

Kevin had been meeting with me every other day to go through some of my books and practice doing some of the service. I was, after a few meetings, able to convince him to help with some of the service, which gave me hope. If something should happen, our little church would go on.

Hope was returning to our home as well. Even the few hours outside each week had lifted everyone's spirit. Not to mention the fact that, for the first time in weeks, we were able to eat meat again. One of the members had a cow that somehow hadn't been killed by zombies, but it couldn't produce any more milk so they butchered it and, unable to eat all the meat before it rotted, offered it to the whole group. They said it was virus free, but we cooked ours well-done anyways. Normally, I would have rather eaten a shoe than a well-done steak, but the whole family devoured it, and afterward, none of us had the urge to devour each other for dessert. Along with food in our bellies, we had a full water tank without poison in it and we were having some of the better days we'd had since the plague hit. I never thought I would look forward to the day when people from church kept me up at night, but after a month of infected making me uneasy, it was a welcome burden.

For all my adventures outside and our newfound confidence in the new world, we still spent most of our time behind locked doors and a barricaded staircase, letting the sun filter in from the un-boarded upstairs windows. I will be forever thankful for Miranda's ability to stay motivated and create work and play for our children. We soon confirmed our theory that a frustrated and tired child was better than a bored and hopeless one, which is why I sat on the roof all week watching for zombies while Miranda and the kids doubled the size of our garden and planted it. Then they sat on the roof and watched while I cursed under my breath, trying to rig up more dew collectors and reinforce our windows.

Inside, we reloaded ammunition from a kit that I got from my father years before and some supplies I got from Kevin. We would share the ammo, so he had no problem letting my kids occupy their time doing it. Miranda taught us all to sew while we brainstormed what resources to stockpile and made plans for a chicken coop.

But it wasn't all work. We also played every board game we had, countless times. We read books, and Luke was able to fill the room he no longer slept in with dozens of models we picked up at the hobby store in the next town.

And, even with our newfound stability, we worried. We worried about family, friends, and our security. Zombies were still coming into town, which meant we needed to be ever vigilant and sweep the area when we went outside. It meant we needed lookouts whenever we were busy focusing on something else, it meant we needed one hand raised high in the air when we saw another person drive through town.

People were out and about more now, more than just for the Sunday meetings. It was common to hear gunshots and car engines in town, so much that some of the time Luke wouldn't run to the window to check out the noise. He did run to the window when we heard the explosion, though.

It shook the whole house. We looked out the back window to see the downtown corner gas station in flames. Miranda convinced me to stay in the house rather than go check out the disturbance, a decision I was thankful for when I saw twenty zombies running toward the flames and black plume of smoke.

I had tried to get the gas pumps working before, but didn't know enough to even get me in trouble. Apparently, someone did. Hours later I went to the pump and saw what, I guessed, was Jordan Thomas' pickup, along with the bones of some twenty zombies that apparently ran headlong into the flames looking for something to devour. I drove by his house and confirmed his death with his crying wife and kids. He thought he could get to the tanks under the gas station, but now he was gone. Another name on the list, another funeral for a Wednesday.

It is a stupidly risky world we live in. We had lived our lives thinking we were so much smarter than the generations before us because we had computers, encyclopedias, medicine, and we knew what bacteria were. But we didn't know how to live. It took me four mouthfuls of gasoline before I thought to siphon gas by inserting a second tube into the tank and blowing air into it. That didn't even begin to encapsulate the issues that I, a man who sat behind a desk all day, had with trying to support every aspect of life for my family. How many curses did I say trying to hook up a trailer? How many cuts and bruises from trying to fix the siding on the house? How many more shouts when I foolishly ran a generator in our garage and almost asphyxiated us all? Life and death was a razor's edge in the new world. I couldn't watch a video tutorial online for anything anymore and I was left guessing and grasping at straws to try and keep things working. However, one thing was certain in the new world: far more than zombies could kill you.

No wonder we prayed a lot. We were careful in everything

we did. We dusted off old user guides and do-it-yourself books that hadn't been opened since the advent of the internet. We had a system when we went looting: Miranda and Val stayed at the truck with the rifle (and phone, recording video) while Luke and I went in with him in his football gear and me with my shotgun. We grabbed odds and ends and canned food out of abandoned houses that the teams and I had cleared. We looked in the stores in the surrounding towns, sometimes never making it inside because their respective city hordes were still rampaging their towns.

One of the little joys was, after clearing a store, letting Val come in and grab a cart and load it with whatever outfits she wanted. Luke's eyes lit up when I told him to get whatever game he wanted that he could run on his laptop that we charged from the generator. That was a high demand item, a generator. The only access to electricity, aside from the solar powered house on the other end of town, in the new world. Some did shy away from them, afraid the noise would attract zombies. But we took the risk and looted one from an empty farmhouse the group had cleared. We used it in our garage after we put together some proper ventilation and soundproofing. We charged our (mostly Valentine's) devices and ran a small freezer to keep some meat in. It wouldn't last forever, unless something changed, and as the explosion made abundantly clear, gasoline was becoming scarcer. But, when you eat canned food for a few weeks straight, you would do a lot for some meat. I still remember what we used to eat before the plague: Thai food one night, Mexican the next, seafood another. Now it was canned beans, canned corn, canned meat. It seems trivial, but when you are trying to survive the psychological scars can add up.

We were spoiled before the plague and the things we took for granted were astonishing. What we would give for air conditioning, for a freezer, for a fan. For centuries people lived without these things, yet we, the spoiled recipients of infrastructure and technology, languished without them. I assume this is why I wasn't terribly surprised when I was asked to do a memorial service for a man on the west end of town who shot himself. His pantry was stocked, he had water, he just didn't have the will to go on.

I made sure to work something into my next sermon about

the gift of life and simple joys, especially the wondrous joy of salvation. I also made a note to savor the beef, even if it was a little tough.

But I knew there was always something that could go wrong, which is why we thanked God each night when we were safely behind our locked doors and boarded up windows. Thankful for our daily bread that got us through, asking the Lord to give us enough to get through the next. Thankful because not everyone got all they needed.

Valentine screamed when we heard the knock on the door. I scrambled out of my chair, knocking the card table over and sending our puzzle to the ground. I cranked a round in my shotgun and turned to the door, but the knocks were too regular to be from a flailing zombie, too consistent to be a rabid infected. I slowly approached the peephole I had bored into our front door and peered through.

A man, probably around my age, but larger and with glasses, stood outside. He had one hand raised in the air holding a handgun, the other knocking firmly and regularly on the door.

I recognized him because he had attended worship the previous Sunday, but I had no idea what his name was. *Man, I need a directory to keep all these people straight.* I had learned early on in my ministry it is better to just be honest and ask a person's name rather than pretending you know it until it gets awkward.

"Opening up," I said loud enough to warn the man on the other side. Then I opened the door swiftly to let him in. He came in and holstered his gun and nodded to my family, who stood peering into the entryway.

"What can I do for you...?" I trailed off.

The man took a second to catch on, he seemed distracted and sad. "Oh, sorry. It's Kyle." And he shot his hand out for me to shake it. "It's," he coughed, sniffed, and took a deep breath to compose himself, "It's my wife, Jenny, she's got an infection and the stuff we been giving her isn't helping, shoot, maybe it's hurtin'—" He choked up.

I turned and narrowed my eyes at Val, who promptly put down her phone and awkwardly adjusted her glasses. Then I put a hand on his shoulder and tried to get eye contact with him. "Listen Kyle, you had to try something and we aren't doctors. That's the—well, it sucks."

He nodded. "Anyways, we don't know much, but it doesn't look good. Would you mind, I don't know, sayin' a few words?"

I turned to Miranda and she nodded. "I'll go get the rifle; we'll be fine."

"Certainly, Kyle, I'll follow you there."

Kyle wasn't lying—it didn't look good. On the west end of town he led me through a door lined with chain link and up a dark stairway. The master bedroom was dark and hot, even with the window open. The candles, like the dying woman, contorted and twisted, while the sickly sweet smell of sweat and death filled my senses. The whole family was in the room with her as she lay in the bed, shaking from seizures, her face twisted in pain.

Honestly, I wanted to turn and run as soon as I entered. I had seen dozens of people die, but this, in the new world, was different. This was not a nursing home, this was not a hospital, this death was not inoculated and carefully controlled. This death was not facilitated through institutionalized unconsciousness.

I should have been ready for it; the family sure wasn't. The kids sat in the corners crying, covering their ears to block out the moans and cries. Kyle reached out his hand to his dying wife, only to have a seizure grip her and wrench her hand away, leaving his empty and unable to help.

But now they looked to me. They looked to me to shepherd them through the valley, as if I was the Lord's rod and staff. Little did they know how scared I was, or maybe they did, my hands were shaking on the prayer book, and even I would jump and stop my prayers when Jenny cried out.

By the grace of God, I got through her commendation, where we offer her over to the hands of the true Good Shepherd, who would see her through the valley of the shadow of death and out the other side to endless day. We prayed, and what tears did we shed when, as we prayed the Lord's Prayer, Jenny mouthed the words along with us! I sang her a hymn; it didn't stop the seizures, but they brought a sound of hope into a place where it seemed there could be none, only cries and sorrow and pain.

Then she died. She convulsed, she spat, she rattled, and half the family drew close as if to help, and half the family drew back in horror. But soon she was still. The room was quiet for a moment while her husband checked her pulse. "I think she's gone," Kyle said before taking off his glasses, grabbing his two kids and sobbing with them.

"And one day you will join her." I added, "Join her in her rest. She is just fine now."

We waited in the room for some time, some were crying more as the reality of her death set in, some were crying less as the trauma of her death wore off. But soon an odor began to fill the room and as the family started to awkwardly look around, I asked them to leave.

As they filed into the hall, I asked them, "Do you want her burned or buried?"

They talked for some time and decided they wanted a burial in the pasture out back. I nodded at her husband and some of the others. "You dig, I will see to this, you don't need to." They thanked me and then most of the men and her kids went out while I donned a mask, changed some of the bedsheets, wrapped her in others, combed her hair, and carried her frail body down the stairs. One of the women held the door for me and I took her out back. Kyle ran to me when he saw me come out the back door and I handed him his wife.

He cried while he carried her to the pasture they owned on the west side of town. He kissed her head, and with the help of some of the men in the hole, he laid her down. Her daughter, she couldn't have been much younger than Val, had gathered flowers from the field and laid them across her, and then we waited.

The shovels were there, the pile of dirt was next to her grave, but who could throw dirt on their loved one? I knew it had to be me. I carefully entered the grave, pulled the sheet over her head and then, with Kyle's help, climbed out. I picked up a handful of dirt. "Ashes to ashes, dust to dust, in the certain hope of the resurrection." We started with handfuls. Handfuls of dirt spotted with tears. And the handfuls turned to shovelfuls and the sobs grew louder, but soon it was filled. The women had made a cross and her daughter banged it into the ground at her grave.

I didn't have a sermon ready, obviously, but it didn't worry me; I simply spoke the hope of the resurrection. Hope in the One who conquered the grave and promised paradise and a resurrection to His people.

I sat at my desk for a long time that night, thinking about that day. It was horrible; it was terribly sad; it was terrifying. But I couldn't shake the feeling that I was glad to be there. I was glad her family was there. In a world that used to be so easy to ignore death, in a world where we never got to see it and its horrors up close, it was so easy to ignore the need for the antidote: the Savior. But no one in that family was forgetting that day, no one was forgetting the horror and pain, and, I prayed, no one would forget to thank God for their daily bread and, even more, for the Bread of Life, Jesus, who gives eternal sustenance.

Shifting Sand

"This is the day that the Lord has made," I said more solemnly than I ought.

"Let us rejoice and be glad in it," the congregation replied. But, once again, I didn't. I wasn't rejoicing. I was torn. Frustrated. Guilty. Jealous.

There were new people in worship, which would normally be reason for rejoicing. One family was the Turners, an African-American family we had met at an old farmhouse on our weekly sweeps. We pulled up into the supposedly abandoned house and immediately knew something was off. There were two trucks in the driveway already. We hopped out of the trucks and cracked off a few shots at the five zombies that had followed us and immediately we were being shouted at from the house. The windows flew open and gun barrels pointed out.

"Woah! There's people in there," Jesse shouted, as he jumped behind his truck.

This wasn't the first time we had come to an old farmhouse and found people home. Sometimes the owners were getting along on their own as old farmers would, not venturing to town, not wanting anything to do with anything beyond their boarded windows and fields. Some of those families recognized us and chatted, offered to trade, or joined us on Sundays. Others fired warning shots at us until we left. One time, we were quite certain that the original family had died and their house was full of squatters. They fired shots at us and, against the wishes of some of the group, we decided to leave it enough alone. There was enough death from the virus, we didn't need to be killing each other.

I feared this would be a similar situation. We all took cover behind our trucks and I got out my megaphone while the people in the farmhouse shouted at us. "Who are you!?"

"Don't shoot. We don't want trouble," my amplified voiced cracked through the air.

"What the hell do you want, then?"

"We came to check on the Redherds, who used to live here." There was silence for a time. "We're from Witherton, three miles north."

"That family isn't here anymore. So you can move on."

Derek stood up. "The hell we will. Where's my aunt?"

At that, the door cracked up and two hands came out first. "Don't shoot I'm comin' out."

I hated the thought, but I knew I had to go meet him. I walked out from behind my truck and met the tall black man halfway to the front door.

"You looters?" he asked, eyeing the guns pointed at him.

"Well, we managed to clear our town and the survivors are checking on people, sharing stuff, and, if the people in the houses didn't make it, then we loot 'em and let families move in to use the wells. Who are you?"

He sighed. "Name's Lonny Turner. We were from the city. Got out just in time. Been living in trucks for weeks, found this place, looked empty." He looked like he wanted to say more, but just shrugged.

Derek still had his gun pointed at him. "Was it? Was it empty!?"

The man looked at him and flexed his jaw as if preparing himself for something he didn't want to say. "No. One zombie, a kid by the looks of it, and a part eaten old couple."

"No way." Derek looked to his wife. "What kid would they have around?" He snapped his eyes back to the man. "I wanna see the bodies."

"Fine," the man answered, then turned to the house. "Roger, go douse those burnin' bodies."

I was thankful the man appeared reasonable, because I was tired of holding my hands up in the air. "Alright, before we go further, let's do something about these guns. No one wants to kill anyone. Let's work this out, let's put the guns down." I turned to my people and they hesitantly lowered their weapons.

Soon a lady came out of the house unarmed and Lonny introduced her as his wife, Lynn. Most of my crew set their guns in their pickups, aside from Derek and Linda.

After a few moments of awkward silence where I tried to figure out what to do next, a few men pulled a tarp around the house and dropped two stinking, smoldering corpses at our feet. Another man brought a third smaller body wrapped in a tarp and placed it gingerly in front of us. Derek hugged his wife and sobbed, the corpses were obviously burned, but even through the smoldering flesh you could see the bite marks and scratches all over the corpses. Their flesh ripped; their guts open.

Derek managed a few breathless words between sobs. "Dumb ol' codger probably let the zombie in, thinking the kid needed help or something."

"Actually," Lynn answered, "we found a broken window and a shotgun on the ground; it hadn't been fired. We think the kid probably broke in and they didn't have the heart to shoot him."

"We can show you," the man said softly.

Derek shook his head. "No, I believe you." He turned to his wife. "D'you?" Linda nodded. Soon, both their guns were back in the pickup.

The man waved and the two guys with him took the bodies away.

"So what now?" Rick said, blinking up at the sky.

The man looked around. "We could really use the place, guys. Really, the city, it's gone."

"What about the military base up there? They ain't comin?" Charlotte asked.

The man laughed. "Those bastards pulled out after the first night. They left us!"

"Is there anything left up there?" Jesse asked.

"The whole place is on fire, the roads are packed to the gills with burned out cars and bodies, and any food is eaten or rotting. The only thing there is about ten thousand zombies."

I even gasped at that.

"How'd you get out?" Linda asked.

His wife, a gentle looking woman with her black hair in a braid down to the small of her back, took his hand and spoke for him, "We were lucky, we lived on the edge. We stayed two days, but knew we couldn't make it any longer. There were mobs of them. Mobs of hundreds. No way we could hold them off."

He looked up again. "So me and mine headed west. South was a deathtrap, you'd just run into thousands of people running from Omaha. North was jam packed, people thinking the winter would come sooner and freeze 'em." He shook his head and said, almost to himself, "How did they hope to last that long, though?" He took a deep breath. "So we went west and circled our way back this direction."

"How was the middle of the state?"

He shook his head, "Dunno, we didn't take the interstate; it was chaos. Car accidents getting traffic backed up, zombies running down the lanes bashing their hands to mush on windows trying to get people. No, we got our trucks and went through the fields. We had to stop every quarter to cut fences, but there were so many distractions nothing chased us too far.

"Been campin' in the trucks as far from roads as we could go. Zombies still found us somehow. Almost got shot by some looters, too, which is why we're a little edgy. This was the closest to civilization we felt like coming. Thought we could supply at your town and still live away from people."

We talked for an hour and met all the Turners; ten of them in all. Derek and Linda decided to let them stay in the house, provided they took a tank of water to town once a week. They gladly obliged. And I was glad to see them show up that fifth Sunday in Lent for the meeting and for worship.

But there was another new face in church. He lived outside Riverdale. The town was demolished, but he survived and was invited to the meeting and worship by one of the people from our town who went by his house looking for supplies. That was why Pastor Barnstock, the Baptist pastor from the next town, was sitting in my Lutheran Service. He was respectful, sure. *But how long until he asked me to help with the service? Or how long till he set up his own service and took half the people from my service who weren't Lutheran?*

We met before the meeting, long before the service started.

One of the members of the Baptist Church in town came loping up with him as if he was bringing me a gift. "Pastor Acton! You aren't alone, Pastor Barnstock from Riverdale is still kickin'."

I shook his hand, but probably stood still for a minute not saying anything. *Shouldn't I have been thankful?* Thankful that a brother in Christ had survived? Thankful that, although we disagreed on things, the greater body of Christ was still living throughout the world? I should have been. But that damnable beast of pride and greed roared in my gut. That same beast that would celebrate when another church's attendance was down. The beast that would puff up with pride when a member talked bad about their pastor. My, how that beast roared within me when I met Pastor Barnstock! It roared and bellowed so rebelliously it was all I could do to try and hide the green envy on my face. I stood there, forcing a smile, while I shook his hand.

Pastor Barnstock, who was normally lanky, looked skeletal now. He also looked mournful next to the beaming man who introduced him. Pastor Barnstock slightly bowed his gray head. "I'm sorry."

I thought about lying and saying I didn't feel put out, but he was smarter than that. I didn't say anything.

"I know this is your thing here," he said, swallowing hard, "but," he looked around and opened his eyes in wonder, "people! And God's people. I just couldn't stay away."

His sincerity brought some tranquility to the greedy beast inside me. This man wasn't much different than me. How many days and weeks was he too afraid to do anything? How many members' well-beings did he pray for, how many kept him up at night, worrying?

"No, no," I finally said, with a bit more conviction than I thought I could muster. "Glad you," I looked over his shoulder at, I presumed, his wife and the adult son she had on her arm, "and your family are alright." And I think I was.

"In fact, some of these people," I nodded to the man next to him, "while faithful believers in Christ, don't confess quite what we crazy Lutherans do." I nodded at the bread and wine behind me on the altar. "Perhaps you can better serve them."

He meekly protested, but the grin on his face betrayed his excitement at my statement. "Well, I don't want to be a sheep stealer—"

"Well, we are both undershepherds of the Good Shepherd, right? And while, of course, division in the sheepfold is never good, which is why we pray for unity, the fact is, in this broken world, people have different confessions. And I think it is better to be honest about that."

At the end of the meeting, when those "enlightened," or "particularly busy" handful of people trudged back to their vehicles, Pastor Barnstock and I both got up and talked about the differences between our confessions of faith.

It wasn't as painful as I thought it would be; Pastor Barnstock, while well spoken, wasn't a theological juggernaut, which piqued my selfish pride that sought to win converts during the time we took turns outlining what we believed and why we believed it. We even took some time to outline some counterpoints, while keeping it cordial and avoiding direct conflict and open debate.

I wish I could say I swayed all the Baptists and Calvinists and Catholics and Pentecostals to continue to worship with the Lutherans, I wish I could say they not only stayed to worship with us, but wanted to publicly join our confession. I tried to tell myself that was the advantage of having Pastor Barnstock around, that people could worship with us because they actually believed what we did. However, the reality was that most of the families went with what they were raised with. Baptists gravitated to Pastor Barnstock, the Lutherans to me, and the rest of the denominations weighed their conviction to the sacraments or what style of worship they preferred. And the beast inside me thundered and raged.

It was still kicking when I began the service that day. Because I knew next Sunday, when we parked another flatbed at the other side of Jacobson field for Pastor Barnstock's service, no doubt nearly half of the people would be over there where they didn't have to sit and sing while others went up to get bread and wine.

Miranda, bless her heart, knew I was struggling without me even having to say anything. That evening she knocked softly on my office door before kissing me on the cheek while I sat at my desk. "You are an amazing pastor. And so what if people want to go to his service? We will be unified in ours and they will still hear about Jesus, too."

I smiled at her and thanked her. And I meant it. But I still stayed up thinking about all the people who would be leaving our congregation for Pastor Barnstock's. But Miranda was right, we would be more unified in our confession, and Pastor Barnstock was a Christian preacher and the people would be hearing about Jesus, even if they weren't receiving the other blessings we celebrate at our church. I tried to force feed these truths to the beast, who only wanted to shout that Barnstock was a charlatan who was ruining my community, challenging me, and poking his nose into my business.

The lack of sleep, fear of a fracturing body of believers, and, as if I could forget, the stress of the constant battle for survival left me in a bad mood the next day. I wound my way down a country lane, driving slow enough not to kick up too much dust, toward Wilbur's shop. He was one of my more absentee members, and, other than checking on his house and shop while we cleared houses, I hadn't really talked to him since the funeral Pastor Barnstock performed before the plague hit us.

I had to siphon three derelict cars in town that morning to get my gas gauge over a quarter full and I cursed under my breath for still driving everywhere. I had a bike in the garage that I could outstrip a zombie on, but I never had the courage to try it. I had seen how far they could run and I wasn't confident I could lose them on the bike. Not to mention the streets covered in rubble and debris, and foot tall grass growing in every lawn and road crevice. One fall and I was dead.

I puttered down the driveway and pulled up short of the barbed wire and reinforced fence outside Wilbur's shop. I thought about honking, but saw the heavy metal shop door crack open. A moment later, Wilbur strolled over toward me, his shotgun on his shoulder. He wore a smile on his face and overalls over his large frame. The old man was bald, but his white beard was noticeably longer. "What brings a preacher to an old fart like me?"

I was out of my truck and scanning the horizon for any zombie followers. I turned to him and smiled as he let me through a pedestrian gate next to his large reinforced vehicle gate. "Well, some preacher stuff and some survival stuff I s'pose."

He laughed and led me back toward his shop. "Well I dunno if I can help, but I'm happy to try."

It took my eyes a few seconds to adjust to the dim shop. The sunlight, already muted by the constant haze, flitted through several skylights in the roof of the shop, which was filled with a few tractors, a classic car, and his crop-dusting plane.

"I remember at Jan Persival's funeral you told me you sometimes make your own fuel."

He set his shotgun down on the workbench and leaned against it. "Sure do. I use oil from shops, but not a lot of shops are up and running anymore."

I nodded. "Yeah, but we in town were wondering if you might have any other ideas of something you can make fuel out of. Corn or something we can get?"

He scratched his beard. "Yeah well that's something, I suppose. But I'd have to experiment and that's not the safest thing to do these days . . ."

It was my turn to laugh. "You haven't used eye or ear protection your whole life, why are you so worried about safety now?" He just smirked at me, so I continued, pleading, "Wilbur, we will make it worth your while. We got water and ammo. Surely there is something we can trade you for it. We just need something that will burn."

He winked at me. "You always were perceptive. Yeah, I'll tinker with it. Get me a few Lutheran beverages and the corn."

"Thanks, Wilbur, I really appreciate it."

"No problem. Now what's the preacher stuff you had to talk to me about?"

"Well, I know you are a personal guy, but I haven't seen you at any meetings or worship, you know?"

He sighed as if he knew the question was coming. "It's scary times, these times, preacher."

"Gertrude makes it out in her station wagon and Curtis with his cane."

He laughed from his belly. "Yeah, yeah, I reckon that's just an excuse. But you know, Preacher, you don't have to go to church to be a Christian. No more than a car has to be in a garage to be a car."

I motioned at the classic car next to us. "What kinda car is this?"

He raised an eyebrow. "It's a 34 Ford. My dad's old car that I fixed up."

"Why's it in here and not outside?"

"You crazy? Even before the acid rain, there's hail and sun damage to worry—" he cottoned on in mid thought and started laughing and slapped me on the shoulder. "Tricky man you are, Preacher."

I laughed with him, "Well, you see my point: a garage doesn't make a car a car, but you know what, it's a pretty nice place for a car to be from time to time. Same for a Christian, at church God's Word works to strengthen us, tune us up, wash us clean, and keep us safe from the things that attack us out in the world."

He smiled and nodded. "Alright, Preacher, s'pose I'm due for a tune up, some of my prayers been a bit bitter since all this started."

I nodded. "I know the feeling." Then I shook his hand. "Thanks for being willing to try making the new fuel, and I'd love to see you in Jacobson's field on Sunday."

"Will do. But first, you gotta admit you had that car comparison ready before you got here."

"Was it that obvious?" I felt my cheeks get warm and he laughed. "Well, let's just say that there's a lot on my mind these days, and one of those things was you. Is that the worst thing?"

"No, I reckon this ol' codger ain't on too many people's minds. So, I appreciate it."

"And even when you aren't on mine, you've got a good Lord who never forgets His people."

I took a deep breath and thanked God as I walked back to my pickup. My congregation might be getting smaller, but there was plenty of work to do.

He Giveth and Taketh

This is the day that the Lord has made," I said as loud as I could without shouting.

"Let us rejoice and be glad in it!" the congregation of about twenty-five replied.

I was talking loud for two reasons. First, because the wind, to my mild annoyance, was blowing so hard against me that I was quite sure the congregation could hear Pastor Barnstock's voice, all the way across the field, better than mine. Secondly, because not even that annoyance could dampen my spirits.

It was Palm Sunday and I was rejoicing as if it were Easter. There were new faces in the congregation. Wilbur was there, but selfishly it was not his face that brought me the most joy. My extended family, which was as good as dead to me, had come to me and their smiling and tear lined faces were in the congregation.

The typical excited chatter during the meeting had fallen silent when two RVs, one pulling a trailer and the other a truck, pulled up next to the field. We all looked around and no one seemed to recognize the rigs, until the doors opened and my family cautiously stepped out. I will never forget a shotgun barrel and a great silver beard coming out of the first rig. I shouted with joy seeing my dad emerge and look cautiously at our ushers with their rifles off their backs and rounds cranked into the chambers.

All weapons were quickly lowered when I raced to him and hugged him.

"Hey, that's Cooper! Pastor Acton's dad," Rick called out.

Seconds later, the rest of my family spilled out. My mom with her long, curly, and graying hair, was fighting back tears when I hugged her. "You never could go an Easter without me, could you, Mom?" She was crying too much to answer. Then I was getting a bear hug from my older brother, Junior. He and his wife and son had joined us from their rig. When I got my head out of his shoulder, he was always a head taller than me, I hugged Kelly, my sister-in-law and my nephew, Emmett. We all embraced, we laughed, we cried. I was never a "call my mother every day" guy, but after months of wondering and fearing the worst, even I cried.

Miranda and the kids caught up to me and fell into my parents' arms and then hugged my sister-in-law, Kelly, with her short brown hair, which the four-year-old boy in her arms, Emmett, shared. We all ducked when the shooting started, and my nephew started crying. Kelly shushed him and held him tight, "Don't worry, Emmett."

I nodded. "Yeah, that's Jayce, just keeping anything that followed you away," I said while wiping my eyes. A dozen zombies had trailed their rigs over the rolling hills.

But soon we were talking again. I had to admit, it was hard hearing about all the loved ones that hadn't made it, or those they didn't know about. They talked about how long it had taken them to get there, how Kelly's family was safe in the mountains of the desert, and how they had stocked up supplies there for a week before setting out for us.

We talked so long the town had already started the weekly meeting when we finally made our way through the field to the flatbed trailers. The townsfolk and members welcomed my family and embraced them, not just for the news they brought from the coast, but because, I wouldn't doubt, it gave them each hope that maybe their loved ones, far from home, were surviving too. *We can live!*

The service, apart from the wind, took on a tone of joy as well. Both congregations, holding the closest things we could find to palm branches on the plains, processed in song to our flatbeds. The children, much like on the first Palm Sunday, sang their praises ("Hosanna, loud Hosanna!") and the choir, with my mother, Ava, sang a beautiful rendition of 'Ride on, Ride on, in Majesty.' Kevin did the liturgy and readings, and I couldn't help but smile through it all. *We were living!*

My joy, no doubt, spilled out into the sermon. Death and gloom, by the grace of God, is replaced by life and reunion. I gave thanks for the sudden, unexpected, blessings of God: that He had brought us together, that He had used us to help and save others, and, even though we all knew there was hardship ahead, that He has blessed us with the One who on the first Palm Sunday, with hardship ahead of Him, rode straight toward it, unafraid. And He rode toward it that we might be seen through our hardship to an eternal resurrection. We had all lost family, but we would see them again, that was the hope of Jesus and the reason we could take joy in the families and friends we still had with us.

After the service, I stood on the stage smiling, smiling because of a reunion with loved ones, because, in Jesus, we had a promise of a reunion on the last day with even more loved ones. Not even Grant, whose foul words were carried on the wind toward where the children played so that a few members had to reprimand him and make a scene, not even Curt, who, after the service, complained to me ("It's too dastardly windy out here, and why can't we sing the hymns that the Baptists did?"), not even they could dampen my mood. So much relief, so much joy. *We can live!*

Most of my members knew my family already from their visits to Witherton over the years and they talked with them about everything, some flattering me for my work leading, others asking for news from their travels across the country. A few other people were introduced to them, including the Turners and various people who attended from other churches in town.

The joy continued throughout the day, culminating in an evening feast in our home. We had meat, well-done, of course, from a newly butchered cow, and my mom made a stew done up so well you never would have known it all came from a can ("This is amazing Grandma Ava!"). We laughed and talked louder than we normally would have ever dared. That night, it seemed like the world was back to normal and there weren't zombies lurking in the darkness outside our windows.

My family thanked us profusely after we refused to make them stay another night in their rigs, which, under normal circumstances would be perfectly comfortable, but not jammed with supplies as they were now. Especially since the kids were sleeping in our room or on the landing, leaving two perfectly good and empty bedrooms upstairs for my parents and my brother's family. We got them set up quickly, but talked and laughed by candlelight for hours, my dad playing a video game with Luke until he fell asleep at the computer, a rare treat since we did not commonly use the generator for his computer. Val was in her room helping Kelly and Emmett set up and commiserating with Kelly about the difficulties of being a girl in the new world. Meanwhile, Miranda, Ava, Junior, and I played a board game in the dining room.

It was like that for days. Nights of joy and socializing with people you thought long gone. People you took for granted for so long.

Each night we would eventually head to bed. I think we were all still scared about the plague and our uncertain futures. The uncertainty was palpable as we spent the day making plans and my dad and brother went around improving the shoddy handiwork on our house's defenses, but for those days, for the first time, we were truly hopeful and happy.

For the most part.

Each night I tucked in next to Miranda who, like every night, had been in bed a bit before me. She would be fast asleep, clutching the picture of her family. I would say a prayer for them and kiss her cheek, which was, every night, wet with tears.

Wednesday came hot, humid, and hazy. The slog of memorials was beginning to slow, though, with half the town missing or unrecognizable we were sure we missed dozens of people. We prayed for mercy in that regard and erected a grave for the "unknown victim." But after only three services that day, the memorial crew of Pastor Barnstock, my family, and a dozen others who helped usher began to put things away. Meanwhile, the families from the services milled about, sharing stories about the deceased, chatting about the upcoming services for Holy Week, or buzzing about which families, inspired and taught by my family, had set off to discover the fates of their loved ones across the country. We all looked up when we heard a gunshot to see what Jayce had put down, a zombie trailing a lone pickup truck. The truck pulled into the field and Jesse got out of the driver's seat. The

137

passenger reluctantly got out of his side and trudged over to us, his head hanging, and hands deep in his pockets.

"This looks interesting. That's one of Grant's friends," Miranda mumbled to me with an eyebrow raised and an armful of wooden crosses.

Thankfully, Grant's friend didn't speak, nor did he have the usual arrogant swagger around him like all of Grant's friends did. Jesse pushed his hair out of his eyes and studied his boots for a moment, before looking up. "Pastor Darren, Tyler here was telling me something, and, well, it seems like you have another memorial to do."

I was concerned, obviously. "Who died?"

Tyler still wouldn't speak, so I looked back to Jesse. He sighed. "Gary Storm. His brother shot him." Even I knew the Storms. Gary was the richest man in town and had the only house with working lights thanks to his solar array. His brother, Dean, only ever invested his little money in alcohol.

"That's terrible," I said, "Is Dean alright?"

Jesse shuffled his feet. "Well, Pastor, that's the thing. He's moving into Gary's house. You know, the big one on the top of the lil' hill with solar power and a well." Dean nor Gary were active in the town meetings, though Gary had come to a few and offered water. "No one saw the body or anything. So, I mean, we don't know."

I looked at them a bit puzzled. Miranda whistled quietly and the people gathered around us began to murmur.

Tyler, his voice shaking, finally spoke up, "I ran with Dean and Grant, and well, they always talked about wanting that house of Gary's . . ."

I'm sure my eyes got wide, since Jesse and Tyler both nodded at the same time. "Yeah . . ."

Maybe Dean didn't shoot Gary because he was infected. Horrified that humanity might not be as triumphant as I thought, I narrowed my eyes. "Find someone to sell me a pig."

Dean had his holster unclipped when a whole contingent of people from the field found him standing on his late brother's front porch. "You guys the police now? Funny, weren't around when I dialed 911." He scowled at Val who had her phone recording. "The press is here too. Great." *How did she get here?*

I looked down. "Dean, we don't want to do this either, but we gotta know."

"What's to know? It was me and him, he was infected and thrashing everything trying to get me. So I put him down just like I have fifty others. It's not like I couldn't tell an infected person from a normal one."

Grant came out of the front door now, along with a strong smell of bleach. "Judge and jury's here I see." He spat on the porch.

"You know anything about this Grant?" Jesse asked.

"Sure do. We all do. Guy gets infected, gotta put 'im down. You all done it, but don't recall a trial for any of yous."

"Yeah, we know." I sighed and turned back to Dean. "It's just that, well, the house is motive."

"Well I ain't lettin' no squatter get it," Dean barked, "or your stupid little council. I'm next o' kin."

"Next of kin still have motive too," Jesse said softly.

"Either way, you can't prove nothing, it was just us, me and Dean. My words against a corpse." He looked me right in the eye. "And you best remember: 'innocent until proven guilty,' if you claim to be so righteous."

"I claim to be no more righteous than anyone, but we do have a responsibility to be just. And it isn't just your word, Tyler says he's got reason to believe you killed Dean, without any infection."

"That little rat," Grant hissed.

Dean turned quickly to Grant and put a hand out. "That ain't no admission." Grant looked down, turning a bit red from anger, *or fear that he slipped up?*

"So, let's get to it," Kevin said. "Show me where it happened, and show me the body."

"Well there ain't no body, I burned it. Like all the infected."

"Bodies don't burn in a day," I said. "Show us."

Just then a pickup with a pig in a crate pulled up. Dean glanced down at the syringe in my hand and his eyes widened in horror. "Uh, uh, nope. This is my property—"

"It was your brother's!" Jesse said, his gun leveled at Dean. "And we aim to see if it's yours now or not."

Three other people walked up to Dean, taking his arms and

his weapons. Grant shuffled off to the side and, for once, appeared like he had no desire to be the center of attention. The whole lot followed me through the house where Dean claimed the fight had happened. The whole kitchen smelled of bleach and a few shotgun pellets peppered the cupboards. Out back, his brother's body was still smoking in a hole not twenty paces from the back porch. I pulled on long rubber gloves and a facemask while the pickup with the pig pulled around to join us.

The body was severely disfigured, but there was enough of it that the people who knew Gary well could identify him. ("Looks like his hair, ya." "And that's his boot.") I hoped there was enough of him for a fluid sample out of the chest cavity cool enough that the virus hadn't been denatured—*if it was there at all*. I looked away as I stuck the long needle into Gary's chest. I cringed when I hit bone, then tried again and got in deep, retching as I sucked out some dark, almost black, blood with some clear fluid. *"Blood and water from his side,"* I thought to myself, shaking my head.

I handed the sample to Linda, who carefully brought it straight to her pig. It bucked, in spite of Derek's strong arms, when she stabbed its hip. She didn't get all the fluid in, but we all knew you didn't need much to turn something. She threw the syringe in the hole and turned back to join everyone else to study the pig, including Valentine, up close recording the pig's reaction. "Get back, Val," I snapped at her, and she, like usual, rolled her eyes and took a half step back. Despite my best efforts, I scowled at Miranda who had come along with her. Luke must have gone home with the rest of the family; they were nowhere to be seen. Regardless, we all watched the pig, except for Dean, who didn't look. Was it because he already knew nothing would happen?

Nothing did.

Dean shot his head up and a slight grin betrayed the fact that he had just thought of something brilliant. "The fire boiled the blood. It killed everything, just like when you boil water!"

I pulled three other syringes out of my backpack. "These were from corpses around town." I selected one with duct tape on it. "This one in particular has been burning a day longer than your brother. If the virus is gonna be denatured in blood, it will be this blood."

I handed the syringe to Linda and she stabbed her pig once

more. It bucked, but she got a good quarter of the tube into the pig. This time Dean paid attention. The pig calmed down after being poked and Dean almost looked relieved. Until the pig started wheezing. Then it fell over. Then it kicked in place. Then it squealed. Then it roared and got up and rammed the cage. And then Derek shot it in the head.

Dean's look of horror, after a few deep breaths, turned to anger. "You bastards are actually framing me, unbelievable." He cussed and spat, some of it hanging in his long and graying beard.

"Keep tellin' yourself that, Dean," Jesse fired back at him.

I sighed. "Go show him the body I got that vial from and ask him if he thinks his brother's blood was boiled more."

"Ya like that is gonna make it all better," Dean raged. "Just know, you pricks, my blood is on your hands."

"Shut up!" I screamed at him. "How dare you say that? You shot your brother and you, and God, and we all know it. You think none of these men had to shoot loved ones? Why didn't we frame them? Because we want your house? Please. I'll live in a house where a zombie's been shot," I gestured behind me, "but that house is full of something worse—murder."

I turned away from him. "Toss him in the town jail after you show him the zombie corpse. I'll feed him and we'll have a meeting before memorials on Wednesday to decide what to do with him."

The guys dragged him away and, while Val went following after, I stayed behind shaking my head. Mostly because I was disgusted that humanity, in our little town, could do such evil. *They can die, we can live, and, apparently, we can murder.* A chink of light on the ground caught my attention. I knelt and, next to the burning body, picked up a silver lighter with a skull and crossbones on it. "Where's Grant?"

Grant, who had been awkwardly attempting to make his large frame as small as possible, mumbled something under his breath when Rick grabbed him by the shoulder. He cursed when Jesse took his gun from his side holster. "What is this now?" Grant protested when Rick gave him an encouraging shove toward me and the smoldering grave.

"Where's your lighter?" I asked him.

"In your hand, genius," he spat.

"You burn this body, genius?"

"He was already dead; I didn't kill him."

"No, but you would know whether he turned or not."

Grant coughed. "Well he was, as I said."

"The blood sure doesn't agree with you, even if Dean does."

Grant, weaponless, fired a glare full of contempt at me.

"Were you going to help cover up Gary's murder? Tell me, was Dean gonna give you a room?"

He looked like he wanted to lunge at me, then, to my horror, reached for the closest thing to him: Valentine. She had come back, she was recording him, her phone out in front of her. He grabbed her extended arm; her phone fell to the dirt while she screamed. Then he was shuffling sideways, our guns aimed at him, at her.

"Don't shoot!" Miranda screamed. While I stood speechless.

Then he knelt down to pick something up. *Please not a gun.* It wasn't, it was a needle from one of the corpses. "Which needle was that!?" Kevin roared. But nobody knew. The world was spinning, Miranda was screaming, and I held her back with one arm while she begged Grant to let her daughter go. My other arm held a shaking shotgun I had somehow, at some point, pivoted off the sling on my shoulder. It was aimed at the ground; even if I could aim, there was no way a shotgun would hit him and still miss my daughter.

Val was crying, her glasses were off her face, her eyes straining to focus on the needle held to her neck. Everyone was screaming and, I don't know if it was seconds or minutes later, Grant stumbled on the loose dirt and I watched the needle plunge an inch into my little girl's neck. It was only for a second and then it was out again, only a trickle of blood to show it ever happened. But Grant had felt it; he knew what had happened. His face was filled, like my daughter's, with horror, and he relaxed his grip. She fell to her knees and he made to run. He didn't make it far before I shot him in the back of the head and he collapsed to the ground.

Meanwhile, Valentine was rising. Thankfully her mother was on her knees next to me, reaching for her girl, because when Valentine got to her feet, she was twisted and turned. Her eyes full of rage, drool running from her mouth, her veins black beneath her skin. She turned to me, she ran at me. But I couldn't do it. *How did any of these people do it?* Did I have to shoot my girl?

She was feet from us when Rick, his cowboy hat flying, dove at Miranda and me, tackling us to the ground. There was a gunshot, then another, and a third. Miranda screamed with each shot. Finally, after some rustling and shouting, Rick got off of us and we saw our little girl, infected, bloody, laying on top of Gary's corpse, dead.

The Death of His Saints

"This is the day that the Lord has made," I said with a quivering chin.

"Let us rejoice and be glad in it," the congregation of forty-something said somewhat timidly.

I don't blame them. It was Good Friday and the sun was getting low in the sky. I was surprised so many had braved the lengthening shadows of our afternoon service. Even more, it was my first service back after Valentine's death and, God bless them, they were all still mourning for her, for us.

Kevin and Miranda tried to talk me out of the service.

"I can do it for ya, Pastor. Maundy Thursday seemed to go fair enough," Kevin said.

"Yeah," Miranda agreed, "it's only been a couple days, everyone would understand."

But they didn't understand. They didn't understand that no one else got to just do nothing after their loved ones died in the plague. Trudy still had to care for her daughter after she had to kill her husband. Kyle still had to work as he mourned his wife. So did Jesse while he watched his dad slowly die from kidney failure. Did they not love their family? Was my grief so much more sincere?

I didn't always think like that, though.

I, to this day, don't exactly remember what happened after Valentine died. Miranda and I sat in the same dirt Rick tackled us into and sobbed in each other's arms for who knows how long. Until suddenly my brother was pulling me to my feet and wrapping me in a bear hug. I know my father wanted to do the same, but he was holding my mother, who was in hysterics. Luke was crying and confused and he ran to Miranda, who clung to him desperately.

"Where's Val?" he asked, his face white with fear.

Miranda couldn't answer, I couldn't answer. It was Junior who bent his tall frame over, put a hand on Luke's shoulder, and took a moment to compose himself. "She's gone."

But she wasn't. She was right there, with black veins and bloody clothes that smoldered away revealing more and more pale skin. That was when I wretched. My sweet girl, twisted, dead, and rotting. "Burn her," I said between coughs. A few men standing by looked around. I wiped my mouth on my sleeve, "Burn her faster!"

Linda pulled a spare gas can from the bed of their truck and, after Derek nodded at her, doused Valentine's body. The thirsty smoldering ashes immediately leapt higher. And then Kelly and Emmett were there bringing sticks and wood from the edges of the property. Kelly laid them as reverently as she could over Valentine. Sometime later they came back with flowers and offered them to us.

We sat in the dirt for hours. Kevin, at one point, shared a reading and a prayer. I thanked him for it, I think, though I don't remember what he said as grief, denial, and shock, like waves, took turns washing over me. I was so angry. At God, at Grant—*I should have made him suffer*—at myself, at Val for going so close. *Stupid girl!* Then that thought made me so terribly sad and guilty. Tears came and went and came again. As we sat there, the sun rose high and the birds chirped in the trees. *How could they go on as if nothing had changed?*

Someone eventually had the sense to pry us away from the ashes after they were covered and crosses were put up. Two of them, one for my Val, one for Gary.

Miranda sniffed, scowled, and shook her head. "My girl buried with a stranger . . ." I agreed. We hated everything about this. Death, we should have known by then, never comes how you want it or when you want it.

As evening drew closer, we found ourselves on our front drive shaking the hands of people coming by before dark to pay their respects. I think I smiled, but I don't know how convincing I was. I stood next to Luke who, bless his heart, was trying to be strong. But as night fell so did his courage. He went inside with Junior, Kelly, and Emmett, who tried to distract him and force some food into him that the rest of us hardly touched.

When darkness fell, the people finally left us alone. But the anger and grief wouldn't. Neither would the crying and sobbing that split through the house. I stood in the upstairs landing. To my right, Kelly was dragging their bedding out of Val's room and moving it downstairs to the office, unable to stomach staying in her room that night. I thanked them for it. Meanwhile, my mother was in there slumped on the floor, crying over Val's stuffed animals that she'd had since she was a girl. My dad sat next to her with one arm around her, the other absentmindedly stroking his beard. He stared at the wall, a bit pale. In front of me, Luke was sobbing with Miranda while she caressed his hair with one hand and crinkled her family's picture in the other. I should have joined them and hugged them some more. But, as sorrowful as I was, the anger still boiled hotter. I hated that all I could feel was hate, which made me even angrier.

I turned away from them, my fists clenched, and tried to take a few deep breaths. All I could see was Grant's head streaming blood, and it comforted me. I knew it should disgust me, so I shook my head. Then all I could see was my scared daughter, I shook my head again. Then it was my infected daughter. Disgusted with myself, and everything, I pulled back the curtains, not caring if a bit of candlelight leaked into the night. The haunting images in my mind were replaced with, right next door, our church, which loomed over us. A cross speared up into the dark and gloomy sky that only a vestige of moonlight dared to show itself in. That night I saw the cross, supposedly a sign of hope, for what it really was: a sign of suffering. It condescended over our mourning house, mocking us.

I was down the stairs and out the door before anyone could protest, before anyone could remind me that our family didn't need another tragedy that day. Even now, I'm still not sure why I loaded my shotgun and marched over to the church. Maybe I needed a place to be angry at God. And what better way to vent your anger at God than shooting up a church?

It was miserably dark when I slid through the front doors of the church on that Wednesday of Holy Week, the day my daughter died. The building was pitch black aside from the dimmest streaks of moonlight that fought their way through the thick stained glass, throwing a blood red shade on some of the pews. I normally crossed myself before a fight, a prayer that the Lord would remember the hunk of flesh that may, very soon, be eaten. But I didn't that night. I thought of Valentine, I remembered her face, screwed up in rage and infection trying to bite us. I walked into the narthex *wanting* to hurt something—kill something. *We can die, but so can they.*

I didn't even jump when the first zombie's twisted and half swollen face appeared in my flashlight beam ten feet from me. That face didn't scare me at all. Only Valentine's did. Maybe that's why I went to the church, hoping, perhaps, that if I saw a few, or a dozen, or a hundred, or a thousand other infected faces I would forget my Valentine's.

As it turned out, there were only six zombies in my church.

As it also turns out, I can still remember Valentine's twisted face to this day.

After I had already killed the six ghouls, my family made it over to the church to try and rescue me. From zombies, from myself. They killed two on their way over, drawn by my shots, but I didn't thank them—*let all the zombies come, let the whole horde wash over me.* After the coast was clear, they tried to talk me into coming back to the house, but I refused. They eventually relented when Junior, knowing I wasn't leaving, dropped off some cleaning supplies and dumped a few bags of our used cans in the doorways so I would at least hear if anything was coming.

I spent hours cleaning the church. I dragged out corpses, I swept the floors, and wet the bloody wooden pews with my tears, bleach, and alcohol. Then, I scrubbed until my own blood flowed. I didn't even look behind me when the cracked double doors of the church opened, part of me hoped it was a zombie. *Devour me and let me join my Valentine.*

But it was Miranda.

"Kevin said he would do the Maundy Thursday service tomorrow," she said almost absentmindedly.

"Good, you goin'?" I responded, still not looking up from my scrubbing.

"No. I think not," she said sadly. "But we are going after

147

my family," she said shortly. I looked up and saw her standing in the candlelight with her arms crossed.

I got up on my knees and stared at her. "Like hell we are. You want to lose more?"

"We are dying here anyways."

I ignored the fact that she was right and headed for my office. I shoved the door open and started bleaching the bottom of my desk where it seemed a zombie had been curling up when not out hunting. "We have people here who rely on us."

"More than your family?" she accused, leaning against the wall of my office.

"Especially my family!" I shouted, hitting my head on the bottom of the desk.

"Well, a right good job you've done keeping them safe."

I stood and threw the bottle of bleach against the wall. There was, for only a moment, a look of fear in Miranda's eyes, but then it was sadness. "I'm sorry. I don't blame you," she pleaded with me. "Please, believe me. There was nothing either of us could have done, it's just this . . ." she clenched her fists almost like she would swear, but looked around remembering we were in a church. "Ugh!" she shouted, tears familiarly back on her cheeks. "It's this stupid, broken world."

"Yeah, well." I tossed the cleaning rag onto my desk. "But I still feel like it's our fault."

"Yeah," she sighed and leaned up against the wall. "I feel that too."

"And so I won't let it happen again. We stay."

She pushed off the wall and took a step toward me. "No, we go. If you want to protect your family then let's make sure we got it all."

I took a step toward her now. "You've seen what this plague can do. We barely survived in a town of 400 people, what are the chances your family survived?"

She stepped back as if I had struck her. Then a moment later stood up to her full height, shouting through her tears, "We don't know! And I need to know!"

"And risk our lives in the process going on unknown roads through unknown towns?"

"You were perfectly happy having your family risk their

lives to come to us, but now you are too much of a coward to do the same for mine."

"I am not a coward!" I shouted as if the volume would conceal the lie. "And I will not leave Luke or sacrifice him on a wild goose chase."

Miranda looked me up and down with disgust. "But you were willing to sacrifice his father tonight. You can take risks when you want to, but not us?" Then she turned around, her homemade skirt swirling the noxious air, and slammed the door behind her.

I slept in the church that night, praying a zombie would take me during the night. But no rattling cans woke me, nor any infected hands and teeth.

The next day was much the same. I cleaned the church, eating only when my mom came and forced me to. I spent hours in that church wiping the pews, scrubbing the carpets, cursing under my breath at the stains, and mostly, at God. At God who let this plague and trial come my way.

Sometime in the late afternoon, the bleach fumes, stress, and exhaustion brought another migraine.

I writhed in the pew for hours and vomited up the scant contents of my stomach on the carpet I had just cleaned. I raged at the Lord, who seemed to bring nothing but pain. I moaned and found myself sympathizing with Job's wife who advised her tortured husband to curse God and die. And with thoughts of anger and wrath, with a desire to die and join my daughter, I laid my head on a hymnal and slept.

It was dark in the sanctuary when I woke, my head mercifully free from pain but still sluggish as I worked my way into a sitting position. That was how I found myself facing the front of the church, the white paraments still hung from the altar, undisturbed since Transfiguration Sunday, which seemed a lifetime ago. Without thinking all that much about it, I made my way into the side room where we kept the linens and, opening the closet, found them still neatly folded. I reached out and grabbed the cool and clean black Holy Week linens and made my way toward the altar.

I pulled up short before going up.

Hours before I wanted to curse God and die. Who was I to

come into His presence when I deserved nothing more than to be struck down for my anger and sin? I stepped back and looked at the black linens marked with nails and crowns of thorns that I held in my hands. That was when I remembered why the cross was a sign of hope after all. My God was a God who suffered. He knows what it's like to feel despair, grief, and pain. He knows, intimately, how harsh this broken world is. Even more, He knows the sting of hell, the curse of God. But He overcame it.

And thanks to that, my daughter would overcome it too. And I realized that if I cursed God and died, I wouldn't join my daughter at all. For she dwells with God in a place where nothing else will harm her. Where she waits until the final day when she will rise again to a creation that is no longer broken.

I bowed deeply before the altar. God had brought suffering my way, no doubt, and I didn't know why. But I did know He still cared, because He had suffered too. And He did it for me and my family. So I bowed, a symbol to show submission, to show vulnerability, as if to say, "You can do whatever you want to me, cut my head off if you wish." If He would take my daughter, if He would take the world as we knew it, if He wanted to take me too, so be it. He is God, He is good, and we are not. Thank God for that. Because He is merciful and has promised us life.

I don't know how long I bent over, but eventually I stripped the white paraments and put on the black. Yes there is suffering, but in a few days these paraments would be white once more— Easter white. How I longed for that day, when we celebrated victory. Our God is victorious, we would be too. And I knelt before the altar and prayed; prayers for forgiveness, prayers of thanksgiving, prayers for guidance, prayers to help my unbelief.

Then I went back to the pews and found the hymnal that had been my pillow not long before and I turned to a song written by a man who had lost children himself: "It Is Well with My Soul."

And it was.

I still mourned, I still do to this day. Miranda and I still had a division between us from the death of our child; there was still fear and hardship and pain. But we had a Savior, and He would see us through this valley of shadow to life eternal—life with my Valentine. So it was well with our souls.

Which is why I marched back to my house to be a father

and husband again. It was also why I battled through a service on Good Friday. It was the hardest service I had ever done, though the sermon was the easiest. How could I not fully realize the darkness and suffering of sin and death? How could I not know the hatred in my heart that deserved that same death? How could I hope in anything other than the One who raises the dead and suffered for me, for Valentine?

The congregation was more supportive than I could have imagined. They thanked me and gave me their condolences. I couldn't help but feel the tragedy that had befallen our family made my ministry more meaningful to them. But the beast inside me riled at the thought, *why should my daughter have to die for them to listen to me?*

On Holy Saturday, when we remembered Christ's rest in the tomb, my family was not at rest. Not emotionally, of course, nor physically. My dad and brother headed north to the old RV sales lot to find replacement parts or a new rig. My mom and Kelly spent the day packing and going over supply lists. And Miranda and I met with Kevin to plan our daughter's funeral for the next day.

We all saw the liturgical irony in an Easter funeral. But the people were gathered, and Kevin and the elders assured us the town wanted to be there for us. Even **Pastor Barnstock** canceled his service and he and his people sat with us on Easter to mourn alongside us. It was a touching and beautiful gesture for them to share our grief on a day of celebration. Especially since they had all lost loved ones too. But I didn't appreciate that until later. I was in a daze, flitting in and out of hopelessness and carelessness, stability and mortal depression, apathy and anger. Still anger. Anger at God, at Grant, at this broken cursed world, at the people intruding on our mourning, even though they were just showing us love, and, of course, anger at myself for not saving my girl.

I could hear Kevin's voice shaking. I should have felt sorry for him, it was one of his first sermons and he wanted to do well for my family and me. I tried to let his words in, to shape me, to curb my broken heart, but instead I was wrestling with myself in an attempt to turn off my overly critical mind. *His illustration was too long and didn't apply in every aspect.* I rubbed my temples. *A verse from 2 Corinthians would have been more applicable.* I pressed my fingers into my eyes. *His delivery was forced.* I had to consciously restrain myself to keep my face from grimacing at times. *Was this man honestly giving us more law?* God's judgment, our sinfulness, my daughter's sinfulness. *Didn't he think we had suffered enough?*

I ran my hands through my hair and pulled until it hurt a little bit. Most of the people thought I was just distraught about my daughter, and I was, truly, I was. But I also hated myself for not being able to just listen to the sermon, I was critiquing it.

But then Kevin's tone changed, pulling me out of my conflicted thoughts and feelings. He looked up from his manuscript on the podium and began to proclaim to the entire congregation, to me, God's wonderful promises in Jesus. *This is why he will make a good Pastor, he loves to share the Gospel.*

He said my beautiful daughter had been claimed by God and united with Him. He proclaimed her death had been swallowed up in victory by her Savior's resurrection. For some time, Kevin went on preaching the beautiful Gospel of God in Christ, the living Lord. Each sentence, like an injection of hope, broke down my infected and despairing heart. A promise of salvation brought tears to my eyes. A promise of resurrection obscured the haunting images of my infected and ravenous daughter. A promise of a reunion with her again made her mother and me embrace. I had never noticed how Valentine's hair smelled just like her mother's until that moment when Miranda laid her head on my shoulder.

The service ended with a blessing. "The Lord will bless you and keep you, the Lord will make His face shine on you and be gracious unto you, the Lord will look upon you with favor and give you peace." I had said it a thousand times. It had been said to me another thousand. But never as I was in such pain. Never had the blessing seemed so ironic, *where was the blessing today?*

Kevin turned and picked up a cross off the altar. The cross of Jesus, who suffered and died, the One who rose and kept His people, even my Val, with Him, whose face dripped blood and grace for her and me, whose peace was not a lack of suffering, but of an eternal victory. *That's where His blessing is, in a Savior.* And we still had a Savior, even in the midst of pain and death.

Kevin marched out into the field, like I had done a hundred times, and staked a cross into the ground next to a hundred others.

152

Pilgrimage

Two days later, Kevin and I sat in my office. As usual, we sipped on some bourbon we never could have afforded before the plague and we had a conversation we never would have had before the plague. After he asked how I was doing and I lied ("Fine, thanks"), we talked theology for several hours as we had done so regularly.

But it had only been a month. A woefully, tragically short amount of time to call a seminary experience. Which is why I wasn't surprised when he raised an eyebrow after I told him I had talked with the elders and they had agreed that, should I not return, we would recommend he take over as pastor of the congregation.

"Well, you better come back, because I don't think I'm ready," he said, swirling the last few sips of bourbon left in his glass.

I laughed. "I don't think so either."

He shook his head and finished his drink in one swallow.

"But in this new world, there is a lot we've had to do that we weren't ready for. The fact is that I, and especially Miranda, are hurting. Bad. She needs answers one way or another. I need to give her this. And maybe a week or two off would be good for me too."

"And if you find nothin'?"

I shrugged. "Then at least I have given her that."

He leaned back and looked toward the bookcase at nothing in particular.

"Look, I still want to serve, I don't think I could really ever

153

stop." I emptied my glass. "But before I got the Call to be a pastor, I took on a calling as a husband. And if I do not care for my family, how can I care for the flock?"

He nodded at my bookshelf and glanced back to me. "Well if you get eaten, I'm assuming I can have your commentaries?"

I laughed. "Kevin, whether I am alive or not, my whole library is yours." I pointed to a new stack of books by the door. "And I got a few of my favorite books from Pastor Mueller's office in Carbondale. It didn't seem like they were being used."

He grinned. "Good, I'll need all the help I can get."

"And you will need a camouflage pastor's stole made for you too. It would fit you perfectly."

He laughed, but then he shook his head and put his hands through his hair. After a moment he looked up and exclaimed, "Don't God's people deserve better than me?"

"Yes. And better than me."

"Well, I mean—"

"I know what you mean, Kevin." I sighed. "But if something happens, I can't give you a degree. And I can't give you four years. You barely know the alphabets of the languages and I don't have all the books or curriculum for the history and the dissertations. But I do know that I have to do this for Miranda, and I do know that God's people need someone faithful and dedicated to learning to lead them and to bring them the Word and Sacrament—to be a pastor."

Kevin laughed. "Yeah. Well, just try not to die."

I chuckled. "I'm not trying to," I gave him a sideways glance, "anymore." He raised an eyebrow at me, having heard about me rushing into the church a few nights before. "Believe me."

We talked for a while and had another class session, this time on the Council of Nicaea. Eventually he pushed his glass toward me, thanked me, put his camouflage hat back on and said, "See ya when I see ya, Pastor." I asked him to shut the door behind him and he did.

Then, once again, I found myself pulling Val's phone out of my top drawer. I watched, once more, the shaky footage of Val walking closer to Grant. *Why do I keep watching this? To punish myself? To find some justification for not saving her?*

I wanted to scream for someone, for me, to tell Val to stop getting closer for a shot. Then I watched once again as the phone fell to the dirt and glimpses of my daughter's frightened face swam in and out of the picture before it went dark, covered in dirt. And then I listened, listened as the screams became more frantic and my shotgun fired—*oh, how that sound made the beast in me leap with joy!* But then the rest of the gunshots came and I cried because I knew they ended my daughter's portion of the story here.

That was also when I decided to continue it for her. I dried my face and I called Luke into the room. I didn't have to call loud in the quiet house before I heard him tiptoeing on the creaky hardwood of the hall toward the office. Months in the new world taught even the children to make as little noise as possible.

The timid boy came into the room and stood in front of my desk, his eyes on the floor, his daylight bravery gone with his sister. I held out Val's phone to him. It took him a second to look up and see what I was doing, another to reach out and take the phone.

His eyes were puffy, no doubt he had been crying. I tried to be brave for him. "Your sister wanted people to know about this plague. I need you to be brave for her and finish what she started."

He turned to leave, then paused. "Is the video on here?"

I nodded. "Whenever you think you're ready. Then come talk to me about it. Promise?"

"Yeah." Then he put his head up, turned, and walked away.

I, also wanting to honor Val's wishes but never good with cameras, picked up a pen and started making notes about our story—this book. A hope that Val's dream would live on, even as she did with her Savior.

On Wednesday, I did a memorial for a man who was attacked by a lone zombie that had bedded down in his back hedgerow. I choked up a bit more than usual, it being the first memorial since my daughter died and also my last memorial before leaving Witherton to find Miranda's family. But I got through it. We told the news of our planned departure to the families that came, though most of them already knew about it through the elders and Kevin. Even in the plague, word still spreads fast in a small town.

By the end of the memorial, most of the town was

assembled for an impromptu meeting in the Jacobson field. Most of the people, we could tell, were worried that we were leaving, though they tried to hide it. "Just a quick trip, eh?" But we all knew there was no one to call for help out there. "Your folks did half the country, they can do to the mountains and back." Even though we all knew the roads were only getting worse. Wilbur, usually a rare sight at church or a meeting, came with a few tanks on a small trailer behind his pickup. As we stood in the field, he motioned over to them. "Sorry for your loss, Pastor, I know I didn't come as much as I said, but I ain't forgot about you." He gestured to his trailer. "There's some fuel I been working on. Take it with you, it should keep you moving if you run short." I thanked him, even though, after a glance at my brother's worried face, the fuel seemed more likely to blast us around the country than keep our engines running.

But even more than any false hope about our travels, I couldn't shake the feeling that the fear and sadness I saw in my members' eyes was because I had now lost someone close to me through the plague. Now they connected with me more. Now I could share their griefs better. Now I was one of them and they were sadder to see me go. Maybe all my talk at memorials about hope in the face of grief, maybe that sounded less fake now that I needed that same hope for myself.

But, at the time, it only made me want to go on the trip even more. Why should they care about my authenticity? The teaching was true or it wasn't. I found myself asking, again, why should I have to sacrifice a daughter for my words to mean something? The whole farewell was a twisted cycle of fear, sadness, guilt, and anger. One minute I bit back bitter retorts to people who only wished us well through fake smiles. The next, when they asked my advice on a few topics, made my pride swell up. They were concerned that Dean, in jail, was taking up food and not offering anything to the society. I told them I didn't have any better options, but strongly urged against killing him, which seemed to disappoint Curtis.

"Pastor, I know I ain't the most agreeable man," the old man said, "but you always gave me half a shake and didn't get us all killed."

I didn't know whether to laugh or cry. "Curt, that was the

worst thank you I have ever heard. But it means a lot, considering the source."

"You always should."

"Go easy on Kevin 'til I get back, will you?"

"Afraid I can't. He's related, you know."

I smiled, shook my head, and did the same to his hand. There were more goodbyes, more complicated feelings, and Miranda, who I am sure felt similarly, followed me through the group. She was crying as she said her goodbyes, but I knew her well enough to see the anticipation and eagerness behind her tears.

The last person I said goodbye to was Kevin. As I hugged him, I choked up. I told him thanks for all the help he had given me and then I wished him well in his ministry should we not meet again; he had been voted in unanimously by the congregation should my vacancy go longer than expected. He thanked me, but I looked away in shame. Because even though I did wish him well, the prideful beast in me wished he would fail. I wanted to be needed by the people, I wanted to be loved and the best. I wanted to be able to say that when I left, it all collapsed.

I spat on Jacobson's field since I couldn't spit on my pride and managed a genuine smile before I walked away from my church family, prayerfully only for a time, to seek family elsewhere.

The next day was a day that the Lord had made, certainly. But we were not rejoicing as we left our home, and, of course, our daughter and a piece of each of us smoldering in ashes. We would see her again. That was our hope.

For all that my pride gloated about being such a leader in town, on the road it was nice to be able to rely on my family who had traveled in the plague before. They knew what to do far more than I. This was made apparent before we even left when I suggested we weld some metal spikes to the frames of the rigs. "Why, so we can drag corpses along the whole way?" Kelly scoffed. Instead, we put cattle guards on to push the zombies, not impale them. I also spent ten minutes hitching up the trailer only to have my dad almost faint because I hooked it up wrong. "We coulda lost all our gas if we hit a bump!" Then he fixed it in two minutes.

Inside the rig I wasn't much help either, the women had a system for cleaning, cooking, and mending that was far beyond me; evidenced when I tried packing a dresser only to find my mother redoing it later. After a half-dozen similar instances, the relief of not having to be in charge began to stagnate. A deep feeling of uselessness and incompetence replaced it, along with dark thoughts. *The church doesn't need me, neither does my family. It should have been me, not Valentine.*

Once we were all packed and I was in the back of my parents' rig coloring with the kids, we pointed our rigs west and took backroads, skirting as far as we could from the city. Not knowing, or caring to find out, what the situation was there.

The trip went much smoother than I had anticipated. The roads were mostly clear of abandoned cars and, though grass was growing tall in the cracks, they were in better condition than I could have guessed, probably due to so few cars traveling on them anymore. We never did find any large hordes in the country, but we did see plenty of zombies, some alone, some in packs.

For hours we rolled on well under the speed limit. A small train of RVs towing trailers and pickups, moving across the plains slow and steady. We stopped only to refuel from the trailer full of gasoline behind my brother's rig, to scout a bridge or piece of road that looked particularly perilous, or at any gas stations that weren't exploded so my brother could try to get some gas. At least on our stops I felt useful, perched on the roof with a shotgun or clearing a dark gas station. *Is killing all I was good for outside of a pulpit?*

I still remember shaking my head to get the vision of Grant's bloody head out of my mind as I sat on the rig couch, Miranda sobbing on my shoulder. I tried to focus on the flowing wild grass attempting to encroach in on the fields of weeds and volunteer corn. Evidently, humanity wasn't the only thing struggling for a foothold in the new world. But the image swam in front of the fields. Closing my eyes only made it clearer. *Why was this man still haunting me? I killed him.* I, of course, had killed hundreds, but never healthy. *He wasn't healthy, he was sick. He was evil. He deserved it.* I comforted my conscience and my pride with these truths. *Or was I gloating in it? Glorying in his busted head?* I fought back the frightful notion that perhaps I celebrated his death more than I mourned my daughter's. I fought back the

158

feeling that something was sick inside me as well. But then I saw a lone zombie running through a field at our rigs. We were past it in a minute. Even Luke and Emmett, who ran to the back window to watch it, couldn't see it after a mile, but it had given me all I needed that day: something to focus on, another twisted face to kill. *They could die.*

We spent the night with our wagons circled at an old, abandoned weigh station off the highway. We took turns on guard duty and I elected for a double portion, happy to be able to contribute something. I found myself on a lawn chair on top of our rig, thankful for the breeze on a summer night. The first part of the watch consisted of me swiveling around and peering into the darkness at every sound or shadow. But my paranoia subsided when nothing came limping out of the grass.

My gaze shifted upward then, at the stars I hadn't seen in months due to the city and our town's pollution. I took a deep breath, the fresh air waking me. I sat there pondering my faith in someone larger than the expanse of a million stars above me and how I had preached that he actually cared for the handful of people left walking on this rock.

Then Grant's head was back again, a bloody wound on the back of his head accusing me, *"You actually believe in some invisible guy up there? If He's up there, He sure don't care about us."*

We are so small, it's true. Our laughs, our jobs, our fights, our deaths. What were they? What were they to the stars and the moon that had seen billions die? Did the plague pique the moon's interest or draw its gaze any closer? Did my hurts and tears and sermons? Did it care of the hatred and violence we carried in our hearts and carried out with hands, needles, and gunpowder? What about the One who made it?

I had no trouble staying awake through my double guard duty.

The next morning, I woke up with sunlight blazing through the swaying blinds in front of me. I stretched and crawled to the front of the rig and saw the mountains tall in front of us. A quick survey of the family's faces showed that the tension of the journey and looming discovery had grown as well.

Hours later, we found ourselves surrounded by pines and clearing the mountain pass into Miranda's family's lake city. We worked our way toward the large town slowly, maneuvering around the abandoned cars on the roads. Her hometown seemed the perfect reflection of my mood: a black haze of smoke hung over the city of about five thousand people. The once beautiful forests that surrounded the mountains were nearly gone. Half seemed burned, the rest apparently deforested and used for who knows what. Fires burned haphazardly about the seemingly abandoned and ravaged town.

It seemed everyone in the rig turned to look at Miranda with wide eyes. She didn't seem to notice; she was staring at the ruined city with her shaking arms crossed and eyes puffy.

Prey

A mile out of town we parked the rigs and loaded into the pickup my brother towed that could more easily maneuver through the chaos on the roads. My mom stayed back with Emmett and Luke. For a moment, when Miranda was saying goodbye to Luke, crying and holding onto her only living child, I thought she would stay behind too. But then she kissed him, grabbed a rifle, and hopped in the bed of the truck next to me.

My brother drove carefully, but with a purpose, taking wide paths around obstacles, sticking to open roads. I remember the town's roadside sign swinging in the wind, "Crestbard, population: 5537." *But how many are left?*

The town was still, aside from smoke from smoldering fires. It was silent, aside from the rumble of the truck engine that should have attracted zombies before we even got into town. The streets were empty of bodies and Miranda hopefully, though her voice still shaky, said, "No bodies. No horde. They must have fought them off!"

My father, in the passenger seat, nodded but shot a sideways glance at my brother that betrayed the same suspicion I had. Sure, there were no zombies, but there was no sign of life either. No gas tanks had been siphoned, no vehicle tracks in the dirty streets. The cars, trees, and wreckage of the city's panic still lay unmoved across the entire ghost town that used to be a city of thousands.

Two miles into the broken and ravaged town, my father, pivoting in his seat for any sign of infected, finally voiced his fears.

"Where the devil is everything?"

"Never thought I'd actually be wanting to see a zombie, this is too eerie . . ." Kelly trailed off, realizing it might have been insensitive to wish the plague upon the city Miranda's family lived in. She awkwardly rearranged the headband in her short hair and went back to looking around at the empty city.

But Miranda didn't notice. She just kept wringing her hands and looking at the vacant, destroyed houses. "Maybe the military came through and took everyone away?"

She looked at me. I shrugged. "As good as anything I can think of."

Then she told my brother to turn. We all stared at the seventh house on the right, Miranda's parents' house. But my little girl wasn't happily swinging from the tire in their front lawn. The tree holding the tire had burned down like my daughter, and only ash and melted rubber adorned the front lawn. The bottom and top floor windows were broken and half the roof had caved in where the front tree, yielding to the flames, collapsed into the home.

Miranda was outright crying now. I had an arm around her and Kelly stood in the bed of the truck to keep watch while my dad and brother hopped out of the truck and swiftly made their way into the house, swinging their rifles and lights into the dark corners.

Five minutes later they came out, guns lowered. Miranda took one look at their shaking heads and burst into more sobs. Obviously, I couldn't sympathize with her fully. Yes, I had known grief and yes, I sat through a month of the unknown, wondering about my family. I knew how the unknown ate you apart, but at least the unknown gave you hope, and now Miranda's hope in the unknown was fading, if not snuffed out altogether.

My brother tried to fan any left back into flame. "No people, but no blood either."

"What happened in this town?" my dad asked as he hopped back in the truck and ran his hand through his beard, thinking.

Kelly, her voice shaking, answered, "Something's moving behind us. And I think I know why there's no people here."

We spun and looked up at seven large wolves ambling down the road after us.

No one had to tell my brother to start driving. When he hit the gas the wolves did too, but now there were over a dozen. He turned down a side street and there were four more. One jumped in front of the truck and, denting the fender, was sent whimpering and flying to the side. I could see, as it rolled back to its feet and limped after us, that its face was scarred and disfigured.

"Hit 'em all!" Miranda cried out in an angry voice.

"Do no such thing," Cooper contradicted. "One busted axle, or any of that blood on us, and we are dead." He leaned out the window and looked at our dragging fender. "Lose 'em."

And Junior tried. For miles we wove through the streets. We hung on for dear life while he maneuvered through burned out cars and jumped curbs to dodge trees or debris. But the wolves could follow our sound. They vaulted cars and fences, cut through burned out houses when we tried to swerve, and with all the chaos on the streets, there was never a straight enough section of road to put them far behind us.

Miranda, on one knee, fired a shot at our pursuers. It was a great shot and one of the wolves rolled on the asphalt until it stopped dead. But the rest of the pack kept chasing. "Why didn't the gunfire scare them?"

I sighed. "Because these wolves don't hunt rabbits and deer anymore, they've been eating people and fighting infected for months." I looked at the now twenty wolves chasing us. "They're hunting us."

"Water," Miranda said, "there's a lake on the north side of town."

Immediately Junior turned left and started weaving his way north, ignoring the wolf that had been trying to flank us and slammed into his door. A few minutes later we had put a little distance between the wolves and ourselves and we could see the lake in the distance.

It wasn't the clear blue I always remembered, it was black and brown and it looked as if twenty boats, barges, and docks had been tied together in the middle of it.

"People!" Miranda screamed with joy.

And she was right, we could see movement on the makeshift water town. People were tending fires on the boats and carefully maneuvering across makeshift bridges between their crafts.

My brother accelerated down the lake's long dock, flanked

by metal and fiberglass dinghies, and Kelly screamed as if he would launch us into the lake. But he slammed on the brakes. The truck skidded to a stop fifteen feet from the end of the pier. "The boat on the left, go!" Junior shouted.

We tumbled out of the truck, not even bothering to shoot at the wolves following us. We clambered into the boat, nearly tipping it. I fumbled with the rope for a moment before Kelly pulled me back and slashed it with her machete.

I got back on my feet and shoved us off the dock. Our rocky little metal boat was in the lake and my dad and brother were rowing hard. I still panicked when I saw how close we were to the pier. "Faster, faster, they're coming."

"We're trying," my brother huffed.

I ducked when the gunshot went off. For a heartbeat, I was worried the people on the barges were shooting at us, but it was too loud. And then there was water all along my side and Miranda was cranking the bolt on her rifle. A wolf carcass bobbed in the water a few feet away.

"Don't let the water in, wipe it off!" my dad screamed. *It's contaminated.* I grabbed my hat, wiped the liquid off me, and tossed the hat in the lake. More wolves were crashing into the water pursuing us, but, between the sporadic shots we sent into a few of them and the ever increasing expanse of water between us, they gave up.

I thanked God after the wolves clambered back onto shore, gave us one last look, and trotted back into the city. But then I turned to what floated ahead of us and started praying some more. I shot a glance at Miranda; her gray eyes were flitting back and forth, scanning the makeshift boardwalk for anyone she might recognize.

"We come in peace," my dad shouted between breaths, then he turned to me. I nodded and took up his task for him. I raised one hand high. "We come in peace. We are looking for family in this town."

Thankfully the people seemed unarmed and, with a wary look at our guns, a few guys reached a hand out and helped us onto the docks.

Miranda was the first out. "The Drews! The Drews!" She pleaded with the people standing around us, ignoring the fact that she was making it hard for us to get off the boat. "Please, any word on the Drews, they're my parents."

Oddly, I think the people found her desperation disarming. They clearly knew we weren't here to raid them.

And then, before anyone spoke, someone shouldered through the crowd. He, like his white hair, was thinner, he looked ill, but there was Miranda's dad, Bryan. And right behind him was her mom, Mary, holding Miranda's niece by the hand. Miranda fell on her knees and cried and they joined her in an embrace on the rocking dock.

The whole community watched as they sobbed, embraced, and then watched as they groaned when news was shared that Valentine hadn't made it, nor had Miranda's older sister Madelyn and her husband. "Sweetheart, I'm so sorry. They left Noelle with us and went back to their place downtown for more supplies when the plague exploded. We tried to look for them, but the horde was too large, the uninfected too panicked and violent, and then the wolves came," Mary explained defensively, but she didn't have to, we all understood. Then she came and hugged me. "I'm so sorry about Val. But she is doing better than us now."

I sniffed and nodded. "Together with Madelyn, Rob, and the Savior."

She hugged me tighter. "Amen."

It must have taken ten minutes, but the people on the docks knew that this was the most important thing for anyone now: to reunite and to share grief. They stood silent until Miranda was back on her feet. "Here, come to where we are staying," her dad suggested.

"Just a minute now." A large bald man, who seemed like he had about three times as many meals as anyone else, stepped forward. "I'm Richard Kettleridge. Kinda put this deal together." He ignored the murmurs from the crowds around him and put one hand in his suspender, the other on his holster. The only gun I could see. "What news from the outside world?" he asked.

My dad stepped forward and Richard took his hand off his suspender long enough to shake his hand. My dad cleared his throat. "Name's Cooper. Nothing good from the outside. We got off the coast just before the chaos hit and have been trying to reunite ever since. Found my son in his small town. They managed to beat their horde and scrape out a life, but it seems most towns didn't."

"So no cure? No military?" a frail looking lady asked.

We shook our heads sadly. "Not that we've heard of," Junior said apologetically.

Richard almost seemed pleased. "But you got supplies, clearly." He nodded at our guns and the truck.

My dad shot me a glance and stroked his beard a bit, he was nervous. "Well, yeah a bit for us to make the trip. But not more than we could live off of."

"Surely that's more than we got and after all, if we excellent people work together here . . ."

Did I sound like this when I asked for shared supplies? It made me sick. *Was I any different than this used car salesman?*

Bryan spoke up, "Look, this is good. We will go with them, Richard. And that's three less mouths to feed, more to go around, and someone can take our craft."

"Not so fast there, Reverend Drews." Richard pulled out his sidearm. And suddenly two more guys who looked more than well fed stepped to his side.

"Woah, we don't want any trouble," my dad said, but he sure had a firm grip on his gun. Junior, bringing himself to his full height, even taller than Richard, stepped in front of Kelly. I did the same for Miranda while keeping a hand on her gun barrel, I knew she wouldn't let anyone take her family from her now.

"Alright, alright." Bryan stepped forward and shot my dad a reassuring glance, as if he knew how to handle Richard, "I think we can work something out here. How about this? These folks will tell us all they know about the virus and any more news. Maybe they show their thanks by leaving us one of these weapons to help with the wolves, of course."

Richard smiled. "Of course."

"And we all might be a little better off."

"Yeah, but I'm still out two good rowers." He looked at Bryan and Mary, who, now that I noticed, was also leaner, sickly even, but muscled.

Miranda, sensing Richard's hesitancy, interjected, "We can offer more."

Richard looked at her with what I could swear was a bit of

lust—the sensual kind I'm sure, but also from greed, thinking of what he could get out of a poor woman desperate for family. But I hoped she wouldn't sell this dangerous man more than we could offer. "You gave me my family back, we can figure out something I'm sure."

"Right." Bryan stepped in between her and Richard like a rodeo clown and a bull. "Shall we?" He motioned over one of the bridges.

Richard sniffed and put his gun away. "Right. After you."

The Fall

We followed Bryan across a small bridge with rope handles and when Junior tripped on an exposed nail, half the people around us started shouting, "Grab on to something!" I steadied myself on a nearby boat and watched as people clutched their loved ones close until the rocking subsided.

"I'm so sorry!" my brother stammered, red in the face.

Richard shook his head as if we were clueless and Bryan, as we filed off the bridge, informed us in a quiet voice, "Life on the water is tense, one person upsetting the rig can send someone else over."

Kelly held tight on to Junior's arm. "That's horrifying. With the virus in there, it might as well be acid."

I thought back to when I played as a kid, jumping on the furniture pretending the floor was lava. A little touch and you're gone.

"It's actually not quite that bad." He continued with his hand on a rope handrail. "There is plenty of virus in this lake but sometimes people can go all the way under and come back up uninfected. Most of the time not, though."

We hopped up onto a party barge and headed across its deck and, more carefully now, across another bridge.

Bryan continued while he led us across the barge. "Best we can figure is that the virus can't live forever in water, it needs a host." He helped Noelle, who didn't need it as young and agile as she was, and Mary over a narrow bridge. "Mind the middle board there, it's rotting." Then he continued as if he was just informing us of the weather. "But the fish that survived the pollution and the animals that come and drink the water keep it pretty well stocked with virus. So we tend to shy away from the edges when we can." Bryan stepped aside and motioned below deck to the small yacht we had climbed onto.

Inside, it was dark, musty, and cluttered as if three people had been living in it for far too long. "Home sweet home." Bryan smiled meekly at us and apologized to Junior who had to hold his head to the side to keep it from hitting the ceiling. Noelle ran off and grabbed a stuffed animal. Mary, a bit red in the face, put some clothes in a box in the corner.

Bryan stepped past her, grabbed me by the shoulder and looked at all of us. "Richard is not an honest man, watch what you say. He will take advant—"

Before he could finish, Richard came lumbering down and seemed to fill a quarter of the room himself. Bryan coughed, forced a smile, and headed off to one side of the room.

Richard wiped his Fu Manchu, rubbed his belly, and eyed our guns, which were lowered. He spoke far too loudly for what the space required. "Alright, let's get this straight. I've put my neck on the line for folks you want to take out of this community. People who work," he nodded to Bryan, "and people who, well," he chuckled, "make this place a little nicer to live in." He eyed Mary. Bryan flexed his fists and glared at the floor while Mary went back to tidying up the dark room as if she hadn't heard anything.

"Alright," I said with a glance at my dad and Bryan. "Maybe we should put out some terms. We want out of here today, preferably soon, and we want to feel safe doing it."

He stepped toward me. "You dare doubt my generosity?" He waved his arm. "Look around, people are alive because of me. The Reverend here," he nodded at Bryan, "should be thanking the Good Lord for me. So, I want assurance from you that I will get a fair deal."

I bit my tongue to stop from telling him that everyone looked terrified and sick in his commune.

My dad stepped in. "Good, no one wants to fight anyone. We've got that settled. So here's what we have on hand to give you: we'll offer one of our guns and ammo, that should help with the wolves, and we got a spare gas tank in our truck. That, plus the fact that you'll have three less mouths to feed, should be reasonable."

"Not good enough." He bent closer to my dad's face. "You give me a week, a week that we can use your guns to keep the wolves at bay while we find more lumber and supplies."

"No way, mister." My brother, taller than Richard, but probably half his weight, stepped forward. "You heard our terms. We got family out there too."

Richard's eyes lit up as if he just found another treasure to mine. "Oh, but don't we all. Even more reason you should help us poor folk—"

Miranda stepped forward now. "Let's not forget the fact that you are making us pay for our family. They aren't slaves. They aren't yours. Maybe we don't give you anything." She brought her rifle around in front of her.

Richard looked like he wanted to hit her, then he smiled and backed out of the room. Once on the deck he called out, "Jackson, Ramirez, these people don't feel like they want to be part of the commune anymore!"

Miranda's family gasped, Bryan went running out after him. "No, that's not what we meant!"

Even I screamed when we heard the gunshots. Afraid that Bryan had been shot, we scrambled out onto the deck to find Bryan alive, but staring defiantly across a two foot gap of water at Richard, who had kicked the bridges down along with his henchmen on either side of us.

They each had a handgun and had shot several holes in the boat's hull. I turned to see if water was in the lower room already, but it was too dark. Mary had grabbed Noelle, who was screaming, and we all huddled on the deck, looking around frantically. Many members of the community were out on their decks and rafts looking at us, but keeping their distance.

"You want to be on your own, you want to spurn our generosity? Then good luck floating free." He waved and smiled at us.

"Can this boat move?" my dad whispered sharply to Bryan, "If we can get to—"

"No, Richard and his two ugly friends took all the gas for themselves."

Richard continued his speech, "I tried to be reasonable, but now it's gonna take a whole lot more to get you out because in your haste to leave," he stuck his lower lip out, "you seemed to have punctured one of my boats." He laughed. "I want a week of labor and all but one of your guns, then you are free to leave."

I looked at Miranda, who was clutching her mother with one arm and holding her rifle in the other. She was angry, she was scared. She had been so desperate for so long and now this man was going to take her joy from her, like I tried to a few days before. Like the joy of her daughter was taken away from her a week before. And I thought of Luke back at the rig with my mother, probably wondering where we were. And I gripped the shotgun in my hand so hard that my knuckles were white.

"What are you doing? We have more guns than you!" my brother said, pointing his rifle at Ramirez to my right.

Richard laughed. "Yeah, but I have you surrounded, and you guys are cowards, never had to kill a person if they wasn't infected, I bet."

But he was wrong.

Which is why he was still smiling when I aimed at his chest and pulled the trigger.

I shouted for everyone to get down as I shot at him, and as I pumped in another round I was jerked around sideways by my arm. Turning, I expected to see someone there holding my arm. And then I saw the blood and felt the searing pain. I looked up at Ramirez, who had shot me, but he had already been shot by my brother and all I could see was the splash of water where he fell.

Behind me, Bryan, though old, had managed to leap over four feet of water and was wrestling with Jackson. None of us dared shoot, but my brother and dad got their balance, cleared the gap, and the three skinny men were able to wrestle the large man to the ground and wrench his gun free. Jackson, even disarmed, wouldn't give up, however. He grabbed Bryan's leg and tried to tip him into the water, but Bryan fell backwards on the deck and clung to a handrail. My brother got to his feet and kicked Jackson hard in the ribs. He grunted and rolled off the edge and slid into the lake.

Not three seconds later the water was boiling. Jackson, as if he couldn't control his limbs, thrashed about, screaming, taking water in with breaths. For all his flailing, he sunk lower in the water.

"He's infected," Bryan said.

Junior picked up Jackson's gun, and, after a nudge from my father, handed it over. Cooper aimed it at what little of Jackson's head was left above water, but a short man with a weeping wife yelled at him to stop. Cooper looked alarmed as the man walked up to him. "May I?" he asked. My dad looked at Bryan, who nodded, before handing the gun over.

He thanked my dad and raised the gun at Jackson. "For the women." A shot rang out and, after a moment, the water was still, save for the ripples skimming far into the lake.

Bryan tossed a rope to Kelly and pulled the sinking boat back close enough to unload the rest of us. He tied the boat off and, with the help of a few people from the barges, offloaded some supplies. Meanwhile, the pain in my arm hit me as the adrenaline wore off. I fell to my knees, not daring to touch my wound, which seemed to be burning. Kelly rushed over, looked at it, and, as sweat started to form on my forehead, fashioned a tourniquet together.

Richard's body lay on its side, facing away from me. The back of Grant's bloody head swam in my view until it rested on top of Richard's. *"Quite the body count there, Preacher man."*

"He threatened my family," I retorted.

"Just admit you like killing people," the wound, moving like a mouth, goaded.

"I do not!" I yelled with tears in my eyes.

Someone shook me and my eyes focused on my family that was surrounding me. "Are you alright, Darren?" Miranda asked.

Then her head turned into Grant's. "No. No!" I tried to pull away from them. I shook my head and when I refocused, her face was Valentine's, but twisted and bloody. *"Why are you killing people, Daddy?"*

I slumped to my side and felt the whole raft spin underneath me. "No, sweetheart, they're zombies. We are all zombies."

I was an undershepherd watching over the Master's flock on a beautiful green hillside. It looked to be about morning and a wonderful orange sunrise was coming up over the horizon. The sandals fit well, as did the robe, and I walked among the sheep, joyfully using my staff only to aid my walking, not to hook any straying sheep.

But then my staff grew heavy and short, I almost tripped. It wasn't a staff at all, it was my shotgun. I puzzled over it for a minute before the sound of bleating and growling made me look up. *The sheep*, something was wrong with them.

They foamed and writhed and then they turned toward me. They charged at me. They had to be infected. So I shot them. Over and over I shot them until I realized they weren't attacking me at all. They were running past me, scared.

Wave after wave of black wolves were coming over the hill, scaring the Master's sheep, but I hadn't protected them. I had killed them. Turning, I watched the few survivors run past me and over the hill. Then I turned back to the wolves, they were so close now. I wanted to run, but I couldn't. *Why couldn't I run?*

And then the wolves were upon me and I would surely be eaten—but the largest one stopped in front of me while the rest ran past, after the sheep. The alpha wolf smiled at me from the corner of his snout. "Well done, brother."

I looked down and I was no longer a shepherd, but a wolf. And I looked in horror at the lambs around me, slaughtered. One was Bertha, the next was Richard, then Grant, and the next was Valentine. I fell on the ground in front of my sweet daughter, but then her face turned to how I last saw it, infected, full of rage, and she opened her mouth to bite me.

I woke up soaking wet and breathing hard. I sat up and nearly cried out from the pain encompassing my wounded arm. It reverberated up my shoulder and into my side. I caught my breath and realized I sat in the darkness of the rig, alone in bed. Miranda must have been sleeping with Luke—because he needed her or because she didn't want to be near a killer like me, I didn't know.

Slowly the hazy thoughts of the previous day came back. I nearly vomited as I saw the smile on Richard's face as his chest caved in. Looks of rage, infected faces, they were nothing compared to that. *And I preached about humanity.* "Well, Richard didn't have any," I told myself. *But did I?*

I shook my head to think of something else.

I remembered the tears of joy my wife shed when she saw

her family again. But then I remembered the fear in Noelle's cries when I started the shooting. I remembered the looks of awe and fear on the faces of my family looking at Richard's body. And then I remembered as I lay on the dock, Kelly trying to help me while, in the background, the people were coming up and shaking hands with my family and Bryan.

Yes, I thought. Yes. We freed them. We freed them from a monster and abuser.

And I hardened my heart against my conscience, against the sin and hate that secretly wanted Richard dead and never asked if there was any other way out of that situation.

I felt even better when I fed my prideful monster inside with self-justification. I told myself that Richard was threatening my family, which was true. I fed the monster, thinking that I had seen one piece of my family lost at the hands of a fool, how could I, as the head of the household, stand for another?

I shook the guilt and doubt away and remembered my father and Bryan leaving the community two guns. I remembered my dad and brother telling the community members how their rifles were zeroed and that they would leave the ammo on the dock so we could leave safely, unsure if any wanted revenge for what we did to Richard and his men. But by the looks on people's faces, they were relieved, not angry. I comforted myself with that.

I remembered firm hands helping me into the bed of the truck. I remembered the gunshots as we raced through town with wolves on our tails, the pain as my right arm would hit the wheel well when we swerved in the road. I remember the tears when Bryan and Junior tossed two smelly corpses wrapped in white cloth next to me in the bed of the truck.

Candlelight flickered in the small hallway and Miranda walked in and sat next to me. "I thought I heard something."

I didn't speak for a while. "Look, he was threatening—"

"We know." She cut me off and took my hand. "No one faults you for what you did. It was a really scary and creepy situation and what you did worked." She came closer and looked at me. "Seriously, you kept us safe." She kissed me on the cheek.

"Then why do I feel like a monster?"

She put her head on my shoulder. "Probably because you had to kill uninfected. Two of them already." She picked her head up and turned to me. "And you are kind enough to know that having to do that isn't good, it isn't fun, it was evil, but evil put upon you by their actions."

"We kill because the infection forces us, and sometimes, I guess, we kill because others force us . . ." I mused aloud.

"Yeah, I think so," she said softly and sadly.

We sat there for some time. I ran my hands through her hair, which looked more dark brown than gold in the darkness. *Everything is darker nowadays.* My thoughts scrambled around between my dream, the pain in my arm, justifications for killing uninfected, and the guilt I felt for the small joy I took in killing them. All the while slowly, thickly, trying to piece together what happened after I was shot.

Eventually she kissed me again. "Get some rest." She headed back toward the front of the rig.

"Those bodies... was that Madeline and Rob?"

She paused, choked up for a second, which told me it was. But then she turned and managed, "Barricaded themselves in their apartment. Probably died of thirst." She took a deep breath. "At least nothing ate them."

"I'm sorry."

"Wasn't your fault," she said curtly.

"You know what I mean, Miranda." I stood up. "Unless you are implying one death was my fault."

She examined me for a minute.

"You do!" I said loud enough to make my dad snort in his sleep. "You said you didn't blame me for Val."

She looked down. "I don't *really*. I was there too and I didn't tell her to stand back either," she said through a sniffle.

I sat back down. "But it's my job to protect the family."

"I don't know what I think about it, Darren." Then she turned and left.

The room was boisterous and there was laughter and the smell of refried beans being heated on the stove. But the rig grew quiet when I stepped out of the back bedroom. My mom came up and hugged me, "How are you feeling?"

I lied and told her I felt fine. Truth was my arm hurt like crazy and my spirit was just as tortured.

"Well, have some food." My dad motioned to the beans.

I made for them, even though I wasn't hungry, mostly because of the people staring at me and I wanted something to do with my one hand that wasn't in a sling.

Kelly cleared her throat. "I'm pretty sure there aren't any fragments in your arm, it missed the bone too. I stitched it up the best I could. It will probably hurt a lot, though."

I nodded. "It kinda does. Thank you, though."

I took a seat on the couch and with my bowl in between my legs I ate some beans and soon the conversation went back to normal. Though it never did stray near the topic of me shooting Richard.

They did talk about how the people on the rafts were going to be fine. They had less mouths to feed and three of them, everyone stiffened up a bit and threw me some sideways glances, had eaten a whole lot. Even more, they had two guns and enough rounds to fight off the wolves, especially after we killed three more leaving the city.

Then they talked about where to go next. Kelly noted that the only other family we knew we had alive was hers, back in the desert. But Mary didn't love the idea of going somewhere that didn't freeze in the winter or have available water. We all knew Witherton was the answer. Homes, support, and resources all added up to survival. Bryan even nodded to me after the decision and said something about how it would be good for me to get back to where I "flourished."

It made me angry. It gave me clarity. My thoughts finally stood still for a moment. I didn't need their charity, I didn't have something wrong with me. Other than watching a daughter die and fighting for our lives, I thought I was carrying on just fine. I thought they owed me, they ought to thank me, instead of treating me like a sick kid who needed help.

I didn't say anything, though I wonder if the flush on my cheeks showed through my, still patchy, beard. I put the beans down and went back to the bedroom. I remember sitting on the bed, watching the mountains fade away while we moved back east. I remember stewing over the reasons I would pull the trigger in both instances again.

But as the mountains grew smaller, I found myself wanting

them to stay on that horizon. *If I was so confident in my actions, why didn't I want to go back to Witherton?* And I realized I didn't want anyone there to know I'd killed another uninfected. *Would they put me in the cell next to Dean?* I could imagine him laughing at the irony.

But I knew they wouldn't, I *was* justified in my actions. But the wounds from these battles were more than the pain in my arm, they were in my heart as well. *What do I do with this joy in violence? What do I do with the gruesome judgments carried out by my own hands, which are supposed to serve?* No, I wouldn't go to jail, but could I be a shepherd of God's people? Or was I just better suited at killing? I was a zombie, a wolf.

They could die, I could kill.
Lord, have mercy.

Absolution

  I didn't talk much as we rumbled down the highway back east. My family was packed in one rig and Miranda's in the other; my brother loaned it to them for the trip east. Miranda rode with them and I couldn't blame her, they had grief and stories to share.

  I slept alone on the couch, giving the bedroom back to my parents, while Luke and Miranda were in the other rig with her family for the night. I could hear my brother rustling around on the lawn chair on the roof and that, along with the pain in my arm, kept me from sleeping. So I laid alone with my infectious arm and thoughts. I began to wonder if Miranda was thankful to be rid of me. I hadn't kept her daughter safe, so now she could flee to her dad to keep Luke safe. *He didn't keep his other daughter safe either,* I thought bitterly.

  That was the night I remembered I had a son. I had been sulking for days, trying to cope with Val's death; who was helping Luke cope? Now I had been so obsessed with my guilt and trying to justify the hate I had in my heart that I almost forgot about the only child I had left. I sat up and looked at the dark rig parked next to us, imagining him sleeping next to Miranda, his hand twitching in hers as it did so often now. A nightmare, no doubt. *Poor kid.* Hardly seemed like the same mischievous child from a year ago. He had to grow up fast in the new world. I probably should, too.

  The next day, I made sure he was with us as we traveled. At one point, after clearing a gas station and finding nothing, zombies or gas, I called him to the back of the rig and set some cards up on the bed. I winced and felt a bit woozy when I put my arm in a sling

178

and shuffled into a cross legged position. We played for a minute, but neither of us seemed to be enjoying the game. I sighed and asked him, "How are you, Luke?"

He gave a faulty smile. "I'm glad we found Grandma, Grandpa, and Noelle."

"Me too, bud," I said as he went back to shuffling his hand. "I miss Val, though."

He stopped shuffling but didn't look up. "Me too."

"Look at me." He obeyed, and I saw his sad eyes, which used to be so full of laughter. I tried to put authority back into my voice. "You will see her again. Jesus makes sure of it." He nodded. "We are a family, we are hurt, we miss some people, and we don't know what comes tomorrow, but we do know we have a Savior and we will be together again someday."

He looked away, sniffling. "Yeah, I know, Dad. But it doesn't make it fun."

"It sure doesn't. But we're still here, so we gotta keep going on, yeah?"

"Yeah," he said, looking back at me. Then he leaned to the side and pulled Val's phone out of his pocket and tossed it on the bed. "If you want to see Aunt Kelly stitch your arm, I got it on video. But you look a little loopy," he said with a grin.

"I bet I did." I laughed. Then I sighed. "Think I still am, to be honest. Trauma and pain meds can do that, I suppose."

His grin faded. "And I watched what happened to Val."

"Hard to watch and hear isn't it?"

He didn't respond, but I knew he agreed.

"I'm sorry I couldn't save her, Luke. I am."

"It wasn't your fault. It was that stup—" he caught himself, "that man, Grant."

"Yes, it was. And he was stupid. And evil. We can be honest about it, as long as we are honest with ourselves."

He glared at his cards. "Then, if I'm honest, I'm glad you killed him."

"I am too," I confessed.

"You might not be able to save her or me, but someone needs to fight for us, for what's right."

"Yes, and as a father that's my job. To fight for you. But it's only a last resort, when they make us pull the trigger, never the other way around."

He nodded. "I hope I can, like you, when the time comes."

"I hope you never have to, it isn't fun. And in the meantime, I think I am going to leave the judgment and justice to someone else."

"Why, Dad?" He looked at me eagerly. "You can do it. You've killed so many!"

I cringed, I'm sure, because he immediately hunched back down. I sighed. "I've killed too many. I hate it, it keeps me up at night. I am supposed to bring hope, and yes, defend the flock, but it's not what I want, not my job, not my Call, to be a professional in violence."

He started shuffling his cards again.

I pulled them out of his hand. "Don't mistake me. I will fight. And someday in this world, you might have to. But if you do, try not to get lost in the vengeance, find some mourning that it had to end that way, and find someone to forgive you for what you had to do, even if you had no other choice."

He nodded. "Yeah, Dad."

I gave him a hug and we wound up playing cards for a while. I even got a few laughs out of him. But eventually my arm started aching so bad that I asked him to leave so I could lay down. I could feel each bump in the road pulling at my stitches and the ambient pain still spread up to my shoulder and down to my fingertips. I groaned and tried to rest, thinking of how I hoped my words would make Luke brave, but cautious against being overcome by the violence of the world.

The rig turned along the highway and I sat up with a lurch, vomited, and fell back into the bed.

"It's infected," Kelly said with a look of horror and shame.

"It's not your fault." Ava, with her long curly hair pulled back and staring at the wound, quickly reassured her.

"Ya, if you didn't look at it and stitch it, he would have died for sure," my brother added, with his arm around Kelly.

I looked down at my arm and saw the tinge of green around the wound. A foul odor filled my nostrils and I could only faintly hear my dad say, "Hang in there, son."

Then I puked and passed out.

I woke up to shadows falling across my face. Not trees, but power poles, and then a billboard. I was sweating pretty bad, but was able to sit up on the bed. My mom quickly came over and forced some water down my throat.

It took me a moment to recognize the small skyline under the hazy sky. "What are we doing in the city, are you guys crazy?"

"We need supplies," my mom said from the bedside. "And not just antibiotics, we've got another family to care for. They're going to get in, stock up, and get out."

My head and arm ached, but I leaned against the pillows and watched as we drew further into the city. Glimpses of zombies walking the streets brought me back to my senses. "No, this is crazy, tell them to get out, you aren't dying on my account."

"Darren, it's been decided," my dad responded, ending my protests.

Miranda and Luke came into the back bedroom. "You got that wound protecting us, so let us do the same for you," Miranda said, with a hand on me to reassure me, or to make sure I stayed in bed.

I thought of thanking them, I thought of trying to stop them, I thought of apologizing to them for the violence I kept finding myself in. But any apologies I might have said died in my throat when we stopped in front of the superstore parking lot. I twisted around, painfully, to see the other rig pull up next to ours. Bryan's mouth moved and I heard his voice cracking through our CB radio upfront. "Looks clear, let's go. Food, drink, medicine."

"Can I come? I'm ready to fight and I need battery packs," Luke said.

"No, Luke," Miranda answered, "This is not the time to worry about video games."

"It's not about them," he mumbled before heading back to the front of the rig with Val's phone.

After much protest, they finally helped me to the front and set me down, with a yelp, in one of the recliners.

"It's a little too quiet out there for having run two diesels through town," my dad said, peering out the window.

"More reason for us to move," my brother said, while he

and Kelly loaded up.

"I agree," my dad responded, grabbing a gun. "Ava, you got the back window. Luke, I need you." Luke stood up tall. My dad gestured to all the windows in the front, "All these are yours. Any movement, you keep us posted on the CB. Got it?"

"Yessir," Luke said and immediately started looking out the side window. My mom picked up Emmett. "Come help me keep watch, big guy," and retreated to the back room.

My dad looked at me. "Proud of you, Darren. Hang tight on this one, though."

Then they were gone. I watched them run into the store along with Bryan. Miranda was with Kelly outside, swirling her long skirt as she turned to keep lookout, her rifle on her shoulder. As I watched her, I kept thinking about my dad's words. He told me to hang tight, no doubt to stop me from doing something foolhardy. *Was I foolhardy?* Fighting a town horde, letting my daughter around the action, cleaning the church alone, firing first on the boat. *I am foolhardy.*

I almost laughed when the realization hit me. I had been luckier than I could imagine. No, blessed. And if the Lord chose to take me because of an infection, then so be it. I just hoped I had helped. *If we get out of the city alive, maybe I had.*

I resolved to be more reserved. But I couldn't deny the fact that my dad's words encouraged me. He was glad that I was willing to do what I thought needed to be done. I held my head up a little higher. But I couldn't help but think that being the best killer around wasn't the ultimate accomplishment. *They could die.* But there was more to it than that, wasn't there? I used to glory in death, was I starting to once again?

The gunfire distracted me. It came from inside the store and soon my loved ones came piling out of the store with two carts full of supplies. My mom and Luke, I couldn't have stopped him if I tried, ran out the door and started tossing the supplies into the rig's storage compartments, while Miranda, Kelly, and Junior shot at a few zombies coming out of the store and through the parking lot.

A panicked three minutes later, my family was scrambling in the rig carrying armfuls of supplies and my father rumbled to the driver's seat and both rigs were off.

"What happened?" my mom asked, back at my side.

182

"Nothing to worry about, Hon," my dad responded as he wheeled the rig around some upturned shopping carts. "A few zombies were hiding in the back, spooked us out of the store, but only a few."

"Think there are wolves here, too? Why else would there be so few?" Luke asked.

My brother shook his head. "No, look around, you see the shoes on the ground, the hats and scraps of clothes. And there was blood all over the store."

My mom's eyes got wide and she reached for Luke.

"He's seen worse and he will yet," Junior said dismissively while he rolled his eyes at our mom. Then he turned back to Luke, "But there were no bodies."

Luke gasped with the realization. "They've eaten everything and moved on."

"But to where?" my dad asked what we were already thinking, while he swung the rig onto the road heading south out of the city.

Twenty miles south of the city we approached a small bedroom community, Canteen, hoping to find more supplies on our way back to Witherton. As we crested the hill, we saw the road was blocked with some mass, the fields were covered as well, not with the green weeds and prairie grass, but a darker weed that swayed and moved.

"Great Scott," my dad said breathlessly. "It's them."

The CB radio lit up, the other family seeing the same mass of a thousand bodies stacked on each other, lumbering into the town. They were still a mile away from us and a road heading west was a quarter mile ahead of us. Instead of risking turning around on an overgrown shoulder, my father revved the engine and we headed for them. As we turned west toward the interstate I saw, oddly, that none of the zombies had noticed us. Perhaps the wind out of the south carried our sound from them.

"Honk the horn, Dad," I said through gritted teeth. Kelly was working on my arm as we traveled.

"Are you nuts?"

"He's right," my mom said. "They're heading south, how long until they reach Witherton?"

I nodded at her. "We can lead them west. I've baited hordes

183

before, just keep in sight until you reach the interstate, then lose 'em."

"And if we break down before they lose our sight and sound in this flatland?"

"We have a truck."

He hesitated.

"They're heading straight south, you either honk or we evacuate the city. They could be there in two days," my brother added.

My dad's cussing was drowned out by the rig's horn.

Luke ran to the back of the rig and shouted with so much fear his voice cracked, "They're coming!"

I hobbled to the back bedroom, wincing when my arm, newly wrapped with antibiotics, hit the bathroom door. Then I looked out the window.

Some people said there would be hordes of millions of zombies running across the continent. Not so. How many people weren't infected? How many died in the chaos escaping? How many died in firefights and car wrecks and fires and explosions and building collapses? And how many infected had died from wounds in this same chaos or had been killed by survivors? No, there weren't millions in a horde, especially the horde from the relatively smaller city of only a couple hundred thousand people north of us.

But that didn't make me feel any better as I watched over a thousand zombies pour out of Canteen. Our rigs headed west at a pace of about thirty miles an hour. Some of us cursing, all of us praying. As we disappeared over the interstate two miles out of Canteen, I still couldn't see the end of the horde following us.

We weren't home long, still unloading even, when Kevin came by. He embraced me so hard my arm hurt. We spent a bit of time telling him and his family of our adventures in the northwest. He filled us in on the past week here, things seemed to be going well and they had record numbers at worship.

Maybe he sensed the beast rising in me, so he assured me it was because of the weather. "Perfectly overcast, just like you always said, Pastor. Too gloomy to go to the river, too good to use it as an excuse to stay in."

Soon afterward, we told him about the horde and we agreed he would immediately go out and let the townsfolk know about an emergency meeting the next day.

With the rigs unloaded and everyone settled, we finally had an evening to spend together, all of us. We somberly ventured into Valentine's room and did some mourning. Then we wandered back downstairs, some of us going to bed after a long, stressful trip, some playing board games, some chatting.

That was how I found myself in my office with Bryan, but it soon became clear that he was doing the pastoral counseling, not me.

"Think my church burned down with my library in it," Bryan said, flipping through one of the books I laid out for Kevin.

"Shame. And your members?"

"Only one family on the boats, but I wasn't exactly holding church for the city barge." He looked at me. "You've done well, I wish I would have done a few things like that."

"Totally different circumstances," I said, sitting down in my office chair. "And, believe me, I got regrets too."

"A dead daughter?" he said, looking at me.

"That's one of them, ya."

"I got one of those too."

"Does Mary blame you for it?"

"Probably a bit. It's—"

"Our job." We finished together.

He pulled two glasses off my shelf and poured some brandy in them. He handed me one.

"Toasting our failures?" I asked, taking the glass.

"Our daughters."

We each took a swig.

He groaned as he sat across from me. "Let's see, what else?" He inspected me for a minute. "Ah. Of course. You regret having to kill two uninfected, or perhaps you don't regret killing them and you regret that feeling."

I scoffed. "You are enjoying this, aren't you?" He laughed a little in response. I sighed. "You always were the counselor." I sat up. "A little of both is the answer."

"I thought so. Well," he set his glass down, "for the first part, just know: no court in the country would ever convict you of

185

a crime. One was a murderer on the run, the other threatening your family."

I nodded and felt a bit reassured.

"But there is another court, another that is still in session in this new world and always will be, is there not?" Out of the corner of my eye, I saw him studying me. "A court that judges the heart and knows all and sees all."

I said nothing.

After a minute of silence, he sighed. "Look Darren, you know what is happening here as well as I. We've done it a hundred times. We convict of sin so that we can apply the healing absolution. Much like we will cut out that infection and apply fresh bandages with antibiotics. So let us not play games."

After a minute of silence, he leaned forward. "We've all got scars, we've all got regrets, we've all got sins, we have to face the reality of this broken world and our broken hearts to find any peace."

I shook my head. "No. We can't. We can't beat this. We've survived this long only to have our humanity destroyed more than the infected's."

Bryan laughed and leaned back in his chair. "Humanity? You think humanity is what we have to lean on?" He ran his hand through his white hair. "You think all the great work you did in here was because of humanity? You think humanity, which has brought about wars and death and plagues for centuries, would be what drags us out of this mess? No, no, we don't need humanity, we need a Savior."

The Savior I had been angry at for taking my daughter, the Savior I was ashamed to think on or call to because of the lust for violence and vengeance in my heart. The Savior who had called me to be a shepherd.

I said it far more clearly than I thought I could manage, my eyes drifted to the boarded up window as if I could see through it, "When I think of those men, I get so angry I want to shoot them again." And then I hung my head. "Lord have mercy, Lord forgive me, Lord give me peace."

I heard his chair scoot on the carpet as Bryan stood and leaned over to place a hand gently on my head. "In the stead and by the command of my Lord Jesus Christ, I forgive you all your sins, even this one."

I smiled for the first time in days, because I actually believed it.

"Your humanity and your heart are black and twisted and deserve nothing but hell. But the Savior who suffered, He suffered and died for you. They are cleansed. Which means you will see your little girl again."

"Thanks."

"It's our job."

"I don't know if it is for me anymore."

"The workers are few, Darren, it would be a shame to lose one."

"'He must be above reproach.'"

He sat back down, thinking. After a moment of scratching his beard, he finally said, "None of us are perfectly above reproach, though, yes, there are things a man can do which means he can't be a pastor anymore, but you broke no laws or a marriage covenant or anything. I'm trying hard to see the scandal here."

There was a long silence.

I finished my drink. "Well, I guess we have work to do then."

"I could use a preacher tomorrow," Bryan said with a sniffle.

"I'd be happy to."

That night, I crept up to our bedroom. "Is Luke asleep?"

Miranda, already in bed, started, then sniffed and wiped her eyes. "Yes, I think so." She put the picture of Valentine away in her robe.

"Can I talk with you a minute?"

She sat up on the edge of the bed and crossed her arms.

"Thanks," I said as sincerely as I could. "I wanted to apologize. I know you deserve some hero, who is always gallant and never does the wrong thing. But that isn't me, Miranda. You know that, right?" I sighed, *what a poor apology.*

She dropped her arms and looked around, the streaks where her tears had been glistening in the candlelight.

I reached out and pulled the picture out of her robe, I was crying now. "I'm sorry I couldn't keep your Valentine safe."

Then she was crying again and slumping into my arms. "No, Darren, no. She was *our* Val. Ours. And I forgive you for everything. Forgive me for being so vile, when obviously you are hurting too."

"I forgive you." And I held her tight.

And for an entire year, an entire year, each night, I asked forgiveness for Val, and she did the same. But for that night, for the first time since our daughter died, for the first time since my broken and twisted heart raged out in violence at another man, for the first time, a couple cried themselves to sleep in each other's arms.

Prepare the Way

The next day I watched Noelle bravely carry yellow and orange flowers, bright against the gray morning, to her parents' graves. Bryan had insisted on digging them in the morning. My dad, brother, and I came to keep watch but after Bryan had broken the ground and his tears that wet the ground had dried we grabbed shovels and finished digging them deep, careful not to toss dirt onto my daughter's grave, not five feet away. *Where her ashes mixed amongst a grown man she never knew.* I don't know why that thought riles the beast inside me, it wasn't his fault, he was a victim too. *The Lord will make her brand new.*

We cleaned up and a few hours later we were back, Noelle laying down flowers as bright as her red hair, and trying to do a verse of "Abide with Me." She had practiced it fine, but then, with her parents lying beneath her, she couldn't do it, and we couldn't blame the young girl. And then it was up to me. Up to me to speak a word of hope to them, like I had done for dozens of other families. But this one was different. It was my family too. My wife's sister, people I'd known for years. It was easy in the sense that I knew they were faithful, I knew they were fine, resting with the Savior and my little girl, but it was also so hard, because grief was there. But not the grief of a parent for a child, I knew that, which is why I didn't do Val's service and why Bryan wasn't doing this one.

A few members who had known Miranda's family from visits over the years scattered around the backyard of Gary's ranch home, which doubled as a crime scene and the center of several hours of discussion in the past week's meeting. Who would get the, albeit diminished by haze, solar power? It seemed so trivial in the old world, but to flip a light switch for light, or to plug in a coffee maker, these things were worth killing for in the new world.

"This is the day that Lord has made," I said as boldly as I could.

"Let us rejoice and be glad in it," came the response, muddled with a few sniffs and sobs.

After the liturgy, a few of the members, along with my mother, sang "Abide with Me" alongside Noelle so she could get through it. And then I preached on Madelyn's confirmation verse, "I can do all things through Christ who strengthens me." It seemed an odd verse for a funeral. A verse often used for sports motivation or passing a test, but what about when you can't survive a plague? Where was the strength there? Did they not believe enough? Were they worse sinners? Was this verse just about winning a gold medal for Jesus? Or was it, as Paul wrote, about knowing there was hope in plenty or in lack? So Madelyn and Rob were in lack. Lack of security, lack of escape, lack of water. But they also had everything they needed, because they had a Savior. And so Paul rejoiced in plenty and in lack, and so we rejoiced, we grieved, yes, but we rejoiced that in Jesus, Madelyn and Rob overcame the plague and dehydration and now rest by streams of still water in the Lord's pasture.

"Are we finally gonna decide what to do with Dean?" a voice in the back of the crowd called out. Another voice joined his. "Yeah, I'm tired of feedin' 'im."

It was such a contrast from the morning's somber service. Now a rare lack of wind left us sweltering in the humidity of Jacobson's field. We'd gathered together to break the news of a coming horde and how we could possibly survive it.

"No, we ain't here to talk about the murderer," Kevin said and I coughed to hide my shock and shame. I knew "murderer" was referring to Dean, but for a terrifying second, I thought he was referring to me. *I'd killed uninfected, too.* The forgiveness was there, but the feeling would take time to fade.

"No," Kevin repeated, "that must wait. Pastor Darren has some bad news to tell."

The reunion with the people of Witherton was bittersweet.

My arm ached and the faces of Grant and Richard still haunted me, but I was able to forget them for a moment when happy faces clapped me on the back. Wincing in pain, I was usually able to return a sincere grin. "Good to be back, good to be back."

Back on the flatbed once more, I cleared my throat and told them briefly of our journey, how we found more survivors (a large cheer came in response), and how I had hurt my arm finding Miranda's family, who had also been greeted with cheers and hugs. But eventually I had to tell them what we saw on the way back. I told them about the horde in Canteen. Afterward, there was such a buzz that we could hardly calm the crowd.

"Are you sure?" someone cried out. Another asked, "Did you lead them straight to us?" Even more asked, "How long do we have?"

Once peace was established again, the rest of the family was able to corroborate my story and Derek stepped forward, nodding his head. "There have certainly been more packs around recently. More zombies coming from somewhere, probably the city."

"Well then, we go around them to the city, if they are all gone?" a lady in the back suggested.

"I doubt they are *all* gone," Bryan said. "There were still some there, and still probably plenty of, ahem, food, in other parts of the city. But we're in the plains, it probably only takes one to see something off in the horizon to lead a pack into the countryside."

"Might save our tails too," Rick added. "I'd rather fight ten packs of a hundred than a whole thousand or more."

Miranda shook her head. "But there is a pack like that. We saw it. And I know we led them west, but if it comes south . . ."

The crowd started to chatter, some suggesting we run, others that we fight, or that we hole up and let them go by, still others that we try to split the pack up.

I tried to clap to get their attention, but winced when pain shot up my arm. Instead, I had Rick, with plenty of experience herding cattle, give a great whistle. I nodded at him in thanks before saying, "My thoughts are we stay and fight. If we run, all we worked for is lost, or at the very least will have to be rebuilt wherever we go. And who's to say a horde of a thousand won't find us there?"

My dad spoke up, "And if we just scatter, we can't help each other like you have been."

Jesse agreed. "Yeah, we stand a better chance together than apart."

"The people in the country can move into town and we build a wall," Charlotte put forward.

"There's no time for that, they could be here any day," Junior replied.

"And we would lose most of our wells," Rebecca added in. "We should stay and fight."

"Are you people insane?" Curtis interjected. "You want to fight over a thousand zombies with a hundred of us, thirty that can fight, and a few hundred rounds of ammo?" He stepped out from the crowd, then slowly hobbled around to face them. "The military ran from the city horde, what chance do we have? We don't got tanks or bombs. I was in a war once and I don't need to see another slaughter like that."

I looked at him. "First of all, this isn't the entire city horde. At least I don't think so."

"Reassuring analysis, General." Curtis leaned on his cane.

"I bet Dad's killed fifty times the zombies you have," Luke, holding Val's phone, shot at him, before Miranda grabbed him and pulled him to her side.

Miranda flushed, still holding Luke back. "What he means is . . ." Her eyes lit up and she turned to the crowd, pleading. "No, we don't have tanks, but we have heavy machinery." She looked at Wilbur, who was standing at the edge of the crowd with his arms folded. "And air support."

"Got any napalm cooked up, Wil?" someone asked.

Wilbur shuffled awkwardly, but chuckled and scratched his beard, thinking.

Miranda continued, "Well maybe not napalm, or bombs but we have stuff that will burn, right?"

My mom added in from the back, "And it isn't like you don't have high ground." She pointed to the large co-op north of us, then turned back to the group. "And from what I've been told, that made a big difference with only three fighters."

Rick chuckled. "Well if we got thinkers like that on our

side, I'll do the fighting."

From then on, the discussion changed, it wasn't about whether to fight or run, it was about how to fight. The meeting went on until darkness began to creep in, not unlike a horde. Eventually the majority voted to stay and pool our resources to defend our town. The opposed, we all agreed, were free to do what they thought best for their families. Three families packed up and left. Two, though dissenting, agreed to stay and help. And after hours of planning, when we were ready to pull our hair out from rehashing the same things over and over, voting on life and death matters, and arguing strategy, we picked a plan and went with it. And the people were off to prepare.

I turned to do the same when Rebecca, with her nails done, a flower in her hair, and still holding a pen and paper, asked me, "So, what about Dean?"

"I don't know, Rebecca. I'm not too keen on handing out judicial verdicts anymore."

Rick clapped me on the shoulder. "A few guilty verdicts will do that I'm sure. But don't worry, me and Kevin here got a plan for Dean."

I nodded, relieved.

"But he could probably still use a preacher," Kevin added. Then he hopped in his pickup and smiled. "And now that you're back, it ain't got to be me."

Aside from being perched high on an RV, I had never been out after dark since my firefight on the front lawn. And I didn't miss it. Walking through burnt out cars, overgrown grass, and buildings was terrifying. Every noise made it seem like we were surrounded by approaching zombies. And with the smoke from the burning towns and cities that hung in the air, we could barely see the stars. It was thick darkness. We had lights, but tried not to rely on them for fear of attracting zombies. It was terrible. But that was the point.

I could tell Dean felt just as frightened, swiveling in his chains at each noise, breathing heavily. But we made it to the Wilson's grain silo a half mile north of town without running into any zombies. We had parked the pickup a few hundred yards away and while Kevin climbed the silo, I uncuffed Dean to let him climb up ahead of me. Rick stood at the bottom of the ladder with his rifle, lest Dean try anything going up or on top of the tower, though if he did, I didn't feel confident Rick would know what or whom to shoot in the darkness. Halfway up my arm started to throb, but I tried to ignore it and the long fall to the field below and made it to the top.

At the top of the tower I cuffed Dean to a pretty large rope that gave him enough room to walk across the top of the silo. There was a lean-to assembled on the top with a tank of gasoline and Rick had hardwired our tornado siren to the top of the silo as well.

"Remember the plan?" Kevin asked. "You see *the* horde, not *a* horde, *the* horde, you hit that siren."

Dean looked at the button under the little lean-to we had assembled on the silo for him.

Kevin added then, "I'd suggest you stay awake, they can use ladders."

Dean gulped, but said nothing.

I took one last look at Kevin, who nodded. "Here's your pistol, Dean." I handed it to him, along with about one hundred rounds.

Then Kevin explained, "In case a smaller horde finds you and you need to buy some time."

Dean, after eyeing the gun for a few moments, looked up at me, shocked I would give him a weapon.

I sighed. "Yeah, I think you murdered your brother, Dean. And no, even if you confess and I forgive you—which I will, by the way, it's my job—you still gotta take the punishment." I waved around at the silo. "And this is it, night watch duty. But one thing I'm beginning to realize is that all of us are twisted and dark and fighting much more than zombies." He looked down. "You lost a battle back in your brother's house." I pointed at the gun I gave him. "I think you'll win this one. I don't know, maybe you'll put a bullet in our backs or one in that rope and just take off. But if your freedom is worth our lives or leaving a town without a watchman, well, let's just say the guilt of that would be punishment enough, I would think."

He sniffed and wiped his eyes awkwardly with his cuffed hands, but said nothing.

I pleaded with him. "Dean, you're on a thirty foot tall bomb, in the dark, with zombies out there. Let me take at least a little burden off you. Is there anything you want to say?"

He steadied himself and glared at me. "Yeah. Why aren't you chained up here too? Word is you killed more men than me."

"He was threatening to drown my family at gunpoint. You wanted solar energy. That's the difference. But, ya, we all got hate in our hearts that needs forgiving." I waited a moment to see if he would respond. He didn't, so I hopped on the ladder. "See you in the morning."

The next days were busy. Spring was turning to summer and, even in the shade of the towering system of grain bins on the south west side of town, we sweated as we unloaded rocks onto the grain elevators, which lifted them to the roofs. There were a dozen people at the top, taking supplies and storing them on the tops of the bins and constructing makeshift shelters and lean-tos. The rocks were being piled up near the ladders to drop on any zombies that might try to climb up after us.

After an hour of loading rocks and bricks from fallen buildings in town, I kept my promise to Dean and went to see him at the top of his tower. I tried to talk to him about his past again, I talked to him about other murderers in the Bible and how there was forgiveness in Christ even for them. But he ignored me and rolled over on his blankets in his lean-to. He fidgeted for a few seconds, trying to get comfortable with the rope still attached to the cuffs on his wrist.

I sighed and picked up his binoculars, scanning the horizon, hoping I would not see a shadow of the horde coming over the rolling hills. Thankfully, I saw nothing but prairie grass leaning in the wind and the ever-present haze on the horizon.

I turned back south and adjusted the binoculars to focus on the work being done in the field between us and the north edge of town. Tractors were burning the precious little fuel we had to dig large pits. We thought of putting punji sticks at the bottom to pierce zombies that fell in, but that would only kill the ones on the bottom layer—it wasn't worth the time. Instead, we simply dug the pits to slow them down and hopefully crush each other. The dirt from the pits was being used to make a small earthen rise outside of town to give the defenders a bit of vision and high ground.

Past the tractors, other farmers were towing out their augurs—long cylindrical helixes used to bring grain up elevators. The farmers and townsfolk organized row after row of them and were busy testing their engines and cutting off any protective screens in hopes of churning up any zombies rushing toward us.

I didn't need the binoculars to see what was going on below me. I leaned off the edge of the tower to see Rick and a few others filling the bin below me with scrap metal, fertilizer, batteries, and anything else that might explode. I looked back at Dean and wondered if this wasn't just a punishment, but a death sentence. We had fastened a zip line for his escape, and I hoped, when the time came, he would be able to use it.

Hours later there was, mercifully, still no horde on the horizon and I could hear my replacement, Jesse, clambering up the ladder next to me. He was an electrician, and when I helped him up, he undid his backpack and started setting up a detonator for the bomb we were standing on.

That was all the encouragement I needed to hook onto the zipline escape. "Be careful," I said as I gladly jumped off the silo and went sliding to the truck where the zipline was anchored some two hundred yards away.

I walked the half mile back into town since my truck was being used to haul bricks and supplies to the co-op. I chatted with some of the workers and waved at Kevin, who was towing his poisoned water tanks north out of town and dropping them every so often in hope of thinning some of the horde out on their way south. Most of the walk, I prayed. I prayed for more forgiveness for my sinful heart. I prayed for healing for my heart, wounded by the loss of my daughter. I prayed for my family and for our town, that He would see us through the coming siege. I prayed for a cure, I prayed for the world, and I prayed for wisdom to help lead the people.

Ten minutes and dozens of petitions later, I stood in the driveway of my house. It was there, at the doorstep, that I finally, shamefully, remembered that after I gave God a list of requests, that perhaps I should give Him thanks. So I gave Him thanks for the day, the time to prepare, the forgiveness He had given, and the chance to be with family again. Most of all, I gave Him thanks that no matter what plague or horde came our way, we had salvation, we had life.

The house was quiet when I entered. I walked down the hall and found Mary sorting packs for the grain bins. "Hi Mary."

"Ah!" She jumped, then blushed. "You scared me, hon."

"Sorry, I should be a little louder considering the times."

She glanced over to Noelle, who looked up from her playhouse, and Emmett, who stirred on his cot, but rolled over and went back to sleep. Mary relaxed, tittered, then said, "No, no, I was just concentrating."

"Anything I can do to help?"

"Sure." She pointed at six packs on the floor. "Those are all set to go up to the grain bins." Then she nodded her head out the door. "And there are lunches for everyone on the kitchen table."

"You're brilliant, Mary!"

She smiled and blushed a little. "I can't fix a car or heal a wound, but I can still help."

"You have no idea how much I understand that."

She smiled. "The girls are at the medical tent at the base of the bins and the guys are at Wilbur's machine shed."

I grabbed a couple of the heavy packs. "Thanks, see you in a bit."

I was sweating by the time I got all the packs and lunches over to the grain bins, where people were hoisting supplies up on ropes. I ducked into the medical tent for shade, some water, and to see how the preparations were coming. I immediately saw my mom, Kelly, and a few other people with some medical knowledge going through all the medical supplies we could find. I waved at one of the Turners and thanked them again for sticking it out with us, even though they weren't from here ("It's our horde, though," he replied with a chuckle).

I almost spilled my water when I went around a table and saw Curtis sitting there. He must have seen my shock because he narrowed his eyes at me. "Yeah, well, I can't turn a wrench or shoot a gun anymore, but I saw enough carnage in Korea, so I'll be here telling the wounded to 'buck up' and 'get tough.'"

I nodded to him. "You do that."

Finally, I made my way across the tent to Miranda. She

smiled at me and wiped her sweaty brow before fishing out another batch of boiled cloth for bandages. "Hey, Darren. How's it going?"

"Just trying to be helpful, you know. Need any help?"

She wrung the steaming water out of some cloths, took a deep breath, and shrugged. "Well there's a system to this; don't want any contamination." She looked away and I knew she probably thought I would screw it up.

I nodded and turned to leave.

"Been by the others?" she asked hopefully.

"Yeah, the guys are at Wilbur's with Linda and half the town, building stuff."

She smiled. "Luke working too?"

"Sure is, they got him driving a quad around."

A look of concern passed over Miranda's face, then she shrugged, "I guess it's better than him spending all day worrying."

"Yeah. But I guess that's what I'll be doing. Not really any time for policies or preaching right now."

"Oh, Darren." She slapped some wet cloth down, then shrieked and tossed it back into the boiling pot. When she collected herself, she looked at me. "You've helped this town more than anyone else around, you do not get to throw a pity party now."

"You're right, I'll go check on Wilbur and pray the fire from heaven comes."

The Siege of Witherton

"Lord, not today!" were my first words, when, three days after Dean was put on the night watch, I heard our tornado siren sounding from north of town. I looked out the window to a dark and misting day.

It was Monday and we had held some quick services the day before, which were well attended, nearly a hundred people between the two services. Whether that was because an imminent battle motivated the people to seek God, or simply because they wanted to hear how plans were going at the meeting, it was hard to say. But few of us lingered after the meeting. Most ran to work in the thick, still, hot air sweltering under a sun baked blanket of smoke and smog. We continued moving machinery, digging ditches, tinkering with tractors, or hauling goods up the large network of grain bins we had not burned down a month before.

But this was a wet, dark morning. I began to doubt if fire from heaven would even help as our family scrambled about the house. We grabbed our bags and ruck sacks and, within minutes, were walking fast toward the grain bins. As I stood in the darker than usual shadow of the co-op and watched the people clambering up, I prayed that, at the end of the day, my memorial list wouldn't be much longer or, at the least, someone would be alive to do a memorial.

I kissed my mother, son, and wife and craned my neck to watch the latter two of them climb up the hundred-foot ladder. Miranda climbed behind Luke, who bravely went upward, one rung at a time. Theirs was the shortest tower, but offered access to the other four bins by a series of catwalks, elevators, and belts. My mom and Kelly, both fighting back tears, didn't follow, they kissed Emmett goodbye and headed to the medical tent, ready to administer aid to anyone before we called retreat up to the skies. Mary came and took Emmett by the hand and after all the hugs were shared, started her ascent with Noelle and Emmett in front of her.

I gave one last glance at the grain bins. They were our fortresses and I was glad I never made it to them a month ago or else we would likely be putting our hopes in the two shorter bins that we had burned down.

My dad was shouting at me to get in the truck, ending my reflections. Without a word, I hopped into the back of the truck and we headed north. We would be the central team and our truck was filled with people I had killed a hundred zombies or more with. My brother rode up front, between my father-in-law and dad; Kevin had his arm around Jayce; Linda and Derek held hands; Jesse looked a certain shade of green, but determined; Rick crossed himself, fixed his cowboy hat, and looked like we were heading to play cards.

We didn't say much as we loaded our guns, though several heads looked up when the tornado siren faded. "It's not a false alarm, folks!" Kevin shouted, "We got the message and Dean doesn't want to call every zombie in the county."

As we approached the north edge of town, I started reciting the Lord's Prayer. Some people spoke it with me, others didn't. I didn't care, I was saying it to calm my own nerves. When the truck skidded to a stop behind the large earthen berm we had made on the north edge of town, we piled out. I picked up my megaphone, fought back a wave of nausea, and shouted a few instructions down the line to the several other teams that could hear. Seconds later, I put the megaphone down and began to walk up the muddy berm.

My stomach twisted and I retched onto the mud. In front of us were hundreds and hundreds of zombies. Maybe thousands.

The horde had found us.

It was a sea of movement. A living mass of undead that waved and rippled when a new sight or sound stimulated them to a slight change in direction, almost like a school of fish that swam with impeccable coordination. But this was a migration, an entire species heading to a new feeding ground. They didn't care that this town wouldn't sate their appetites for a minute. They didn't care about our hopes and dreams and all the work we had done. But then again, the virus didn't care about theirs, either.

I suddenly wished I had said more to Miranda and Luke. I pictured them on the grain bin, dropping a rock on my twisted face. I shook my head—the thought was making me sick again. I suddenly had to go to the bathroom and puke at the same time. I was gasping for air.

Then there were gunshots from the south. It was probably Miranda and a few other good shooters picking off some lone zombies from the countryside attracted by the siren. *They're fighting, I can fight.* I swallowed hard and stood up taller. "The victory has already been won," I told the team, "so we might as well go down swinging."

Kevin nodded and my brother gave an "Amen."

The ten of us stood and stared at the approaching mass of flesh. We managed to tear our eyes off our impending tribulation when we heard a rumbling behind us.

Donald, Jesse's dad, still looking thin and yellow, cracked his tractor door open and gave us a grin with a few teeth missing. "Like my tank?" His tractor had plates welded over the hydraulics, razor blades on the fenders, and bars over the windows.

Jesse whistled and, despite everything, I chuckled. "Not bad. But remember, there's only one God and I don't care what you're driving, it ain't you."

He laughed. "Yessir, we'll stick to the roads."

"We'll . . . ?" Jayce began until three more such tractors rolled around the corner. Linda gave a hoot and Derek saluted the men brave enough to drive into a thousand zombies.

They headed north toward the horde, which, even through the haze and mist, was beginning to become clearer as they began to congregate around Dean's tower not far north of us. As if the sight of the twisted, rotting mass wasn't disturbing enough, their scent had made its way ahead of them. The fetid smell of decay had lingered for weeks, but today it was worse as a thousand unkempt zombies, feasting on flesh and rot for weeks, bore down on our town. I pulled my bandana up over my face and made sure my shotgun was slung securely on my shoulder.

A team of men and women on four wheelers were already

out ahead of us, turning the augur motors on and starting their metal helixes spinning. Their engines attracted some of the horde, but Dean was busy shooting his pistol off and making a ruckus on the top of his tower, which kept a teeming mass of hundreds at the base of it. Any zombies that went after the four wheelers found themselves falling into a twelve-foot pit.

Then there was us. Beside me were the guns, someone had been wise enough to put them on tarps to save them from the thin layer of mud the mist had created. Behind me was a table full of every type of ammunition, color coded to the guns that could shoot it. There were boxes upon boxes, from precious hours and miles and gallons of fuel as we sent out runners to far off towns to raid their stores. I cringed thinking that, even with all of it and with perfect accuracy, there wasn't enough for each of the zombies. *Would it be enough? Did we have a prayer?*

But before that prayer, there needed to be one for Dean. Daylight was breaking now and I could see Dean's figure on the grain bin ahead of us. In the binoculars I could see him walking around the top, periodically firing a shot or dropping a rock down the ladder. He also had an impact wrench and was taking the last few bolts of the ladder out. After a few minutes, it came crashing down into the zombie mass.

His only way out was the zip line fastened to a truck some two hundred yards out. I prayed it would be enough and almost bloodied my lip from guilt. Yes, his punishment was to be bait, but once again I wondered if it was nothing more than a death sentence.

I clicked on the radio. "Well, Dean, you found them."

"Damn right. There's a ton of them, man. Maybe over a thousand. I don't know about this."

"Yeah. But, hey, thanks for the heads up."

He laughed. "Bah, they woulda found me anyways."

"Well, they sure did, so might as well do your part of the plan. Think you got enough around you?"

"Honestly, I don't know. But they aren't hurtin' anything yet I don't think. I can hold off a little longer."

"You're braver than I am. Bail when you feel the need, meanwhile keep them interested."

"That I can handle."

I heard his pistol go off and faintly, carried on the wind, a yodel.

A minute later, Pastor Barnstock came running. He leaned up against the pickup, wiped the sweat dripping from his short gray hair, and wheezed, "Wilbur has not got his plane off the ground. It was too hazy and misty before. He thinks the fire should be able to go once the dew leaves the grass. Maybe an hour or two?"

"Can we hold that long?" my dad asked. "Surely some of them will come to town before then."

"We can't do this without a crop dust. No way. We have to hold." Kevin began to pace.

Over the next half hour the teams from the east and west reported in. The horde was so big that the edges were more interested in the town than Dean, and our pits were beginning to fill with zombies. Soon they would be at the augurs.

"Dean could bring them in," Junior said.

Almost as if he heard my brother, Dean's voice crackled over the radio. "Guys, they're getting toward my truck. I think I have to go."

I clicked mine on. "Fuse it and get out now."

He didn't respond, but the group of us on the dirt bank watched him through binoculars. It was hazy, but we could see him attach himself to the zipline, then dip back into the hut and fiddle with the fuse. After a minute, he was yanked violently out of the hut. I turned my binoculars to the truck and saw a group of zombies on it already. Then I saw one rip the zip line from where it was tethered to the truck. The rope, Dean's only escape, fell limp to the ground.

I slammed my binoculars down, my mind racing to try and think of a way to save him.

The radio cut me off, Dean was laughing and sobbing in it. "Don't even think about comin' to get me, Preacher. I'm a goner."

"Dean, you have to believe me, I didn't want this."

"And for some reason, I do believe you." He laughed, then was silent for a moment. When he clicked back on, he said, "Hey Pastor." He sobbed. "I did it. I shot him, I didn't mean—I mean, it wasn't—oh what does it matter?"

"Dean, listen to me, I know someone who forgives and gives life, even to murderers."

"Nah, it ain't that simple."

"But it is! Do you believe Jesus two thousand years ago hung up on a cross, dying to save you? Do you believe that actually happened?"

"Yeah, a far greater man than this one hanging out here to die."

"Then I forgive you all your sins in the name of the Father, and the Son, and the Holy Spirit."

There was a pause before he spoke again, softer now, "Tell me about those other murderers."

I chuckled. "David didn't just murder, he broke all the commandments, and he had his punishment too, but just like yours, the Lord took away his sin. And before him was Moses—"

The silo exploded. Forty feet of screws, fertilizer, gasoline, car batteries, aerosol cans, and anything else we could think of that was combustible or would damage a zombie burst outward into the crowd of hundreds and hundreds of zombies climbing on top of each other to get to Dean. The blast shook our clothes from a half mile away and any zombies that weren't immediately blown up were doused in flames for nearly fifty yards.

We would have cheered if one of our own wasn't among them.

"Godspeed Dean, I'll see you at the feast," Kevin said and with a tear in his eye, slapped me on the shoulder and then clicked the safety off his rifle.

Dean's fight was over. Ours was not. I don't know if the next half an hour went by in a moment or if it took an eternity. The horde, once it found nothing to eat at the explosion site, turned south, attracted to our town full of four wheelers, auger engines, smoke, and gunfire. The mindless zombies sprinted straight into the twelve-foot pits. A hundred must have fallen in and never made it out. But then the first pit was filled and the zombies climbed out and sprinted straight into the next trench. Two pits filled with hundreds, but hundreds more raced across the fields toward us.

"Hold your fire!" Kevin shouted, though no one had fired a shot yet. We knew to save every bullet and let the augurs thin them out. The spinning helixes groaned when the first zombies ran into them. Most of the zombies sucked into the augers died, several had their limbs sheared off and they continued their pursuit toward us missing a limb. The more athletic zombies leaped over the augers and raced toward our dirt mound.

Jesse swore when he saw his hopes in the augurs, like mine, were misplaced. Not only did they fail to stop the fastest zombies, most of their engines gave out, or their pins busted after a half dozen zombies clogged them.

Kevin, smartly, had us stagger our fire into the faster zombies so we wouldn't fill one zombie with twelve rounds. But that only lasted a minute, soon we were all firing volleys of gunfire into them. Even I was shooting a rifle—I honestly couldn't miss. I sighted a fast zombie, missed him to the right and took out the knee of one behind him.

After I emptied my magazine, I went to help Bryan at the table loading for the others. Even though I could hit something in the mass of zombies, the other shooters could be more lethal. I cranked round after round into magazines until my fingers bled, and still we kept reloading.

Over the screams and gunfire, I could hear the two other teams east of us had begun shooting as well. My fingers were on fire and slick with blood by the time Bryan and I reached the bottom of the ammo cans. The relief our fingers got gave us no joy as we crawled to the top of the dirt mound and saw there were still waves of zombies crashing over the bodies of their fallen and wounded kin.

The first zombie I saw was a teenage girl with dark blonde hair just like Valentine. I slung my shotgun off my back and raised my gun. "Lord, have mercy," I whispered right before someone shot the girl off her feet. I shook my head, picked another target, and sent them crumbling with a blast of my shotgun. In about fifteen more seconds my tube was empty and I stepped back to fill it with shells once more. I glanced down our line and saw both the teams from the east had moved closer to us. Apparently, the teams realized there was no need to stretch so thin down the line, the zombies wouldn't pass up such a noisy attraction. It gave us more condensed fire and slowed their attack, but opened us up to being swallowed and surrounded by the horde.

As soon as my eyes went back to the charge, I saw a wave of shotguns rip the zombies with pellets, buckshot, and slugs. The carnage and power was sickeningly awesome. The stopping power staggered zombies back into each other, but it only slowed the charge for a breath. The amazing firepower we held in our hands seemed to dwarf in front of the mass of flesh constantly surging toward us, and the awe was replaced with fear in that moment. Fear that nothing our hands could do could hold back the darkness.

I stepped back into the line and fired another tube. For five minutes blood, guts, screams, and blasts filled my senses. We must have killed hundreds, I think we even pushed the horde back a few yards, we were killing them so fast. But then our pockets were empty and the zombies had no fear of the wall of corpses they climbed over, nor of our smoking barrels.

A small mercy was served when, after our guns stopped firing, a few hundred zombies turned after the next loudest thing they could hear: the tractors rumbling down the road. Still to this day, I know we would have been dead if not for the tractors. Rolling hunks of metal crushing down waves of zombies.

The ground was wet with dew and blood, so the tractors stuck to the highway, but their roaring engines attracted large crowds of infected. After their first pass, they lowered their buckets, not to kill, but to clear the road ahead of them of the corpses. This, of course, killed dozens more, who raced toward the tractors. I looked up from searching the muddy bank for unspent ammunition to see a few zombies climbing on the tractors, pulling at the bars, trying to get in to the drivers. But a dozen more were cut by the welded blades, and the large machines bounced as they crushed corpse and living zombie alike into the pavement.

But not all of the zombies chased the metal bait. Some were clearly more interested in the uninfected food in front of them. Kevin shouted at us to fall back off the dirt mound and we gathered our poles out of the back of the pickups. We each held long, sharpened pieces of wood, pipe, or anything else we could find. I held mine tight and readied myself for the melee. My father was beside me, Bryan and Kevin to my right. Jayce had been commanded to start the truck should we need to retreat and to my left was Derek and Linda. *Where was my brother?*

I broke ranks to look down the line. My brother, usually so easy to spot in a crowd, was nowhere to be seen. "Junior!?"

My father grabbed me and threw me back in line. "He's fine." We heard the roar of an engine behind us. "In fact, there he is now."

One of the RVs came billowing down a dirt road that led toward the horde. My brother was dangling out the side door. When he got close enough to the horde, he hopped and rolled up next to us while the rig bounded up the berm and flipped over into a mass of zombies, crushing dozens and lighting a few more on fire.

"Brilliant!" I said as he grabbed a pole and joined us in the line.

"Yeah." He spat on the ground. "Not gonna solve all our problems, but we sure don't need it if we don't survive this." He nodded behind us. "Them either."

A few of the older men, even Curtis, had tied ATV throttles down and sent them racing into the horde. One hit a pothole, swerved and crashed before it got there, one went straight in and barreled into a few of them. But at the very least, they distracted some. *Some* would never give us much relief, however.

Soon the older men were back on the few ATVs they had saved and heading back to the grain bins. Soon after, two men down the line dropped their poles and ran south for the towers, one was a member, the other I hadn't seen much of. I swallowed a shout of rage and instead forced myself to say, "Let them go, no one made any oaths here. But we can't run forever, we must fight, for each other, for the people on the towers, for—"

Looking back, I should have felt embarrassed that a horde of zombies interrupted my gallant speech, but no one cared, we were all too scared, and so we shouted and screamed and drove our poles into the first wave.

We poked and prodded at the zombies racing toward us. Every zombie I speared reminded me of the first one I ever killed, poor Bertha, impaled in front of me. I thought I was scared then, with just one. Now there were more. Always more. You stabbed one and by the time your pole was free of their chest two more were coming in.

Our pathetic melee lasted not even a minute. We dropped the poles or left them stuck in ribcages when Kevin shouted to retreat. We scrambled into the pickup truck, our boots, slick with mud and blood, making us falter. A zombie grabbed my dad's leg, but Jesse made it nimbly into the truck and already had his machete, which meant a zombie lost his arm. With the high ground, we beat on the horde with our knives, hammers, axes, crowbars, and bats.

But they kept coming. The truck was rocking back and forth. I stumbled and looked up to see Kyle and Pastor Barnstock driving their team off to the bins. A quick glance over my other shoulder showed the Turners were pulling back as well. I steadied myself and swung at a hand reaching for me. Then the truck rocked again and Jesse, fighting next to me, was pulled over and gone before any of us could register the fact. Kevin stared blankly at where Jesse had stood a second before and shouted, "Go! Drive!" Then he, eyes still staring where Jesse had been standing, slumped to the bed of the truck.

Jayce sat in the driver's seat, stunned and pale, looking far younger than I had ever thought of him. He still had acne and his eyes looked like a child's, wide with fear and roaming between where his dad sat and where Jesse disappeared. *This boy should be worrying about sports and girls, not this. What have we done to him?* My dad dove through the open back window and tossed him aside. A few seconds later, my dad gunned the truck and spun the tires on dirt slick with blood. The tires finally got traction and the truck lurched; a zombie had Derek by the wrist at the same moment and he was pulled over the tailgate into the horde. It took Bryan, Junior, and me to hold Linda back while she struggled to reach for him. She screamed for him while we drove south, outrunning the horde.

I watched blankly at the hundreds of zombies, now inside our town, chasing us.

I was a fool. A fool to think we could fight this. And I was angry, angry at myself for getting them killed, fighting a battle everyone tried to tell me we would lose. And I was angry at God. We had made it so far for so long in this hell. I had done so much, so much in His name and this was His thanks? A city horde destroying everything I had done. Where was His fire from heaven? Where was His mercy? God, please, I prayed, please give us *something*.

And He answered.

He answered when my dad was swerving around a derelict car and our front tire blew out, sending the truck rolling.

The world turned upside down and there was metal scraping, glass and bone shattering, grunting and shouting. I readjusted my bike helmet and saw I had been thrown from the crash. I took a selfish second to see that I was not seriously injured. But better men didn't even do that. My brother was wrenching my dad out of the driver's seat already. Bryan and Rick were trying to lift the truck off of Linda's twisted body. Kevin, no longer sobbing, was helping Jayce, whose bone was sticking out of his arm, to his feet. I will never forget Jayce, his face white with shock, staring at his arm and laughing.

But the zombies kept coming.

In a weird moment I still can't quite explain, I saw the horde seem to slow down and the beast inside me roared. Roared because it knew what I had finally discovered. That this was never about me. The Call to this little town, the struggle to survive, the battle, the Church, the world, and universe. It wasn't about me.

I think we all have a hard time admitting that we aren't different, we aren't the one who the world revolves around, we aren't the one who gets to never die. And how much more arrogant is a pastor? The Church was not mine, it was God's. He had seen it through persecution and trial and He would see it through this plague; truly the gates of hell would not overcome it. The Savior had won for us salvation, He had established His Church and He would see it and His people to a brighter day, with or without me.

With a strange joy and courage, I prayed that, though He didn't need me, He would do it with me. I prayed He would use a broken, selfish pastor like me to help His people.

I picked up the megaphone that had rolled to my feet. "I love you guys," I said through the megaphone, while I ran away from the truck. I glanced back at the truck to see my dad, free from the cab of the pickup, struggling to chase after me, but my brother held him back. "Tell the others I love them too." Then I ducked down an alley after I saw the majority of the horde was following me.

In a half second of bold joy that my plan was working, I taunted the horde behind me. "Haha! Come get it!" But then I saw they were gaining on me. "Oh—"

I ran.

I ran and when I thought I could spare a breath, I shouted in the megaphone. After I made the alley, I turned and headed north, better to give the wounded as much time as possible to get up the grain bin. The zombies were gaining on me, their energy was endless. One in the front tripped and a dozen collapsed over it, but it only got me a second of a lead because there were a hundred after me. Even worse, they were bursting through yards and alleys at me.

I kept running, my legs growing uncoordinated. If I kept going I would fall, if I slowed they would catch me. I was at the north end of town when I saw smoke rising ahead of me out of the carnage. A tractor, once green, but now red, stormed toward me. Donald waved at me as he drove past and buried his blade into the horde behind me. *I wonder if he would wave if he knew his son, Jesse, was dead.* The zombies that the blade didn't hit—the horde took up nearly the whole street now—turned and chased the tractor, but a handful were still after me. I ran again and clambered up an oak tree, which must have been sickened from something in the groundwater because, even though it was late spring, it had few leaves.

Between kicks at the few zombies climbing up behind me, I watched Donald turn his tractor around for another pass. I could also see over our dirt berm to where the pits writhed with dying zombies, there were still dozens out in the fields, some crawling and wounded, others walking in a daze, apparently uninterested in the sound of the tractor engine for one reason or another. Others were still racing toward us.

I shouted and cursed when I kicked a zombie below me in the face, but, feeling no pain, it latched onto my foot. It growled and tore at my leg until I could shake it off. And I climbed higher. But more had seen the commotion and they piled on one another high enough to grab branches. I went higher, sweating, scared, and when I reached the top, I knew they would get me eventually.

But perhaps the people from the truck ("Those that were still alive," I thought bitterly) made it safely to the grain bins; *that would be worth dying for.* I comforted myself with the fact that I would find out someday, when I saw them again. The zombies climbed higher and the northern road we were on filled with zombies and I wondered if they had enough rocks on the bins. Did they have enough food to outlast this? Or were they doomed to an even slower death than me or Donald, whose tractor was beginning to grind and groan?

But my thoughts were drowned out by the growling and hissing below me. There were thirty of them clambering up the tree, falling and hitting the branches on the way down. Others inching closer so that I, swaying in the weak limbs on the top of the tree, threw kicks with my boot at their heads. But then there were too many for my foot to handle. They grabbed at my legs, they tore at my laces, the tree creaked and groaned under the weight of all our bodies.

I fought my losing battle for a few minutes and when my boot was wrenched off my leg, I decided to jump. Maybe if I landed in the mass it would be quick, less painful, maybe they would do so much damage I wouldn't get infected and march along beside them.

I crossed myself and prepared to jump when the explosion happened. It wasn't large, but it was loud, like a car backfiring. It came from the tractor, I was sure, but I was more focused on the mass of zombies at the bottom of the tree that found it more interesting than me. Dozens of them ran for the tractor, some jumped out of the tree, and others, using their peers as a ladder, fell down the tree, crashing on each other.

Suddenly the five zombies still hanging on and still interested in me looked a bit more vulnerable. I began kicking with my other boot, and jumping to an outer branch, I caught on, letting it lower me a few feet nearer the ground, and let go. I crashed into an overgrown lawn, but never felt a thing. I was running. Through a house's busted out picture window, up the stairs, and out on a balcony.

Donald's tractor was stationary, he swiveled the bucket back and forth, knocking over zombies. Apparently, they had done enough to damage it so it couldn't drive. I thought of shouting to distract the zombies, but it wouldn't have worked. Instead, I said a prayer for Donald and tried to ignore the pounding on the door behind me while I tried to think of a way to get to the grain bins. It didn't seem possible, not with the mass of zombies on the road, not with several of them spotting me and racing to get to the house. Not with several of them breaking down the door behind me.

But then fire from heaven came.

211

Not exactly. It was Wilbur with his crop-duster. The roar of the propeller distracted the zombies as the plane flew down the street, dumping its volatile and flammable mixture on the teeming zombies. I stepped back under the eaves of the house to stay dry.

Donald kicked open his tractor door, sending two zombies flying. He shot a handful more, then pulled his sickly frame, with some difficulty, up to the top of his tractor. He raised his hip flask to me, took a swig, and threw it at the zombies. Then he pulled out his lighter and flipped it into the mass below him.

The fire spread like nothing I could have imagined. Zombies ran wild with the flame and set *everything* on fire: trees, houses, and, most importantly, each other.

I could just see the top of Donald's head over the raging inferno fueled by a hundred zombies around his tractor. I saw his torso silhouetted in flames and I will never forget seeing the old man cross himself, raise his pistol, pull the trigger, and tumble into the inferno. *Now he was with his wife and son once more. And his Savior.*

I fought back tears from sadness and guilt that he would die for me, from shock, from fear, from the acrid smoke that was everywhere. I wiped my eyes, waved goodbye to the zombies sticking their heads through the hole they created in the door behind me, and hopped off the balcony. I picked my boot up from under the, now ablaze, tree I was in, put it on my foot, bloody from broken glass, and set off back to the south.

Several zombies saw me, but most of the horde was on fire and, while they could still move, couldn't see or hear much, at least I assumed, since I ran through the horde without drawing too much attention. Halfway through I ditched my trench coat that had caught fire. By the time I made it to the grain bins, the whole north side of town was on fire and even the most resilient zombies were succumbing to the flames.

A few hundred still teemed around the grain bins, but none were by the ramp we had fashioned from elevators that started several hundred yards away. I climbed up the long ramp and was greeted by hugs and cheers and a few curses from my dad.

But the joy was short lived as a hundred people mourned those who died in battle and watched half the town they grew up in burn.

Exile

"This is the day that the Lord has made."

"Let us rejoice and be glad in it." The congregation was small, mostly because people were busy defending ladders and situating themselves on the top of the grain bins. But I was doing memorials and they knew where to find me.

I had my back to the north where half our town burned, blazing so bright I could easily read the names I had scribbled in my notebook. Twenty five of us fought on the berm, only seventeen of us returned, though not all of the missing were dead. Some, too ashamed to come to the grain bins, fled the town completely. When I returned, I was covered first in hugs by my family, but then with questions.

My family made it back, that was the best news of the day for me. Everyone who survived the truck crash made it as well. *Poor Linda.* I comforted myself, knowing that she was with Derek and no longer at war. Kevin was in tears while he watched his son writhe in pain from his broken arm. Kelly and my mom tended to him and had splinted his arm. My dad sat silent, no doubt feeling guilty for crashing the truck. We all slapped him on the back and said it wasn't his fault, but those wounds needed time, and even time wouldn't heal it all the way.

Junior and Bryan were off throwing rocks down their respective ladders and for a moment I sat down next to Mary. She was distracting Luke by having him peel potatoes under a lean-to. On the metal roof next to him, Noelle and even Emmett leaned into her while she read one of the stories we brought up the bin. Luke shook his head when the story ended with "happily ever after."

"That's a lie," he said.

Mary looked at him for a minute. "Well, yeah, not every story ends happy."

Luke looked at her. "Does ours?"

"Well, honey, I don't know, but I know God has seen us this far, and we have each other."

"Not Valentine." He glanced at Noelle. "Not Uncle Rob and Aunt Maddie."

Mary looked at me with watering eyes. Then she sighed, "Luke, Noelle, and you too Emmett, you know way too young that most happy stories lie. In this world things get old, well, not even that anymore." She chuckled sadly. "In this world things get sick and they die." She put her arms around the two little ones. "But there is one story that is real and it is good. So good that it changes so many stories and makes them good."

"Does it make ours good?" Luke asked.

"Yes, dear. It sure does."

"Can you tell us that one?" Emmett asked.

"Well, you've heard it many times before, but I would love to." And she went on about the One who suffered and died and rose, so that we might too. That was the happy ending we needed, it was the happy ending the people needed while they sat scared and watched their town burn.

That's why the dozens of people who could fit on the slanted grain bin roof sat and watched their town burn while I did memorials for the people we had lost. Telling the people of the hope of the Good News, the happy ending, the reunion and feast promised by our risen Lord. There were tears, and there didn't seem to be a lot of hope, but I didn't blame them, it was a difficult evening to rejoice in. Some of our loved ones had died. A hundred zombies growled and screamed below us and the smoky skies made the air thick and the sunset brown. We were enveloped in fear. But most of us were alive.

I had done half the memorials when we heard screaming on the next grain bin. I awkwardly said a few more sentences before stopping and deciding to go check out the commotion with a few others. Screaming and wailing wasn't abnormal on top of the grain bins, neither was fear or grief, but this wailing was persistent and pleading.

By the time we got across the narrow catwalks to the next grain bin, the screaming had died down. A mother, I recognized her from the grocery store, was reaching out to her son who had, apparently, just been hauled back onto the roof of the grain bin.

Gertrude, who was there before us, saw the puzzled looks on our faces and said quietly to us, "Jason tripped, and before anyone could do anything, he had rolled under the railings. If he hadn't caught the ledge so his dad could grab him, he'd be gone."

The grain bins had pretty steep angles on them, most of the kids were strapped in, but many of the adults wandered the grain bins without restraints and we couldn't keep the kids leashed the whole time.

As the mother clung to her son so tightly it seemed the boy couldn't breathe, his father tied a restraint to his belt – not without giving me a withering glare and mumbling under his breath. No doubt he blamed me for their son's near-death experience.

I never finished the memorial services that day, but headed back to the grain bin my family had set up on. I sat on a bucket, pulled out my notebook, and thanked God I didn't have to add one more name to it. I don't know how long I stared at the names I had shakily etched in, fighting off the reality that, maybe, if I had made another decision, maybe they would still be alive. *Derek, Linda, and Jesse.* Those names hurt. Eaten alive or crushed because of a plan I made. *They would still be alive if we ran.* And we wouldn't be stuck on grain bins with half our town on fire and only bricks and rocks to whittle down the last hordes of zombies. Then a raindrop plopped onto the notebook.

That was when I started to cry. I turned away from the people even though I didn't really care what they thought. We were all grieving, we all had to make decisions, decisions that cost people their husbands, wives, and daughters. "O, Val . . ."

"Hey, Pastor. Hey!" A gravelly voice demanded my attention.

As if it wasn't enough for him to interrupt me on a Sunday morning as he usually did, today Curtis decided to interrupt me in my grief.

With one hand on a railing and another on a cane, Curt

shuffled over to me. "Listen here, now. You brought us up here and look around, people are nearly dyin' and if we don't—"

Curt rattled off a few more complaints, but I wasn't listening. His whining had transformed my grief into anger. At that point, I suddenly didn't care anymore. I didn't care if they all tossed me off the grain bin, just as well, the peace at the bottom would be welcome.

I stood up and, in front of the twenty other people crammed on the grain bin, rounded on him. "You think I don't know Curt? You think I don't know that my decisions led to this? Well I do. I get to live with it the rest of my life. Live with the fact that my calls got all these people killed today. Do you even realize that I, as a pastor, have to give an account? And to God, not to some crotchety old man."

Curtis gaped at me.

"But dammit, Curt, someone has to make a call. Or we wind up like all the other towns around here. You seen 'em? There's nothing left. And I never said my calls were always the right ones, the Good Lord knows they aren't, but someone's gotta try something!

"And I'm not above criticism, but for crying out loud Curt, it sure would be nice if for once, just once, you did something other than whine and complain and grumble. It must be so easy to do that when you aren't the one who ever has to do anything. I mean, when have you actually done something? Ever?"

He stammered for a moment, "Well, I, uh, can't—"

"That's right, you can't! You can't get out, you can't get your own water, you can't board your windows, so you know what, we did it for you. And the pathetic thing is we were kinda happy to do it, even as you moan and whine about how we do it wrong or too slow the whole time. Get a grip, Curt. And do us all a favor for once and give us a break."

He shook his head. "This is no way for a pastor to speak."

"And what do you know about being a pastor, Curt? Week after week after month after year of complaints, of funerals, of pews getting emptier. Day after day of praying, of counseling people, trying to help them, only to watch them completely ignore everything you suggest and then blame their ruined marriage on you. Night after sleepless night, just hoping, just praying you could reach someone, but they got more important things in their lives than eternal life to worry about. Night after sleepless night of going over conversations in your head, wishing you had said something different, worrying if you had pushed someone away. Hospital call after hospital call, watching terrified people, trying to give them some hope to cling to."

A crowd was gathering now, but I didn't care, so I kept going. "You want to know what I worry about? A whole bunch of people I never cared enough to reach out to. People I was too afraid to talk to. I've been lazy and I've been too much of a coward to speak the truth because I didn't want to push anyone away from the Church. I worry about how I take my frustration out on my family, who don't deserve it. So, by all means, come on over and tell me how I've been wrong and how it should be done. Tell me you don't need me. You would be right. God doesn't need me, His Church doesn't need me."

I stepped closer to Curt. "But remember how you didn't want a pastor around when you're sick and dying. Because maybe you won't have a pastor somewhere up late at night, losing sleep because he is worried about you and praying for you. Maybe he won't have a stress headache because he won't be worried about saying the right thing in a gentle, loving way as to not push you away, but to help you grow and find hope. And maybe someone won't come by and give you the only medicine we have left, the medicine of the Gospel."

There was silence for a while, aside from the rain hammering on the metal grain bins. I sighed. "You don't like your pastor, Curt, that's fine. But a whole lot of people used to hate the police, but boy wouldn't we like to have them around again. You don't want me as your pastor, whatever. Sure would save me a lot of trouble."

He didn't say a word. Neither did anyone else.

"Memorials resume tomorrow." Then I turned on my heel and headed through the rain to the next grain bin.

Mercifully the rain only lasted an hour or so. In the middle of the night, I sat by the ladder listening to the growls and hisses below me, mindlessly dropping a brick down when the noises seemed to get too loud. I didn't even bother to look down, mostly

217

because it was too dark to see more than fifteen feet down the ladder, as this one was situated on the south side of the grain bins, away from the fires still burning in the town. But I also didn't particularly care much about anything. The thunk of a brick or rock on a zombie's head was satisfying at first, as well as the commotion they caused as they fell. But after a few hours, I hardly noticed the sounds anymore.

I felt relieved that I had finally spoke my mind to Curtis, but I dreaded the conversation when I would have to go reconcile. I did go too far asking "when have you actually done something? Ever?" So I would have to apologize for that. But the rest of it was true, said too rashly, yes, but true. Still, I would have to remind him that I did care about him and I was his pastor and would be happy to see him if he ever needed anything. The beast inside me raged that once again I was wasting worry on Curtis, but I forced it back down, this was my job, even more, my Call from God's Church. *How bitter and sad is a pastor who hates his people? God's people.* I would go apologize for not speaking the truth in love and make peace with him tomorrow.

I would also have to check on Jayce and Kevin. I could tell by how silent Kevin was that he, along with my dad, felt bad about their decisions and actions during the fight. They would want some reassurance and Gospel that, even though their actions weren't wrong or sinful, we have a God who died to cover our shame. I wish I had someone to speak those words to me, I could use them. "Physician, heal thyself." I chuckled as I tried to take my own words to heart. It kind of worked, but never as well as someone else's words. God didn't make us to be alone, physically, emotionally, or spiritually, I realized. *Maybe I should talk to Pastor Barnstock or Bryan.*

I silenced another too loud, too close growl with a brick.

I would need to thank those guys too. They fought for a town that wasn't theirs and they helped attend to the hurting and mourning. The beast riled a bit at giving Pastor Barnstock praise, but it didn't growl too much, he was a good pastor, he spoke of the cross of Jesus. So did my father-in-law. That night I wished every man was a pastor so that the good news would permeate this night filled with heartache and fear and smoke. But maybe I just wished every man was a pastor so I didn't have to do it anymore. There would be less sleepless nights and stress headaches. Less frustration in meetings. Less peace-keeping duty. Less worry about others and what I could have said differently. It would be so nice. But I knew that if something needed to be said, I would open my mouth and say it, come what may. I shook my head, leaned it back against the railing, and laughed; maybe I couldn't run from this call if I wanted to.

Another growl too close.

Thunk.

Was that my fiftieth of the night? Only a hundred more to go.

After another hour of bitter thoughts, my mom came over and sat next to me.

"Next shift isn't for another hour," I said.

"Nope. A mom's shift never ends." I could only see the silhouette of her long curly hair, not her face, but I was sure she was smiling.

I chuckled. "Thanks Mom, but I don't much feel like talking."

Her silhouette nodded. "I know. I didn't come to talk, you know I'm not as eloquent as you. I just came here to be with you."

I smiled and turned so I could lean my back up against hers. "Thanks Mom."

Another hiss down the ladder.

Thunk.

My brother shook me awake from my lean-to, where I was trying to catch up on sleep after my shift at night. He pointed over the side. "Is it just me or are there more of them?"

I rubbed my eyes, winced away my headache, and looked over the edge at a hundred zombies banging on the sides of the grain bins. "Man, after dropping rocks on them all night long, I think there are." Miranda fussed with Luke's hair ("Knock it off, Mom."). "Must be the smoke from town, probably visible for miles."

"This town hasn't stopped smoking all spring, but I s'pose you're right." The plumes were higher than I'd ever seen them.

The meeting that day was long and contentious. Anyone who had fought the day before wasn't anxious for another confrontation, including myself, and scared to initiate our plan to get off the silos. The other part of the group was desperate to. Acid rain started up again halfway through the meeting and that didn't help anything, either.

"It's miserable up here. It's windy, wet, hot, and I want to go see what's left of my home," they said.

"But it's safe for now and we have supplies, and we are thinning them at the ladders," Rick replied.

"Then why are there more of them down there?"

They had us there. But ultimately, the rain, even though it made everyone want to leave more, made us stay. Kevin, *it was good to see him talking again,* finally ended the debate. "We're gonna have to get them with fire. Can't do that with the rain. Let's wait another day."

"Assuming we don't start jumping off before then," Rebecca, her makeup smudging from the rain, mumbled as she finished the minutes from under her umbrella.

She had a point too. The constant banging, the screams, and groans and moans were driving us crazy. The best of us were irritable, the worst and most fragile shutting down or, like Rick's sister, Vickie, needing to be restrained.

That was also the moment I realized why, in the midst of a fight for survival, Rebecca spent so much time on makeup, hairstyles, and clothes. So much of this world was now out of our control, but she was still in charge of a few things, as trivial as those might be. She was fighting back in her own way each time she did her makeup or ironed her clothes. But, on those grain bins, I could tell even she was faltering.

Which is why I was so relieved that Charlotte stood up on the apex of the grain bins with a slightly forced smile on her face. "We can do this! We have earplugs on our bin and, if you start getting loopy, find someone to talk to and something to make you busy. Keep the mind going, keep the mind positive, and we can last another day."

Miranda, Ava, and Mary, together with Gertrude, put the church choir back together on the largest grain bin. The sweet sound of hymns took the edge off most of the growls and it only took a few minutes for most of the population to congregate nearby, seeking some solace in music.

It seemed like we were up there a month and most of it night. The dark sky blocked the sun and made it set early and rise late. But we did our watches, I did memorial services, and the girls, by request from Gertrude, sang a beautiful hymn at the end of them, a pristine contrast to the growls below us. Even Vickie seemed to calm while the music rolled over her.

But it was only three days. Three days until, mercifully, a dry morning advented upon us, burning off the dew, drying us, and, more importantly, the zombies below us. The pack's numbers had dwindled slightly in proportion with our supply of bricks and rocks that fell on their heads. But we had little ammunition left, less food, and even less patience.

We lowered raw meat down on ropes to get the hordes congregating, then we doused them in whatever propellant we could stand to lose and set them on fire. Once the flames were high, we tossed meat at random off the towers to get the zombies moving. In their scrambling for a bit of meat, they spread the fire amongst themselves and anything else in the general vicinity.

We waited until most of the zombies gave in to the flames and, when we would rather risk facing them than the possibly melting grain bins, we climbed down the elevators. Two dozen zombies met us at the bottom, but with careful aim, we were able to put them down with the few bullets, rocks, and arrows we had left. We cheered as, finally, the remnants of the city horde were cut down. We had won.

A group of wounded, mourning, and weary people came off the grain bins. But we were alive. It felt awkward, after being so bonded in life and death for days, when we just tipped our hats and scurried away. I shouted out something about a meeting and to ask if there were any who needed houses. But it seemed most people had moved into acreages with wells or, having watched their neighborhood burn, found arrangements while on the bins. I thought a moment how tempting it may have been for those outside town, like several families, to simply hole up in their home, rather than come and fight. But so many stuck with us. *Humanity? Or something more?* A love for neighbor, a sacrificial love like the Savior showed. That's what got us through. Sure, you didn't have to be a Christian to survive the plague, nor did you have to be one to help your neighbor, I would be long dead if it wasn't for the help of unbelievers, but our quirky little band of people in the middle of the plains owed so much to the Savior, who gave us hope and strength. Any love we showed each other was truly because of the greater love He showed for us.

It was the same Savior who got us through the next months while we wept tears for loved ones that we missed, while we worked together to rebuild what had been destroyed, while we ran the battle through our heads over and over again, wishing we had done some little thing differently. Our Lord was the One who forgave the past and helped us more forward. He was the one who helped us to see that, even though our battle with the horde was over, when it would have been so easy to settle in and hide in the new world, we could keep looking for others to save.

Church Militant

"This is the day that the Lord has made," I said to the congregation of sixty-some people.

"Let us rejoice and be glad in it," they responded enthusiastically.

And indeed, we were glad in it. Because, for the first time since the plague had started, frost lined the windows of the church. A hard frost, still holding even at ten in the morning when we started the service. A frost sure to hold any zombies that bedded down for the night in place for good.

A fire roared on the wall opposite the altar in the church. We had the stone fireplace and chimney put in as part of the many winter preparations we had made in town. Two churches survived the fires and plague: the one I had been called to and the Baptist one down the street, which other Christians were gathering in at the same time.

We worshiped and thanked God that we had been seen through the Summer of the Plague, as we called it. We rejoiced that we were in the "sterile zone" behind our large, city-wide fence—at least the parts of the city that survived the fires. We celebrated that we had made it to winter, where nothing could walk unless it had fur, feathers, or fire. But we, as on every Sunday, still mourned. We prayed for mercy to see us through a winter like none we had experienced or been taught to live through before. And we prayed for mercy in a world, where all across the north, infected people, but people nonetheless, were freezing to death without even realizing it.

Even a zombie that instinctively huddled in some warm house or hollow wouldn't last long in the winter. They couldn't hibernate, they had a desire to feed above all else, they would go into the cold and die.

The summer months had flown by. But standing in our church on that winter morning, it felt like we were years removed from those terrible nights on top of grain bins. We seemed like completely different people than the ones who came off them wounded in so many ways.

But we had made it, by the grace of God. I won't waste a lot of time talking about how we prepared for life after we fought the horde. There are a hundred books out there since the outbreak to study survival. We did all the normal stuff. We rebuilt homes and we built walls around the town. We dug wells, harvested stoves from houses, gathered wood, and cured meats. We harvested and stored seed for planting, we scrounged up some solar panels.

We did all of that. But we did so much more. We made the difficult choice to let God's forgiveness have the final say over what we'd done. Kevin for not calling retreat earlier, my dad for rolling a truck because of a blown tire. Myself for what I did on a sinking boat, for what I didn't do the first two weeks of the plague, for what I did to Grant, Richard, and Dean, for not protecting my little girl. Some of them were sins, some weren't, but they still hurt, they still left shame and pain. So we preached and heard the good news of our forgiving Savior and we shared that forgiveness with each other. We worked, harder than putting up some fence—that was easy—we worked to live in the forgiveness of the Savior. I still feel the guilt and pain, my feelings haven't caught up yet, but they'll get there sometime. In the meantime, I keep acting and living what I know: I'm forgiven. Blood cleansed.

We had so much to be thankful for. But that is not to say everything was great. We almost lost my brother to an infection when he cut his arm building up our town's front gate. Miranda dreaded every mosquito she saw, since no one knew for certain if they could spread the virus or not. No one talked about what we would do if someone got appendicitis or worse, though Kelly and my mom were reading every medicine book they could find and had successfully delivered a baby in late July.

When I was a child, I was afraid of every bump in the night, and that was when I had nothing to be afraid of. Luke did. He still sleeps in our room, but even then, not a week goes by without a nightmare from him. I don't say that to shame him—he's no coward. He has seen and faced far more than I ever did at his age and he does it head on with his sister's camera still recording.

The three grain bins that survived the fires were stocked with supplies should we need them and, after the fence was completed, we searched every single house, rooting out the dozen zombies still lurking in our town. We established a night watch rotation and I never slept so soundly than that night, when I finally felt like a zombie wouldn't be walking right outside our windows.

And it would have been so easy to stay like that, with our families living next door to each other on a little lane a block from the church. It would have been so easy to seal the city gate to all but the people we knew in the country that came in to do business or bring us water.

But our Lord promised us that He would be with us to the end of the age, and, even though it seemed like it, the age hadn't ended. His promise was still true, which meant His commission to go and baptize and teach wasn't over. Which is why a town of a hundred and eighty-seven people with three pastors and a seminarian—Kevin was still studying—worked to share the Word of hope in the new world.

The interstate, ten miles away, was more deserted than not, but there were still traveling who knows where, people who, like us, were scared. We set up a water station, gated to keep the zombies out. We painted the billboards with hopeful messages, reminding people not all of the survivors would kill them in their sleep for a tank of gas. We set up large fenced enclosures with padlocks and keys so people could lock the gates on the inside.

And we draped everything in the Gospel. Not just verses, but papers with answers to the questions we had struggled with for so long: "What do we know about the virus?" "How could you believe in a God who lets this happen?" "Is there any hope?"

And once a week we would find that someone used some water or the fenced-in campsites and we would refill the water tank and replace the locks. I'm sure many people drove right on by, terrified it was a trap, though the beauty of the plains is that they could see no one was around for miles. And about once a month it seemed someone would trek the ten miles to come find us. Most wanted something. Most had their sob stories, but we all did in the new world, so very few of those got us to open the front gate. Instead, we handed supplies out to them: some milk from our cows or eggs from our chickens (kept safely penned inside the gate), some meat from our freezers run by solar power, or some water. Whatever they needed. We also gave them a Bible and a prayer before we wished them well on their way. At first it felt like we were shilling the Gospel out through survival resources, but most of the people, in a world so harsh, were genuinely interested in why we didn't take advantage of them in their desperation. And so we spoke the hope that was in us.

Some we let stay in a fenced in area of the compound. The first one was a guy who had picked up some water and a Bible and, discovering I was a pastor, rambled on about the Spirit and how he'd been sober for real long, though oddly not long enough to get the smell off him.

He stayed two nights with us, being sure to, as politely as possible, mooch supplies off us while continually reminding us about his second cousin who was a pastor. We wanted to help, so it didn't bother us, but when he continued to insist that he should be allowed to play with the kids or take watch on the gate, we politely invited him to leave. When he, instead, called down curses on us for being so hateful and judgmental, we less politely, at gunpoint, encouraged him to move on back to the interstate.

But that was the risk we took, some more willingly than others, of course. We could have taken the signs down to keep us safe from raiders and moochers, but we would not hide the Master's coin. If a hundred people took advantage of us and our supplies, maybe one of them would remember it was the crazy Christians who tried to keep them safe, who tried to help them. And maybe they would remember why we helped them: because Christ has helped us and given us life everlasting. If just one of them remembered that, it would be worth all the risk, it would be worth the sleepless nights, mourning those who were mad at us when we were only trying to help.

One man who stopped by the front gate asking for supplies

pulled a small trailer behind his truck. He seemed genuine; genuinely afraid of us, but after we didn't gun him down and talked to him for a while, he seemed genuinely thankful. He accepted our water and gasoline and wiped away tears of gratitude. A few minutes later, I was showing him how the gate worked so he could stay the night in our shelter when his trailer started rocking. The trailer creaked and the screams inside were terrifying. We leveled our guns and he put his hands up, crying, "Please, no, it's not what you think." He asked me to peer through a window and a second after I did a bloody, clearly infected boy slammed his face against the window trying to bite me.

"It's my son," he sobbed. "I know what I should do, but I can't!" He leaned against the trailer as if he could comfort his rabid son through it. "Please don't hurt him or me."

Turned out he was heading west, stopping at every city and military base, desperate for a cure for his son. All summer he had been searching. We wished him well, gave him what he needed, and of course, reminded him of the message he and, God be praised, his son knew before he was infected, that Jesus gives life and eternal healing. But then we told him he couldn't stay here. Nothing infected inside the gate, even the visitor lockup, that was our rule and we stuck to it.

He understood, said he would maybe camp at our enclosures by the highway for the night, and shook our hands as he readied to head off, at least with a tank of gas and water. "I don't know how to thank you," he said.

"I know," Rebecca said from the top of the fence, "if you find your cure, come right back here and let us know."

We laughed as the man tipped his cap to her. "Will do."

There were other visitors, each a different case, each a different story, each a different context, and over the months some earned our trust and the town welcomed them inside our walls. One of the families was with us in church on that first frosty morning. I smiled as I shook their hands, along with Kevin, who had preached that Sunday, and was glad that another family could join us on our challenging, but important mission to provide safety, community, and light in a dark world.

After church, Miranda's family and mine, as always, walked across town to where Gary's large solar powered house once stood. The smoking hole had been filled in and knowing our daughter's ashes were in the backyard, upon Charlotte's suggestion, Miranda, Kelly, and our moms had turned the whole plot into a memorial garden. Miranda held my arm tight as we meandered the gravel pathway between the newly planted pines and flowerbeds that, in the summer, would be full of wildflowers. We walked past the hundred memorial crosses that had been relocated from Jacobson's field. We stopped at Jesse's. *He was right next to me, I could have reached him if I was looking.* I shook my head. *He's just fine now.* It was the same when we passed Derek and Linda's crosses, and Dean's. Bryan and Mary cried every time we stopped by Madelyn and Rob's, I cried when we went past Valentine's. We walked in silence, aside from a few sniffs from cold or sadness. Soon we had wound our way back to the street and turned to give a last glance at our memorial cemetery, complete with a sign and, though it was covered in frost, a display case with my notepad in it. Full of names of people who didn't make it as far as we did.

It was easy to pity them, though, oddly, when I thought of the toils and dangers and fears still around us, perhaps it was easy to envy them. But that wasn't right either, death should get no glory. God should. And He called them to Himself when He willed, He would do the same for us. In the meantime, He had work for us to do.

That was when the church bell started ringing.

Not ours or the Baptist Church down the road. It was the bell from the burned down Methodist Church that we moved to the front gate of the town. It was rung by the watchman when strangers were approaching.

By the time we reached the front gate, the strangers, spotted far away on the plains, were only a quarter mile away. I didn't need the watchman's binoculars to see that it was a military convoy of seven Humvees with mounted guns.

We all stood dumbfounded for a moment, not sure whether to be excited for some civilization or terrified about a militia that could wipe us out.

"Prepare for the worst," my dad suggested.

Rick spat his chew over the fence then agreed, "Yeah, full routine."

And without another word, the gatehouse guns were out.

The men from town clambered up to the top of the gate and chambered rounds. The women and children were whisked away to their homes or the vehicle garage, ready to flee out the back gate if needed.

On top of the wall, we watched the convoy draw closer. Sweat trickled down my brow in spite of the cold day. They didn't have any tanks, thankfully, but each mounted gun, I had no doubt, could shred our wooden wall to bits. "If they want to fight, we ain't winning," I said somberly, "so you guys should leave. If they are peaceful, it's all the better."

"If anyone is leaving, it's you young'uns," Pastor Barnstock drawled. My dad and Bryan grunted in agreement.

In the end, no one left. Some of us probably should have, but the convoy was already at the gate, their mounted guns trained on us, not to mention the ten other rifles that soldiers, who had piled out of the Humvees, held. They at least had American flags on their shoulders, which gave me a bit of hope.

A stocky black man got out of the lead Humvee and, like he had no fear of the guns in our hands, addressed us. "I am Sergeant Clemson of the US Army. We were told that there may be people here sympathetic to our cause, which is to return law and order to this state."

"How do we know you ain't lying?" Kevin shouted down.

"By the simple fact that I have not ordered my troops to blast your puny wall into shreds with you on it."

We looked at each other, nodding. "He's got a point," my brother said out of the side of his mouth.

"We're just a small town that's trying to survive and help some people on the highway," I said, feeling a bit awkward holding a shotgun. "The guns and wall are, well, you know the times."

"Indeed, we do," the Sergeant agreed. "A man with an infected son told us we might find you here. Do you know such a man?"

"Yes, came by a few weeks ago," Lonny Turner called down.

"Yeah, bad news is we don't have a cure, the good news is the Denver horde has been cut down and we are expanding our influence, looking to bring some order, clear hordes, and rebuild."

229

He sized us up for a moment. "No big hordes come through these parts?"

Jayce puffed his chest out. "You better believe one did, over a thousand, and we cut down every one."

Clemson looked at Jayce, puzzled, but perhaps a bit impressed at Jayce's courage. "And how did you manage that with those hunting weapons?"

Curtis, who had finally caned up to the gate through the crunchy grass, shouted through a hatch in the wall, "With a whole lot of will, pain, and loss. Go check the field of burnt bones north o' here if you don't believe it. Maybe make you think twice about threatenin' us."

Clemson nodded at him and whistled. "I can see how that one survived." He stepped closer. "But it doesn't change the fact I need to search your premises."

We looked at each other, perhaps it made us look guilty, but we hadn't had government help for eight months and it sure didn't seem like it could be real.

Kevin finally spoke up, "I got women and children in here, so forgive me if after half a year of zombies, raiders, and wild dogs, I am a little hesitant to let you in." He paused and shrugged. "Is there some form of ID, or something you can give us?"

"Understandable, understandable," the man said, while he kicked a pebble on the road, thinking. Then he looked up at us. "Tell you what. You've got seven guys on that wall? One of you come down here and I'll show you some papers and then you let me and three of my men inside to look around." He waved at his soldiers to stand down. Their guns dropped. "That's the best I can give you."

We looked at each other and nodded. "Deal," Rick called out.

I gave Clemson the tour of town with Junior and Jayce. A few other men tagged along, including Kyle, out of caution or curiosity, I wasn't sure. The older guys, honorably, insisted on staying on the wall in case anything went wrong. We explained the best we could how we got here and what our plan was as we searched the barns, the churches, and garage. We walked through the streets while people peered through their blinds at us. After a while, the panic of potential raiders seemed to give way to the hope of civilization and order. We developed a small throng of families and kids, Luke, Emmett, and Noelle included, who followed us around. Several men introduced themselves and Clemson chatted with them kindly. He even tossed one of the kids his gloves, which were clearly too large for the young boy, and didn't mind when Luke started recording on Valentine's phone.

When we walked out of the Baptist Church, he lingered for a minute and I got the impression that he had been in one before. "So you're risking your necks to tell people about Jesus?" He rubbed his chin. "Where do you do the witch burnings and the sacrifices?"

I smiled a bit, I'm sure. "Hey, I know you've probably seen some gross stuff in churches with this plague, but don't mistake that for actual Christianity."

He nodded and started walking again. "Yeah, yeah. I know, it's just hard to believe now . . ."

After an hour or so, we found ourselves back at the gate. "Alright, everything seems up and up here, I would encourage you to put an American flag out." He nodded to one of his soldiers who fetched one, folded up, and placed it in my dad's hands. "We want people to know that this is still a country, we still have laws. Though, of course, certain ownership laws are being reinterpreted now." He nodded toward the houses. "Furthermore, we are trying to rebuild outside of Denver. Do any of your people here have any experience in medicine, in research or engineering, anything like that?"

Junior cleared his throat. "I can turn a wrench and my wife's a paramedic."

Clemson raised an eyebrow. "That's something. Want to make a difference in the new world?"

My brother looked at me for a moment, then dropped his gaze. "I don't know."

I grabbed my brother's shoulder. "First of all, this man is not just some wrench monkey, he can fix *anything* with a motor." Then I turned to Junior and gestured around at the town. "Junior, you don't have to do this, this is my dream, and you've risked and done enough for it. You do your dream if you want. I'm sure you and Kelly could do amazing things with their resources."

He kicked a rock and sighed. "Yeah, I s'pose."

"Besides, Denver is about halfway between your families, even mom couldn't complain that much."

He nodded, then turned to Clemson. "Sergeant, if it's all the same, maybe I can come visit on my own terms in a few days. Gotta talk some stuff out first."

"Sounds good, son." He gave him a sheet of paper with directions and information on it.

"Give me an extra," Junior said, then turned to me and smiled. "Wilbur can fly and is pretty good at making things explode."

Clemson nodded. "Sounds like someone I could use." Then he studied us for a moment. "Anything else? Contractors, developers, electricians?"

We looked around for a minute. "We've got pastors."

The Sergeant chuckled for a moment, then cut himself short with a cough. "Oh, you're serious, sorry."

"What's the suicide rate like, even in your camps?" I asked him.

He cleared his throat and studied his shoes.

"That's what I thought. This world got a whole lot darker this year. Well, we know One who is the Light. We've got people suffering, who have had to kill their infected loved ones, we've got people who've eaten and done who knows what . . . we offer forgiveness, meaning, and hope."

He nodded. "Just didn't think anyone believed in God anymore."

"This didn't all come from nowhere, Sergeant. Somethin' made it all. And, I can agree, that Something sure doesn't seem worthy of worshipping when He lets a plague hit us. Until you hear of how that Something, that God, has faced all the same: abandonment, forsakenness, rage, pain, wrath, and death. But then He conquered it, rising again. And it's not a fairy tale, real people in real places saw it and died for it, because they knew that He gave them a share in His victory. And couldn't we all use a little victory like that? A promise to see our families whole and healed again? That's what He gives us." I paused to stop myself from choking up, thinking about seeing my daughter again, not twisted and broken, but beautiful and smiling once more. "If you want to face this broken world with guns and laws, certainly, do your thing.

232

But there is stuff even that can't fix. Our God, who died to make all things new, can. So, see if you've got anyone who wants to be a chaplain, and if you got anyone who is, well, you know where to send 'em for some training."

He patted his papers against his hand, thinking for a moment. "Well preacher, I s'pose my men, and this world, probably could use a Good Word . . ."

Afterword

Everything about the plague was fast. It turned the infected fast and once they were turned, well, they were fast too. The chaos and death that swept the world was fast, and, while the months seemed to last forever, up here it was all over come wintertime and the survivors were left to pick up the pieces of the shattered world.

There are a few things we can be certain of in the new world. First, we know the virus is out there. The frost may have killed the hordes in the north, but the ones in the south rage on, while, even in the north, the virus lays dormant somewhere—in some animal or well. We can also be certain that humanity itself cannot overcome this, since humanity itself is infected with a virus that leads to greed, thirst of power, lust, and envy. But lastly, we can be certain that there are people out there who need us. Well, not us so much as the God we proclaim who offers cleansing and healing and purity and life. If you want to learn more about that message, come find us.

If not, I hope this little book, in accord with my daughter Valentine's wishes, brought you a glimpse of what life and death was like for our small town and family in the zombie plague. You are welcome to view her and Luke's footage at the Witherton Seminary.

Our Seminary has one of the largest libraries on the continent, gathered and preserved from churches and schools around the country. While we cannot boast of national accreditation, we do have a dedicated staff of teachers and pastors who know what it is like to minister in the new world. We offer classes on biblical languages, Church history, preaching, exegesis, ethics, and we offer more classes as our staff grows and specializes in their areas of interest.

*Tuition is negotiable and paid by service hours on the night watch, in the farms, or garages.

If you are brave enough to seek us out, and crazy enough to preach or serve the Word of God in a broken world, take the only north-south interstate that still remains through the plains until you see our signs. Then drive east until you see the steeples.

Jesus lives and, therefore, so will we.

Made in the USA
Monee, IL
01 March 2023

28527217R00142